CARNAL DESIRES

Celeste Anwar

Erotic Paranormal Romance

New Concepts

Georgia

Be sure to check out our website for the very best in fiction at fantastic prices!

When you visit our webpage,you can:

* Read excerpts of currently available books
* View cover art of upcoming books and current releases
* Find out more about the talented artists who capture the magic of the writer's imagination on the covers
* Order books from our backlist
* Find out the latest NCP and author news--including any upcoming book signings by your favorite NCP author
* Read author bios and reviews of our books
* Get NCP submission guidelines
* And so much more!

We offer a 20% discount on all new ebook releases!
(Sorry, but short stories are not included in this offer.)

We also have contests and sales regularly, so be sure to visit our webpage to find the best deals in ebooks and paperbacks! To find out about our new releases as soon as they are available, please be sure to sign up for our newsletter (http://www.newconceptspublishing.com/newsletter.htm) or join our reader group
(http://groups.yahoo.com/group/new_concepts_pub/join) !

The newsletter is available by double opt in only and our customer information is *never* shared!

Visit our webpage at:
www.newconceptspublishing.com

Carnal Desires is an original publication of NCP. This work has never before appeared in book form. This work is a novel. Any similarity to actual persons or events is purely coincidental.

New Concepts Publishing
5202 Humphreys Rd.
Lake Park, GA 31636

ISBN 1-58608-656-1
© copyright Celeste Anwar

Cover art (c) copyright Eliza Black

NCP books are available at special quantity discounts for bulk purchases for sales promotions, premiums, fund raising, or educational use. For details, write, email, or phone New Concepts Publishing, 5202Humphreys   Rd.,   Lake   Park,   GA   31636, ncp@newconceptspublishing.com, Ph. 229-257-0367, Fax 229-219-1097.

First NCP Paperback Printing: 2004

Printed in the United States of America

Other Titles from NCP by Celeste Anwar:

Beauty Ravished (Dark and Dangerous Anthology, now in Trade
Paperback)
The Color of Twilight
Your Every Desire

CARNAL APPETITE

Chapter One

The heavy bass pounded the air of the club as lights flashed to the deafening techno beat. Glowsticks twirled in the semi-dark. Dancers twisted in sensuous movements to the throbbing tempo that suffused their limbs. The floor was thick with scantily clothed, sweaty men and women rolling on X and other erotic drugs.

Curling wisps of smoke and artificial mist hung over the crowd, clinging in the half darkness like a lover's touch.

It was Saturday night--and it was crowded. The club, Inferno, was the most popular night spot in the city since the blue law had been lifted. For the unwary, the naive, it was sometimes the last stop they ever made.

Across from the dance floor, shielded from the flashing lights and the near ear-splitting music, tables stood for those resting from the dance--or those interested in pursuing more carnal delights.

Cloaked in shadow, Raoul Etienne followed the movements of the dancers, two fingers of scotch sitting untouched before him on the scarred, wooden table. His gaze unwavering, he fingered the rim of his glass, watching one woman in particular--the same woman he'd come to see night after night. Clara. He'd learned her name the previous night when a friend had called out to her. His ears had perked immediately to the sound of her voice, as husky and seductive as its owner. Raoul caught glimpses of her through the crowd as she danced and tossed her hair, two shades too red to be natural but mesmerizing nonetheless.

He sensed movement to his left, and Navarre Lyssandro strode forth and sat beside him without a word. Navarre scowled as he followed the line of Raoul's gaze. Raoul ignored him, unwilling to cease his vigil for a moment. He hadn't since he'd discovered what had happened, and still that bastard had managed to mark her a second time. He would not allow it again.

"You've been here all week, just watching her. How long will this continue?" Navarre asked.

Though the music drowned out Navarre's words to other listeners, Raoul heard him just as easily as if there'd been no music at all. Raoul didn't spare him a glance. "It is the third night. The third mark."

"You are certain?"

"I can smell it, practically taste it on my tongue." He paused a moment, then said, "She does not know Danior has marked her."

Navarre sniffed the air, looking at the dance floor. Past the sweat of many bodies, the smoke, the liquor, he caught the faint scent that he had missed before. Navarre was silent a moment, contemplating the weight of this discovery. "Better you take her against her will than he?"

Raoul turned fierce eyes on his friend. "At least she would not die," he growled, menacingly low, then remembered to whom he was talking. He forced his raging blood to calm as if thrust into an icy river. It did no good to be angry at his friend--he was only pointing out the obvious. But if Danior Blake took her again tonight, she would cross over into the un-dead, into the festering world of the vampire. Already he saw her lagging endurance. He knew not how the vampire had enticed her here, but it was moot. The damage had been done.

"You would have her as your *femme entretenue*? You know she could never be your mate. She is not of our kind."

"I need no permission to keep a woman, nor do you need remind she is not *louve*." Not *wolf*.

Navarre remained stone faced regarding him. He leaned forward, propped his elbows on the table and cocked his head toward Raoul. "I know your true motives, *mon ami*. I should stop you. It's foolhardy coming to his lair to take the woman."

"That never stopped us before." Raoul picked up his glass and threw back its contents in one swallow.

"No, it hasn't."

Raoul grinned, wolfish. "You hate them as I do, as do we all." He stood abruptly, pushing his chair back with a scraping rattle.

Navarre leaned back and stretched his arms behind his head as he watched him. "You could start a war."

"Then let it begin."

* * * *

It was impossible for Clara Falkner to be unaware of the strange man's attention. At every turn, she could feel his gaze roaming her body as palpable as a caress. It was intimate. Almost ... hungry. And she enjoyed it. Never had she been a woman to garner admiring glances from a man. The chill of goosebumps made her shiver despite the cloying warmth of many bodies pressed close.

He'd been watching her for the past two days---ever since she'd arrived at Inferno with no knowledge of how she'd gotten there. It could be her memory loss and lethargy were just coincidental with the stranger's regard, but for some reason that teased the edges of her brain, she didn't think so. And it merely intrigued her all the more.

In the movements of the dance, she casually turned to peer through the haze to where she knew he sat, watching her. He was talking with another man she hadn't noticed before, this one as fair as *he* was dark. He seemed to sense the moment her gaze alighted on him, for he looked up and caught her staring. Clara felt a shockwave jump between them as their eyes met.

She looked quickly away, breaking the contact, then glanced back when she thought it was safe. The hairs rose on the back of her neck as she saw him rise from his seat and stride purposefully across the room, allowing nothing to distract him from his goal.

Her mind immediately conjured an image of a wolf moving in for the kill.

And he was coming for her.

She knew it as surely as she knew her own mind. The scene seemed to play before her like a movie moving in slow motion. Agonizing seconds ticked by.

Her heart pounded in her chest, her blood pumping furiously through her veins, throbbing deafeningly in her ears. She knew she should run, knew she shouldn't be so fascinated by the stranger, but she couldn't. The dance was forgotten. Clara ceased moving at all, became deaf to the music thumping in her ears ... and ignored that warning, inner voice that had shielded her all her life. Unable to do anything, she could only watch him move toward her with the confidence of a predator claiming his quarry. The throng parted unconsciously at his approach, allowing him an unobstructed path straight toward her.

Despite his height and muscular breadth, he exuded a predatory grace that was unnerving. The black mesh shirt he wore left little to the imagination. Rather, it enhanced the bulging muscles of his chest and the rippled abdomen that tapered down to his lean, leather encased hips. A silver ring in his nipple, barely hidden by the mesh, glinted in the flashing lights. Strands of long, black hair fell across his forehead, over his broad shoulders, drawing her gaze. On another man, it might have appeared effeminate, but there was no mistaking his masculinity. And Clara had always responded to men with long hair.

Eager to study his face, which she'd been fearful of looking overlong at before, she lifted her gaze, past full, kissable lips and his straight nose, until she met his eyes and was caught. He held her like a trapped bird, hypnotized. The amber orbs almost seemed to glow with an inner fire. She was helpless to look away from him.

Inexplicably, she could feel her heart slowing its rapid tattoo, calming as he reached for her. He placed a hand behind her waist and pulled her flush against him, against the hard bulge of his erection. She was instantly aroused.

Sound returned, fear and excitement, as the music swelled and he moved with her in the dance. Clara draped her arms over his shoulders, rolling her body against him, her breasts pressing tantalizingly against his chest with each rocking movement. He cupped the cheeks of her ass, grinding his hips into her, spreading her legs. Clara gasped as he rocked his erection against her sex, clinging to him. She was blinded to anything but his eyes, boring into hers. Her short skirt rode high on her thighs, and she felt moisture creep into her sex with his rough abrasion.

The tempo quickened, and he responded by holding her closer, moving into her as if he'd take her there on the dance floor, standing in the midst of a crowd. His faint, musky scent had the allure of something wild, savage. He bent his head to her neck, rubbed his faintly whiskered jaw across her sensitive skin, and nipped her earlobe with sharp teeth. His tongue was rough against her neck, tasting her. His breath hot against her already feverish skin, she shivered from the sensations, welcoming the alien feeling. Never had she danced this way before ... or allowed a man such intimacies. It was so close to making love, she thought she'd collapse from the delicious agony his proximity aroused in her.

"Leave with me," he whispered into her ear, rocking his hard groin against her for emphasis, leaving her in no doubt of what he was asking. She tightened her arms around him in response, weakened.

Was it a request? A command? Her senses reeled with unfamiliar lust. She was past the point of caring about anything but satisfying that ache between her legs. Clara nodded, and breathless, said, "Okay."

He straightened from her, almost smiling. She felt suddenly chilled without his body pressed tightly to her, and wondered briefly if she'd gone insane. He took her hand before she could change her mind and led her off the dance floor toward the back exit.

No one took note of their passage or barred their departure. They were quickly outside, pushing through the outer door into a dark alley. The heavy, metal door slammed shut with finality behind them as they exited, silencing the raging cacophony of the club. In the quiet, Clara felt almost deaf from spending hours inside.

Sanity was slowly returning, despite her best efforts to keep it at bay. She shouldn't be doing this. She wasn't the type of person to have a one night stand, to go off alone with a strange man whose name she didn't even know. It was insane to trust him--but she did. Unfathomable as it was, she wanted this like she'd never wanted anything before. And she wanted him.

He turned abruptly, faster than she could blink, and pushed her into a darkened doorway before she could react. He propped his arms on the door on either side of her head, blocking her outward view. She could only see his eyes, shining gold from some light beyond her line of vision. Clara froze, mesmerized, unwilling and unable to fight.

"I've wanted to take you since I first saw you."

She couldn't deny the thrill that raced through her at the husky admission. His voice was incredibly deep with a hint of an accent. Perhaps French? The low timbre made her tingle in all sorts of forbidden places. He leaned forward, his mouth mere inches from her own, teasing her when all she wanted was to taste his kiss. Her lips parted of their own accord ever so slightly. She held back, waiting to see what he'd do, eager and afraid all at once.

Closing the gap separating them, he touched his lips to hers, slanting his mouth across her lips. Clara startled as a jolt of pleasure vibrated along her nerves at the contact. He growled and cupped her jaw, forcing her mouth open as he plunged his tongue inside. Greedy, demanding, he tasted her, sweeping his tongue through her crevices with a slow, thorough glide.

She sucked his tongue with near desperation and felt when the change came over him, when need overrode everything else. He'd been holding back before, though she hadn't realized it.

He growled low in his throat and crushed her against the door, trapping her to the feel of his body, of total domination.

Clara moaned, clutching at him, needing more. Her knees went weak, her legs became as supportive as rubber. She draped her arms over his shoulders, pulling him closer as he guided a knee between her legs.

She clamped her thighs against him, reveling in the hard feel of his leg pressed intimately against her. It wasn't enough. She'd worry over her doubts later. Right now, she needed his cock inside her.

Clara broke the kiss and he latched on to the base of her throat, sucking at the tender flesh. He was driving her crazy, and they'd shared no more than kisses. "I want you," she gasped, running her hands down his back to cup his tight buttocks. She dug her nails into the leather, and he grunted with pleasure.

He lifted his head, looked at her. "You are sure, *chere*?"

Clara nodded and tugged at his waistband. It was all the prodding he needed.

He kissed her again, nibbled her lips as he hurriedly unbuttoned her blouse. He popped the remaining buttons off as he ripped her blouse open to devour her. Trailing searing kisses, he traveled down her jaw to her collarbone, sucking at each new discovery until he reached her breasts.

Clara groaned as he pushed her bra aside and drew one breast out from its lacy covering. Frantic to feel him inside her, she didn't want him to take his time, but when he closed his mouth around her nipple, she forgot her objections. He sucked the small bud hard, teasing her with his teeth and tongue, with heat and wetness. He was greedy, rougher than she normally allowed. She felt as though he could consume her whole and she'd never utter resistance.

"You are so *tres doux*," he murmured huskily against her flesh. So *very sweet.*

He pinched her other nipple, toying with her breast as he reached his other hand beneath her skirt. Peeling her drenched panties down her thighs, he let them drop down her legs to the ground. Clara kicked them off her feet. Fingers shaking, she proceeded to work at his fly, anxious to ease her craving and have him fill her. The hard leather fly resisted her efforts.

Recognizing her struggle, he pulled away from her long enough to unfasten his fly and free his cock from his pants. Clara reached for it, curious to feel his size even if she couldn't see it in the darkness of her position. He groaned and tilted his head back as she wrapped a tentative hand around his thick length. He was enormous. Her slit grew wetter as she thought of him burying his huge cock inside her.

"Protection," she said, near breathless with wanting.

He nodded and dug in his pocket until he found a foil packet. Tearing it open with his teeth, he slid the thin rubber over his erection.

Clara pulled at his hips, urging him forward. He hesitated a moment, and she could feel his body tremble with tension and energy, as if he was debating with himself the wisdom of this course. His hesitation only made her want him more. Desperate beyond belief, Clara lifted a leg and wrapped it around his hips, drawing him to her, weakening his resolve. He shuddered finally, the battle he'd waged within over. Giving in to her demands, he grasped her thighs in his strong hands and spread her wide open. Cool air caressed her nether lips with shocking fingers. She trembled, waiting.

With a strength she'd never experienced, he thrust his full length inside her, his strained passage eased by her own soaking juices. She could feel every rigid inch passing inside, so hard and tight. He settled his mouth on hers, muffling her cries of pleasure as he pumped his cock inside her, grinding his pelvis against her clit.

Clara couldn't marvel at his strength in holding her up. She could only think of taking in more of him, of taking in all she could hold. She hooked her calves under his buttocks, urging him on. He pumped into her faster, harder, rocking her against the door with near bruising force.

She didn't care--could only feel the ecstasy mounting in her every nerve with each grinding thrust. Clara threw her head back as pleasure ran through her veins with each coarse stroke, leaving her trembling and weak. He dragged his mouth down her throat, sucking at the curve until he'd left his mark of possession near the small, healing wound she'd gotten days earlier, piercing her skin slightly with his teeth. He slid his cock in and out of her soaked pussy.

She hovered at the edge of ultimate release, ultimate agony. Clara dropped a hand and massaged her clit, craving the fall. She stroked herself roughly, slipping in her own juices until the orgasm took her in one liquefying climax. She screamed then, her muscles contracting around him as he continued thrusting inside her, faster now, shorter strokes as he rode her to his own completion. Her pussy continued to quiver with the orgasm, building to another as he continued. Clara moaned, the pleasure exhausting and thrilling all together.

He kissed her, hard, arms shaking and tense, hands gripping her as though he would fall without her anchoring him to this world. With a great shudder and a heaving sigh, he came. His cock twitched inside her, the thin rubber no protection against the potency of his release. He dropped her legs to the ground and collapsed against her, breathing raggedly, leaning heavily against the door.

Clara hugged him tightly, enjoying the feel of his hammering heart against her breasts--fast and powerful as a wild beast's. Her own pulse and breathing slowed, returning to normal. The pleasure still surged through her veins--her clit throbbing with the intensity of her orgasm-- distracting enough to stall thoughts of remorse for a time.

A chill wind suddenly burst through the alley. It howled through the narrow passage with the ferocity of a train bearing down on them. Newspapers and other debris caught in the current whirled through the path past them, twirling as though caught in the force of a cyclone.

He broke away abruptly to look into the darkness and fastened his pants as he walked away to stand in the middle of the alley. Pale light shone down on him, casting fierce shadows across his face, illuminating the tension evident in his body and rigid stance. He appeared ready to pounce at the slightest provocation.

Clara shivered and pulled the edges of her blouse together, smoothing her skirt down over her thighs. Something was wrong. Leaning back against the door, she felt inexplicably weak, as though she would faint. Her skin felt feverish despite the cool air, and she didn't think the cause was their rigorous love-making from moments before. The eerie feeling taking hold grew by the minute, stronger and stronger. Her sight had narrowed down to a single point of focus, and she grasped at the vision of her lover to keep her afloat.

The sudden stillness of the night was broken by his voice, startling her.

"Danior," he said, speaking into the yawning cavity of darkness before him, a single word that sent chills traveling up her spine despite its simplicity, for she'd thought them alone.

There was such depth of hatred in his voice--she would have had to be deaf to miss it. She never expected he would get a response.

"Am I interrupting?"

Chapter Two

The man stepped from the shadows like a cliché from a bad horror movie. Only nothing about this scene made Clara feel like laughing. An immense feeling of terror pervaded her senses, brought on by the man who'd seemingly come from nowhere. It was an unreasonable reaction, but something about him struck her as frighteningly familiar. The memory of the strange wounds she'd discovered while showering inexplicably came back to her, flashing in her mind's eye like a haunting vision.

A long, black cape concealed his body, making him appear to almost glide toward them. Equally strange, it took her a minute to realize the wind did not stir his hair or clothes. A chill ran down her spine at the sudden insight. She shook it off, determined not to allow her imagination to run wild.

The scope of her sight began clearing as he neared them, but her breathing was harsh in the ensuing quiet. She had to fight for every breath she took and could only stare in mesmerized horror as the two of them faced off.

A struggle for dominance, for power, was taking place between them, she knew, though neither uttered a word. Unseen energy fairly crackled in the air. She half expected them to lunge at each other's throats, but after a few minutes of tense waiting, something gave and the cloud of morbidity lessened enough to breathe and think once more.

Clara gasped as a rush of air entered her lungs. Attracted to the sound, the man glanced directly at her for the first time. Darkly beautiful, inky hair framed a face of sharp angles, but his full lips softened masculine edges. His skin was pale enough she wondered if he had an allergy to the sun like a child she'd once known.

A buzzing began in her ears as he stared at her, creeping through her brain like spider webs. Unconsciously, she took a step forward from the shelter of the door frame, releasing the edges of her blouse as she dropped her arms. Air struck her exposed skin. Becoming aware of what she was doing, she shook her head, trying to dismiss the probes tickling her mind.

He smiled, sensuously chilling, and the humming stopped. Clara hastily buttoned her blouse, uncaring if it was straight or not. She swallowed hard. *What just happened?* she wondered.

"You've taken my cherry, Raoul. I admit I hadn't expected such audacity near my abode," the stranger said suddenly in a softly seductive voice, returning his attention to the man who had so lately ravished her with pleasure.

Raoul. It sounded archaic. Clara didn't wonder at the strangeness of his words, rather that she now knew her mystery man's name. The knowledge had barely settled in her mind before she was caught off guard by Raoul's response to the man.

Hands clenched as hard and tense as his body, he looked capable of rending a man to pieces. Harsh, almost feral, he said, "I've given her the first mark, Danior. There's nothing you can do."

The finality of his words made Clara shudder. This confrontation should have struck her as ridiculous, but there was nothing farcical about the two men squaring off. Reaching up, she tenderly touched the bite Raoul had left on her neck in the throws of passion, so close to the wound she'd discovered yesterday. She'd ignored the small pain then, but did he think it entitled him to something more?

"I have only to drain her life's blood to cancel your marks," Danior responded.

Enough of that! "What the hell are you two talking about?" she demanded, anger and fear mingling as one.

"A small matter, nothing more, my pet," Danior said, keeping his eyes trained on Raoul.

"I'm not your ... anything. Or *his* either." Her brief insanity had landed her in a hell of a mess. It was past time she got out of here. Scraping through a confrontation was better than sticking around and being murdered. The proximity of the club wasn't enough of a safety net to suit her nerves, even if there was a chance others could come out the back exit as they had.

Clara straightened her resolve and pushed past the both of them, giving wide berth but exposing her back as she walked by. It couldn't be helped--it wasn't so bright that she couldn't *not* watch where she was going. Spraining an ankle wouldn't help her out run them if they gave chase.

Air rushed through the alley as it had earlier, and someone--Danior--laughed harshly behind her. Clara glanced over her shoulder as she quickened her pace. Only she and Raoul remained in the alley. *Oh shit. Breathe. Just breathe.* She ran. This was too freaky. She half wondered if she'd somehow been drugged and hallucinated the entire episode.

Heels clicking rapidly with hollow sound on the pavement, she raced through the remainder of the alley, looking wildly around as she dug her keys out of her pocket. She just wanted the safety of her car--to go home. Dashing through the floodlight at the end of the alley, past the club's entrance, she headed for the packed lot where she'd parked.

Raoul caught her at her car. Clara gasped in surprise when he grabbed her. She hadn't heard him over the deafening thump of her heart, hadn't expected him to be so fast, so close. One minute she was alone, and the next, he'd spun her around and trapped her against the closed door. Her keys clattered as they struck the ground, knocked from her hand in the tussle.

Raoul closed his large hands around her biceps in a vice grip and pressed his hard body tight to hers, caging her so that she couldn't move ... unless he willed it. She struggled a minute, realized it was less than useless to fight someone so much larger, and relaxed her back against the cool metal door.

"What do you want?" she asked belligerently, forcing herself to breathe deeply to calm her racing heart. She could act brave when she needed to. She'd talked her way out of worse situations, and she was eager to put this night behind her.

"I'm afraid I can't allow you to leave," he said with soft menace.

"I'll scream."

He leaned in close, until his mouth was inches from her own, teasing with his nearness. His breath warmed her skin, making her lips tingle with awareness. She thought he would kiss her, but when he did nothing, she was strangely disappointed. He was close enough she caught that wild scent that drove her insides into turmoil and filled her with instant lust. She couldn't remember ever being so ... animalistic before.

"You would have screamed already if you'd planned to, *chere*."

What? She'd been so focused on his mouth, she forgot she'd said anything. "I still could."

"But you won't." He rubbed his thumbs against the soft sides of her breasts in a manner that soothed as much as it teased. Her nipples tightened inside her lacy bra, and she suddenly had too much clothing on. She squirmed under the touch, and he pressed his hips harder against her as a warning. Any closer, and he'd be inside her. She bit her bottom lip, hating her responsiveness to him.

"There's over a hundred people inside that club. Someone will come," she said softly, unwilling to concede defeat.

"You know very well no one would hear you over the music. Besides," He paused a moment, his smile feral as he pulled back slightly. He passed a lingering look over her breasts, exposed by the hastily fastened blouse and her position. "No one heard your cries of pleasure."

Heat suffused her body, flushing her skin pink under his gaze. Her breasts felt heavy, swollen. She longed for him to massage the ache away. "Don't look at me like that," she said, attempting to bolster her anger.

"Tell me you don't enjoy it...." He smiled knowingly. "You can't lie to me ... I can smell it."

His voice was soft, almost apologetic in tone. But the look in his eyes belied that impression, dared her to contradict him. Clara remained silent. It was the truth. She swallowed hard as the realization hit home.

"What are you going to do with me?" she asked softly, almost afraid of the answer. There was a dangerous allure, a restrained savageness, about him that had captivated her from the moment she first saw him. She *wanted* him to brand her, to take her god only knew where. And that was the most frightening realization of all--even if he was mixed up with some lunatic.

As an answer, he shifted against her, almost nestling between her legs, as if he knew exactly how much she wanted him. And damn the consequences. The thin, silk skirt she wore was little barrier to the bulge of his arousal pressed hard into her. Moisture gathered in her sex with the insistent contact, tickling her swollen labia. She tilted her head back, closing her eyes, resisting the urge to moan, and suddenly remembered she hadn't put her panties back on. A flick of his wrist, and he could release his erection, take her there on the car. She shuddered.

"I want you to come with me."

She looked at him, and her clit throbbed at the look in his eyes. Her mouth was instantly dry. Clara swallowed past the lump in her throat. "I ... can't. This is crazy. I don't even know your full name, who you are...."

"It's Etienne. Raoul Etienne."

"Clara Falkner. I *thought* you sounded French." It seemed ridiculous to have this conversation now, after all they'd shared, after the strange confrontation the two men had had. Jeez, could she be any more inane?

Clara wanted to dig a hole and cover herself with a rock. This man had had his tongue and cock inside her, and she'd not even had the grace to discover his name first. Her family would be so ashamed at her behavior. She hadn't decided if she would bury the memory yet. It was hard to think past the fog of lust he inspired in her, with his scent still on her skin, with his erection pressed intimately against her and her own body begging to be filled by his cock once more.

"Cajun," he said succinctly, bringing her back to the present. "Danior still wants you. You will be safe at my place, Clara. Allow me to take care of you."

Staring into his eyes, she felt her willpower wavering. She was just about ready to say yes to anything he proposed. She'd begun the night with insanity. Shouldn't it end that way as well? Instinctively, she knew he would not hurt her, so what was the harm in living out her fantasies?

Lost in thought, she said nothing. When she didn't answer him, his face grew serious. His eyes darkened and his brow furrowed. In a voice chill with certainty, he said, "If you do not come, you will die tonight."

* * * *

Raoul saw his words had provoked the appropriate response in her. Her face paled, and her eyes grew wide with dawning fear. Danior had scared her--he had reminded her of that fact. If she'd known the truth about Danior, about what *he* himself was, she would likely be terrified. He wanted her to be afraid. Fear was the ultimate survival tool.

She seemed to remember herself after a moment and clenched her jaw tightly.

Raoul's face darkened with irritation. He tightened his hands on her arms but she continued to look at him unafraid. She had him to thank for her ease of mind, though she didn't realize it. Had he not broken the vampire's mind marking, she would have willingly gone wherever the bloodsucker asked and been completely susceptible to his every suggestion.

He had made a mistake not taking her from this place to start with, to goad the vampire so near his lair. But when she'd begged him to take her and wrapped those sweet thighs around his waist, he'd been unable to resist sinking into her depths. And still he'd not had his fill of her. A mere human woman had tempted him and clouded his reason. It angered him to lose his control ... and it was deadly.

Danior had given them a brief respite for some unknown reason. Raoul couldn't risk that he would not return with back up. He could only fight so many before succumbing. Clara wouldn't have a chance in hell. He wanted to shake her, make her realize the danger.

If he'd had time to place the remaining marks on her, she would not be so foolishly defiant now. She would be bound to him, would crave his touch as she would no other. His cock hardened unbearably at the thought of laying his claim to her.

Beneath her bravado, she was still anxious, still afraid, and the heady mix only increased his hunger for her. She couldn't know her heightened adrenaline was as enticing to him as the musky perfume of her desire. Couldn't know that he was dangerously close to losing his chained beast after confronting Danior. He could not afford her fear right now, and did not want to fight her. "I am the only one who can protect you. I swear, on the blood of my heart, I will not harm you."

His sincerity pierced her stubbornness. "I'm regretting this already." She sighed and closed her eyes, shaking her head once before looking at him again. "I'll go with you. But you have to explain everything to me."

He nodded once and released her. "You'll learn more tonight than you ever wanted to know."

* * * *

Clara was surprised when they reached his car, not expecting that he would drive such a costly vehicle. He was a large man, well over six feet tall, and the black viper fit as though made for him. A custom job on an already expensive car. Luckily, wealth had never impressed her like it did some people, and she was able to be at ease in the luxury vehicle.

Lights flashed as other cars drove past them on the lighted streets, busy with late night traffic.

She hadn't noticed before, given all that had happened, but now that she had some leisure and at least dim lighting, she could see he was covered with scars. Deep gashes rent his forearms and exposed shoulders, pulling toward his back to disappear under his mesh shirt. They were old enough to have healed completely and faded into the color of the surrounding skin. She wondered just how extensive the damage was.

"What happened to your arms?" she blurted out without thinking and cringed at her callousness. She touched a gentle fingertip to him, fascinated, traveling along one long scar that curled around his biceps. It was smooth and felt no different than his whole skin. "It looks like an animal got hold of you."

He glanced at her then back at the road, his look unreadable. "Something like that."

He didn't seem a man to talk much, but she sensed she'd struck a nerve, and with good reason. She shivered, thinking of what he must have gone through. Her heart ached with empathy for his suffering. "It must have been painful."

"Yes."

She burned to ask more but fell quiet when she saw where he was taking her.

They headed to an expensive residential neighborhood, enclosed in the city for convenience, where she knew the lots cost in the tens of thousands due to their location and illusory seclusion. For the first time, she wondered what he did for a living.

He pulled into the only road in or out and stopped at the gate briefly before a guard waved them through. Old fashioned street lamps lit the way through the heavy woods, and they passed several immense houses before he pulled into the drive of an old style Tudor.

The tension was thick in the intimate space.

She'd remained silent as long as she could bear it. She still wasn't ready to drop his accident. She knew instinctively that it was something she needed to know. "Would you like to talk about it? About the accident?"

He parked in the front and turned off the car. "Some things should be forgotten." Palming his keys, he got out of the car and opened the door for her.

"And some things you can never forget."

He gave her an angry look, then headed up the path to his front door. She had to practically run to keep up with him. He took so long to respond, she'd begun to think he wouldn't even bother answering. "You wouldn't understand," he said finally.

"Try me," she said, a little breathless as they stopped in front of the door.

"You don't belong in my world," he said gruffly as he unlocked the door and held it wide for her to enter.

"You've just invited me inside...."

Chapter Three

Could he risk telling her the truth? That the monsters of the world's nightmares actually existed in a shadowy, secret society? She wouldn't believe him. No one did until it was too late to listen to the warnings. He'd never worried about people heeding him before, but he found he *wanted* her to believe him--not just think he was some psycho.

Had he not been attacked, all those years ago, he himself would still be ignorant and deny their existence.

He could warn her, tell her what had happened to him ... and what Danior had done to her. But that wouldn't mean she would listen.

Clara waited in the foyer, watching him expectantly with her soft, hazel eyes. She perceived too much. There was a vibrancy about her spirit that was difficult to resist ... or deny. That, and she was too damn beautiful by half, a woman built for loving. Being so close to her incited him to a raging lust he was hard pressed to control. Small wonder that Danior wanted her for his own.

"Follow me," he said finally, resigned, leading her into the living area that opened off the front entryway. A two story cathedral ceiling stretched above them, the hewn wood warm and inviting in the soft yellow light of a central chandelier. Here was as good a place as any to divulge his secrets.

He picked up a remote and hit a button. Instant fire roared to life in the fireplace.

Sitting near the blaze in an overstuffed chair, he stretched out his legs and bade her sit across from him. He stared at the fire, waiting until she was settled before beginning.

"Seven years ago, I was on the force, heading up the case of the Necro-ripper."

"I remember when that happened. I was in college, we were all terrified."

He nodded. "We thought we had him tracked down to the swamp. Had every available officer out there scouring the area, set up a perimeter and road blocks, the works. He wasn't getting out. He'd taken another girl, you see...."

He turned his gaze to her, watching her reaction. "My partner, Jim, and I had discovered some tracks. I never got to radio the finding in. Something fell from a cypress, slashed into my back. My left arm was nearly severed in the struggle. The last thing I remember was seeing Jim's head floating next to me in the water, and then blackness."

Clara looked about to speak, but Raoul held his hand up, stopping her. "I woke up in the hospital a week later. They'd found the Necro-ripper. Put about three dozen bullets in him. But the damage had already been done to me. I ... *changed* the first full moon...."

She looked confused, unsure of what to say. Her hands fidgeted in her lap, wringing the bottom edge of her blouse. "I ... I don't understand."

Watching her steadily, he held her rapt with his gaze so that she couldn't look away. "I was infected, *chere*. By a very rare virus. So rare, it's become nothing but a myth, or a tale to scare children.... Lycanthropy ... a werewolf."

* * * *

Clara laughed. What he'd said wasn't the least bit humorous, but the horror he described, the conviction in his voice.... Her body hurt as though she'd lived through it, and her gut reaction was to bleed off the fright in the only way she knew how. She was disturbed to hear her hysteria so plainly, but she couldn't help herself. After only a moment, she went quiet, confronted by his dead seriousness, his silence.

"I'm sorry," she whispered, ashamed at her lack of control. It had been a hell of a night. She rubbed her eyes with her fingertips, covering her face with her palms, unable to bear meeting the condemnation she knew he bore her. What she'd done was unforgivable. She'd been brought up better than that. But how could she have suspected he would tell her something so ... so outrageous and impossible to believe? She expected any minute some cameraman would jump out and surprise her with the knowledge she was on Scare Tactics.

"It's understandable, *chere*."

That only made her feel worse. Worse still, her gut told her he wasn't lying. She couldn't believe that he would lie about something so horrendous--not when his voice held the pain of truth. Not when confronted with the evidence of his extensive scarring. There had to be *some* explanation for it, but at the moment, she couldn't fathom what it could be.

"This is crazy," she said finally, her voice muffled by her hands, still cowardly trying to hide her shame.

"Don't make me show you, Clara. I don't want you to fear me."

Dropping her hands to her lap, she looked at him, struck by his tone and words. He was just as beautifully masculine to her now as when she'd first seen him. Hearing his admission, however crazy it sounded, hadn't changed her desire for him, her desire to know him. It was insane to have such strong feelings when she didn't know him, but he provoked a powerful response in her that she'd never encountered before.

"I would never fear you," she said with conviction, feeling it to be true. Obviously he was attuned to action, but as a foil for violence, not an aggressor. He'd been a police officer before. It that was true, it would explain much.

"You can't know the future." He looked into the fire, his jaw hard.

No, she couldn't, but she knew her feelings of the moment. She wanted to go to him, to soothe his torments, but she dared not right now. He seemed ... distant, troubled. So she did nothing but sit there, watching him. He excited her, but he didn't scare her, intense as he was. Still, there was one inconsistency she hadn't considered. "If you're a ... lycanthrope, how can you wear that?" She indicated the ring in his right nipple. "Isn't it silver?"

He smiled darkly. "I like a little pain mixed with my pleasure."

The low timbre of his voice vibrated along her nerves like an electric current. Heat flooded her, pooling between her legs. She shook herself mentally, trying to get a grip on her emotions. It was frightening how easily he could play them. Maybe he *was* more dangerous than she realized ... just by sheer potent sexuality....

"I know you don't believe me. You needn't worry. I will still protect you from Danior."

She felt better moving on to a different subject. It allowed her to gain control of her libido--before her brain was fried. Better not to dwell too long on his *disease* ... or her reaction to him. "Who is he?

He watched her a long moment before finally saying, "He is a *vampire*."

Clara shivered, unexpectedly chilled by this admission. She should have known better than to ask. She was reminded of that eerie wind that hadn't touched him, how he'd seemingly vanished. No, it just couldn't be. Still, Raoul's contempt made her curious. "You say that like you hate ... them."

"I do, as do all of my kind."

She couldn't fully believe him--it was just too far past the realm of believability--but suddenly she was fascinated. The paranormal had always captured her imagination. She'd spent more hours than she cared to remember reading horror books through the night. "Why?"

"They seek to control, to drain us. Our blood is like a drug to them, addictive, potent, rare. I have never met a natural born shape-shifter, but even those who were once human are scarce. Men rarely survive their attacks--women, almost never."

From a scientific standpoint, it made sense, just based on old legends and stories. Lycanthropes were like superhumans. It stood to reason that their blood would be more powerful, and highly prized by a vampires, who subsisted on blood. And also that it would be difficult and painful for a human to survive such vicious attacks, which would account for the rarity of such a race, to the point of lack of evidence to support their existence in modern society. She supposed most who were attacked were ... eaten. Clara swallowed hard, ill at that possibility.

Still.... "Then I'm not the target. He'd want you, if what you say is true." It seemed like sound reasoning, based on the information he'd provided and her own deductions. And if they were enemies, it was only natural to fight it out. They were men, after all, even if all the paranormal mumbo jumbo could be believed. Oozing testosterone and highly territorial.

The look on his face told her something entirely different. His brows drew down as he frowned at her. "You felt dizzy in the alley when he was near? Like you would faint?"

What did that have to do with anything? And how could he know? She swallowed past the lump in her throat. "Yes. Yes, there was this horrible buzzing--"

"You have two marks on your body, do you not?"

She nodded slowly. How could he know about that? A chill ran up her spine, forcing goose bumps to rise on her skin. Despite wanting to believe the contrary, she was beginning to doubt conventional reasoning.

"He has given you the first two marks of what is called the triad: the mind, body, and lastly, soul. Anyone with the knowledge can invoke the spirit in three hallowed areas of the body and bind it to their own ... for a time.... It can weaken or strengthen, depending on the match.

Danior has been preparing you for his new ... companion. Surely you've heard the old legends: on the third night of blood-letting, a human dies. And the next night, they are reborn a vampire."

Clara raised a tentative hand to her neck, feeling the small wound, and the new one beside it. It couldn't all be true ... this was just ... too much to believe. The memory loss, the fatigue--was it possible? She felt like she'd entered the twilight zone, and Inferno had been the gate into hell.

"I can't remember what happened two days ago, not yesterday either...."

"He rolled your mind to make you forget. Easy enough to do once the mind mark has been invoked."

"I feel ... tainted somehow. Dirty." She shuddered, rubbing her arms rapidly for warmth. The thought of someone invading her mind and making her forget horrified her. She hated losing control.

Raoul stood and offered her his hand. "It's late. I'll show you to your room."

She took his proffered hand and rose, but shook her head at his suggestion. "No, I'm not ready to sleep. I ... I need to get warm. To feel clean again."

"The bathroom is up those stairs, to the right. You'll find everything you need in there."

A tense moment passed between them while he held her hand, and she thought he would kiss her rather than let her go, but finally he released her. Walking away from him, it took effort not to turn around, but her neck prickled and she knew he watched her go.

She was thankful he didn't follow, but disappointed too. She needed time to think about what he said, about the implications, and yet she also craved comfort and security. The kind she could only have in a man's arms ... in Raoul's arms.

Finding the bathroom just as he described, she entered the cavernous space. A whirlpool, cast in black marble, encompassed one entire corner of the luxury bathroom. In another, a huge shower stood that could easily have accommodated half a dozen people. Shower heads dotted the glossy marble walls. Plush black towels hung within easy reach on silver bars just outside the glass doors of the shower.

Clara stripped off her clothing, dropping it in a pile on the floor. She was reluctant to wash the comforting smell of him off her skin, but needed to cleanse her body and spirit of the taint holding her mind. That man *had* enthralled her. She couldn't deny it, no matter how much she wanted to. She didn't understand how it was possible, but she did know Raoul had saved her.

Stepping into the shower, she closed the door behind her then turned on the water, running it until heated. It took her a few minutes to figure out exactly how to use the shower, but after several tries, she finally managed to turn on just the overhead faucet.

The water was almost too hot as it rained down on her, but the heat banished the chill that had settled in her marrow. She stood there several minutes, just soaking up the heat and wetting down her body.

Grabbing a nylon loofah, she squirted bodywash on it and began lathering her arms. There was a soft click, and cool air flooded the space as the steam was sucked out. She turned slightly and glanced over her shoulder, surprised to see the shower door open ... and Raoul standing inside it.

Chapter Four

Raoul closed the door as he stepped fully inside--too close for Clara's mind to continue functioning as it should. The enormous space shrank around them, until he stood mere inches away from her. The water seemed cool compared with the heated look he ran in a lingering pass over her body with deliberate thoroughness.

Her skin tingled from his leisurely once over, as if his hands stroked her curves. Clara forgot to breathe. Her heart stalled a moment, and then its pace quickened to a raging tempo. Thought fled along with all the reasons why she shouldn't get involved, shouldn't give in. It didn't occur to her to try and cover her nakedness. All she could do was stare at him.

Naked, his skin glistening from the escaping steam, he was more magnificent than she'd ever imagined. She'd always been able to admire a well honed body but had never really been aroused by looking at nudity. Raoul inspired instant lust.

The muscles of her sex clenched as a rush of liquid desire saturated her labia. An ache started low in her belly, an ache that could be cured only one way.

The nipple ring drew her eyes, and she was reminded immediately of what he'd said--and how it had made her feel. Hot. Hungry. Ravenous to taste him and tug his nipples with her teeth. She drew her eyes down his wide chest. A few scars curled around his ribs. His scars were a part of him, a savage badge of power. Her fingers prickled with the need to caress them, to touch every hard muscled inch of his body. She resisted, wanting--no, *needing* to see all of him.

A trail of dark hair traveled down his rippled stomach, guiding her to his cock. His erection was impossible to miss in the well trimmed thatch of hair surrounding it. His rigid member was thick, standing straight out from his body, and long enough she could easily wrap two fists end to end around it. Veins bulged along its length, his skin stretched impossibly tight. The cock head was swollen and large as a plum, it's color a deep red that looked hot to the touch. And she wanted that heat deep inside. She grew thoroughly soaked gazing on him, imagining him ramming his cock into her.

Raoul moved toward her, and she tore her gaze from his erection looking up at his face. He smiled, as if he knew she approved. Silent, watching her with unmistakable heat in his amber eyes, he reached slowly for the loofah, treating her like a skittish doe, and took it from her lax hands. He dropped it to the bed of the shower.

Taking her hands, Raoul pressed her palms against the heated marble. She watched as he squirted soap into his hands, and then he moved behind her where she couldn't see, out of the water. He slid against her, his body as wet now as her own, nestling his hard chest and stomach against her back until his cock pressed intimately into the crevice of her buttocks.

Clara bit her lip at his contact, craving more. She dug her fingers into the marble until her knuckles turned white with the effort not to turn around and jump him. Eager to know what he would do next, she held still, waiting with tensely.

He kissed the curve of her shoulder, and she tilted her head to allow him easier access. Nipping her with his teeth, he moved soap slickened hands up her braced arms to her breasts. Her nipples tightened unbearably as his palms skimmed over them, making her breasts feel heavy and swollen. She squirmed under his teasing touch, and he grunted low against her neck, cupping her breasts. Slippery with soap, he massaged them firmly, pinching her nipples hard between his fingers.

Clara moaned, pressing into his hands, desire uncoiling in her belly. She was more than ready for him, could feel her juices tickling her nether lips. "Please," she whispered, begging as she rubbed her ass against his cock. His hard erection twitched against her sensitive cheeks.

"So soon, *chere?*" He sucked her earlobe into his mouth, flicking it with his tongue before kissing the hollow behind her ear.

"Yes. I want you inside me. Now."

She felt him smile against her neck.

"I'm afraid I can't accommodate you just yet, *petit.* I'll end your torment soon. For now, you must keep your hands on the wall," he said in a voice that brooked no argument.

Clara groaned in frustration but obeyed him.

Raoul moved down her back, dragging his teeth and tongue over her wet skin, licking up the water droplets that collected on her body. His hands moved down her ribcage to her belly, lathering her and teasing unbearably with his nearness to her pussy, fingers massaging just above the hairline. He reached the top of her buttocks with his mouth and pressed kisses across the top, at the base of her spine.

Clara startled when she felt his tongue slide down the cleft of her buttocks, then jumped in shock when he nipped the underside of one cheek. He sucked at the tender skin, and she felt something building inside her at the odd sensation. It was a forbidden area--she'd never allowed a man to ... kiss her there. She hadn't known her cheeks could be so sensitive. She shook at the feel of his sharp teeth grazing her neglected flesh.

He broke away and nuzzled her nether cheeks, his breath hot against her. "Spread your legs for me, Clara," he demanded, his voice hoarse, hovering on the edge of control.

Clara trembled and moved her legs slowly apart. Something wet and hot pressed firmly against her *taint* while he slipped one hand down to massage her inner thigh. She felt as though she was being groped by two men, handled everywhere she wanted most. She jerked as his fingers slipped through the hair covering her pussy, teasingly slow, just shy of where she wanted to be touched the most.

"Raoul, please....," she said hoarsely, unable to bear the torment.

He flicked his tongue against her and delved deep with his fingers until he found her swollen clit. Clara moaned, biting her lip as he rolled the small nub between his fingers, moving his tongue higher up her slit, until he plunged the liquid smooth length inside her depths.

A gasp tore from her throat, and she pressed her forehead to the wall, tilting her ass toward him, unconsciously begging for more. He pushed his tongue further inside, curling it in her tight passage, then withdrew to lap at her juices and the sensitive edges of her hole. His fingers found a tempo with her clit, alternately rubbing and pinching with faster and faster thoroughness.

A pulse beat in her sex, climbing with each stroke. He broke away from her cleft, and she felt the loss with aching clarity.

"*Ma doux* ... my sweet. You taste so good," he said, his voice muffled against her inner thigh. He sucked at her labia, pulling at the outer lips and moving toward her thigh.

Sliding his fingers down, he plunged two inside her, keeping his thumb rubbing hard against her clit. Clara shook as he moved in and out of her, bucking against his hand. She was going to cum. She could feel the orgasm build with every stroke, trembling on the edges of her climax.

It took her with a suddenness she hadn't expected. Her inner muscles gripped his fingers. As the orgasm ripped through her, she felt his teeth sink into her thigh. Clara screamed, the pain and pleasure mixing as one.

Sated and gasping, she collapsed against the wall. Slowly, her breathing returned to normal, though her cleft still spasmed. He stood behind her, kneading her ass cheeks.

"I'm not finished with you yet," he growled softly.

"No," she said weakly, "I don't think I can take any more." The orgasm had left her weak and her appetites appeased.

"You can. And you will." Kissing and suckling her neck, he turned a knob and the wall units of the shower came to life, spraying the length of her body. The water massaged her breasts and belly, sensually bringing her back to life and washing away the evidence of her arousal. Guiding her, he moved them both until a jet of water sprayed directly against her sex. She moaned at the liquid assault to her sensitive flesh.

She heard him squirt more soap out, and after a brief moment, felt the nudge of his cockhead between her ass cheeks. He slipped down, slowly opening her folds.

She wasn't moist enough, she knew, to accommodate his huge length. Biting her lip, she expected pain and braced for it. He pushed his swollen cockhead past her tender lips and thrust fully inside her.

Clara gasped as he slipped with little effort inside, his way obviously eased by the soap. She was exhausted ... and dismayed to realize he'd rekindled her desire.

Placing his hands over hers against the wall, he pumped his huge cock into her, lifting her up with each powerful thrust. The water pummeled her clit with the vibrating power of a machine, driving her closer and closer to the edge.

He cupped her breasts, massaging her hard, grinding his hips against her.

Raoul was so huge and tight, she thought she'd burst from taking all of him in. Each stroke nudged her cervix. Just when she thought it was too much, that she couldn't take any more, he pulled out and began again. Faster. Harder. Deeper. Ramming his cock full hilt inside her again and again. Clara shook her head, crying out as he bit her neck and sucked her with bruising force.

The climax flamed through her veins, and still he drove into her, groaning against her neck, whispering French into her ear before plunging his tongue inside. Her clit spasmed with the continued assault, torturing her with another wave of pleasure.

Groaning, he worked into a frenzied tempo, and she could feel the power of his climax building even as her own radiated through her veins. He groaned hoarsely against the back of her neck as his cock pumped its seed into her until he was completely drained.

He collapsed against her, pressing kisses along her shoulder. Clara moaned as he pulled his heavy length from her body.

He turned her around and pressed her into the wall, crushing his mouth against hers in a fierce kiss. When he pulled away, her lips felt tender and swollen. And she'd thoroughly enjoyed every second.

Smiling wolfishly, he guided her to the overhead faucet and they rinsed away the sweat from their love making, running their hands over each other with playful thoroughness. Clara wondered if it was possible to become addicted to another person, and knew if so, she was hopelessly hooked.

Raoul patted her down with a towel until she was dry, then he scooped her into his arms and carried her into his bedroom, which was located right next to the bathroom.

The room was equally large as every other in the house, and a bed dominated much of the floor. He set her feet on the floor and drew back the comforter, revealing black silk sheets.

Clara climbed in and he followed, spooning her as he cradled her close and wrapped his arms tight around her. Secure and comforted, she felt positively glowing. He'd succeeded in taking her mind off horrible possibilities, but slowly the fear began creeping back, though not as strongly.

Determined to put it from her mind, she closed her eyes and sighed deeply. She'd just drifted off to sleep when she felt Raoul tense behind her. And then a voice whispered in the room.

Chapter Five

The bed dipped as Raoul rose, and she felt the loss of his heat instantly.

"You violate the pact entering my home, Danior," Raoul said.

Shivers skittered up her neck like spiders' legs. This wasn't possible. Was she having a nightmare? Clara scrambled to the side of the bed, fumbling for the switch on the lamp, clutching the blanket to her chest. She couldn't see her hand in front of her face. How the hell could Raoul see anything?

She really didn't expect him to be answered, least of all by the man from the alley. There was a harsh laugh, too cold to be Raoul's. "You broke the second mark, Raoul. Did you expect me to do nothing?"

Light washed through the room as she found the elusive switch. She gasped and felt the blood drain from her face. The dark stranger, Danior, stood in the middle of the room. The hair rose on the back of her neck, chilling her. This couldn't be a nightmare--nightmares had never felt so ... real.

"You can't have her," Raoul growled, tensing to spring at him.

Clara watched in horror as his hands changed. She rubbed her eyes, hoping she was wrong. But she wasn't. His fingers grew, lengthening to half again their original length. Black claws sprang from his fingertips, curved and glistening in the weak light.

"So it's war you want," Danior said softly, his voice strangely deep.

She tore her gaze from Raoul to Danior and saw that he had changed as well. His teeth had elongated, his canines forming double fangs she'd only seen before in horror movies.

It was true. Everything Raoul had told her was truth.

The two men slowly circled each other in the wide space, each of them watching for weakness. Hands darted out for quick strikes, but each time the blows were blocked, resulting in minor wounds.

"I thought you would be better, Raoul. Those legendary skills of the wolf have grown lax I see," Danior taunted, chuckling as he swiped a hand across Raoul's biceps, leaving thin bloody slices.

Raoul grunted, landing a punch to Danior's ribs. Bone crunched audibly from the force. "I thought I'd take it easy on an old timer," he said, grinning like a mad man.

Clara hated this, wishing it was over, but terrified to know the outcome. She almost suspected they were enjoying themselves--if not for the seriousness of the situation. She gasped with each bloody contact, expecting a death blow to be delivered any moment.

Something changed in Raoul at her small gasps of surprise, as if he'd finally awakened to reality and realized their danger. Half crouching, he braced his legs, tensing for the jump. Growling deep in his throat, Raoul rushed Danior with a suddenness that stole Clara's breath. Danior caught the force of his movement. Raoul caught him by the throat, slamming him against the wall until it caved in under the pressure.

Plaster rained down, dusting them with white powder. Danior grinned and dug his fingers into Raoul's arms, forcing his hands open. Dropping to the floor, he pushed Raoul back, slicing into his chest with nails sharp as blades.

They moved with dizzying speed, so fast their arms were blurred with the furious movements. She couldn't keep up with them, couldn't bear to look away. She thought briefly of calling for help, but who could pull a werewolf and a vampire apart and not die in the process?

Raoul slashed his claws toward Danior's neck, but the vampire ducked, catching the blow in the shoulder. Retaliating in the blink of an eye, he came up with his own sharp nails, slashing into Raoul's neck.

Clara screamed as a bright stream of red gushed from the wound rent in his neck. Raoul staggered from the blow.

"No! Stop this, please!" she cried. Danior looked stricken, but she paid him no heed, her eyes only for Raoul. She jumped off the bed and rushed to him, pressing her hand to the wound.

Chest heaving, he bore her touch. His amber eyes were hooded and unreadable, his jaw muscles flexing.

She watched him steadily, unwilling to break contact. "I am yours, Raoul. I belong to you and no other." Slowly, the blood stopped flowing, the wound healing beneath her fingertips.

"The lady has made her choice, Danior," Raoul said gruffly, his eyes never leaving hers.

"So it appears," Danior said behind her.

"Perhaps another time, *mon ennemi*."

"I look forward to it...."

The heavy tension suffocating the room lifted as his words trailed off. The window burst open and cool air rushed inside, the curtains fluttering in the current.

"He's gone, *chere*. You can breathe again." He smiled and kissed her nose.

Clara laughed softly, the darkness that had clouded her mind gone. She looked down at herself and then at him. They were both a bloody mess, but she didn't care. All she wanted was to feel Raoul, his heartbeat, and know that he lived ... that he was real.

She pressed her palm to his heart, reveling in the pounding tempo.

Raoul bent his head and kissed her softly, bringing her to tingling awareness. He broke away rather than deepen it, and cupped her cheek in his palm.

"Will he come after us again?" She had to know and couldn't help asking.

"You made it plain you did not want him, so I think not. But did you mean what you said? Can you love a werewolf?"

She felt him tense imperceptibly, expecting her rejection. His vulnerability made a thrill race through her, singing in her veins. "I'm willing to give you my all," she said through a grin, touched.

Raoul smiled wolfishly. "Good. Let's take another shower," he said, winking.

The End

CARNAL KNOWLEDGE

Chapter One

"Hold it, bitch."

Kaeli Jackson stopped instantly at the mouth of the dark, narrow alley, a chill creeping up her spine at the mugger's high, nasal voice. The door to Inferno was only thirty odd feet away, but she'd never make the run in her heels. She hadn't gotten decked out in a year, and she'd break something if she tried it. The bass from the music pounded outside--there was no chance they'd hear her scream or anything else. She was on her own.

The mugger moved up behind her. "Damn you're phat, bitch." 'PH' phat he meant by the tone of his voice--he damn well wasn't commenting on the size of her ass. She didn't want to tell him phat went out a year ago. He pinched an ass cheek and she gritted her teeth, biding her time, hands clenching.

He snickered and released her. "Gimme your purse." He wrenched at it on her shoulder and she slipped it off, dropping it on the sidewalk from his grasp.

"Oh, I'm sorry. I didn't mean to," she babbled like a helpless female, glancing down and watching him stoop to grab the purse. His hand snaked out, and she lifted her foot to grind her heel into the back of his hand--the meaty part near the thumb. Blood welled instantly. His high pitched scream rattled her eardrums. She twisted, grinding him into the rough pavement, knocking him back on his ass with a shin kick she'd learned in KardioKick.

He sat back, clutching his hand to his chest, crimson rivulets streaming down his arm. Kaeli got her first look at her would-be attacker. *A damn punk ass kid.* Why were they always kids? Quick perusal of the pavement confirmed he didn't even have a weapon--stupid damn kid. Hell, even she packed in these neighborhoods, not that it had done her any good.

"What the hell are you doin' robbin' people when you ain't even got your pubes yet, brat?"

He glared at her. "For the hell of it, bitch."

Kaeli crossed her arms over her chest, narrowing her eyes. Should have known it by looking at his gear--baggy britches and tight, long sleeved shirt, a chain on his waist. He had skater extremist written all over him. Just like a damn extremist--it was getting to where they'd do just about anything for a rush. "Fair enough."

She bent and snatched his wallet off the chain. He didn't try to stop her--still nursing his wound. He'd live, that was sure.

"You can't rob me! That's not fair," he said in a whiny voice.

A sure sign of immaturity. "Insurance, brat. Now get out of here. You're damn lucky you wasn't brandishing or I'd sic the cops on your ass right now."

He continued glaring but scrambled to his feet and backed away until it was safe to run.

As he disappeared around the block, Kaeli sighed, wondering if it had been a wise move. She knew he was priming for prison, but she'd put enough fear in him maybe he wouldn't do anything else tonight. She'd make a call to the cops once she got inside and turn his wallet in--not that the cops would do anything more than spoil an already marvelous night.

As it was, she wouldn't be surprised if he was taken in and sued *her* for hurting him in the mugging--it was the American way, after all.

Kaeli had just turned back toward the club when clapping came from near the dark alley's entrance. She halted and tensed, expecting renewed attack. Maybe she had gone crazy....

"That was an entertaining show, petite," a deep, rumbling voice spoke from the shadows. Gooseflesh raced over her skin just listening to it.

"Who the hell are you?" She couldn't help being defensive. She'd just been attacked, after all. She put the kid's wallet into her purse, slipping her hand on the butt of her gun.

"You don' need a pea shooter for me."

She startled inside, tightened her hand on the butt. How the hell did he know that? Lucky guess was all. Had to be.

He chuckled and moved into the light. Kaeli's breath hitched, and if she hadn't been frozen in place, she'd surely have melted at the smoky look the stranger passed over her. Thought became chaotic, sluggish as she did a once over and went back for more.

Blond. Golden. Adonis. He looked like some bad ass metal band member--a lead bass guitarist. Long, wavy hair trailed down to his chest, muscles but not breadth hidden beneath a tight black T-shirt that tormented her. He had classical features: squared jaw, dimpled chin, straight nose, and smiling, full lips--but the combination tantalized when Grecian statues left her cold as the marble used to carve them. The man oozed bad boy like people expelled carbon dioxide--and he was definitely just as dangerous in too great a quantity.

Tribal tattoos twirled about his muscled arms, and painted on leather pants completed his ensemble. She tried to look away, but her eyes stayed rooted to his groin. Couldn't go any farther than that bulge, thumbs ... thumbs hooked in his pockets, framing his groin like a picture. It was one of those subtle moves all guys did but few could pull off because they didn't have the package. This one definitely had it goin' on.

He sauntered toward her, that cocky stride that couldn't help but garner any straight woman's attention. "Navarre Lyssandro."

Kaeli gaped at him. "Huh?" Once she'd seen him, her mind had blanked beyond the need to procreate--fast. NOW.

Someone that damn sexy was nothing but trouble.

Navarre chuckled, standing just inside her comfort zone, crowding her until she took a step back. He leaned against the lip of the alley, leisurely running his gaze down her body. She shivered, the tips of her breasts tingling with imagined contact.

"You asked who I was, I tell you. Navarre Lyssandro."

He had an accent. Damn his hide, he had an accent! French and Southern rolled into one tantalizing package that had her near salivating. She shouldn't lust after a stranger like this--it was completely foreign to her. Kaeli glared at him, unwilling to concede defeat to a damn Cajun. "What are you doing here?"

"Meetin' a friend, chere. You goin' tell me your name, pretty lady?"

Never in her life had anyone accused her of being a lady. "Kaeli Jackson."

"Kaeli," he said, savoring her name like choice wine. It sounded so much better on those lips.

She swallowed and offered her hand like an automaton. He shook it, his hand warm, callused ... lingering. She withdrew quickly, palm itching to know more of him than that brief contact allowed. She never drank, but tonight she needed something cold and hard to quench her libido.

Anger was good. It kept her head vaguely clear of confusing thoughts when she concentrated on being outraged. "Why the hell didn't you help me when that kid attacked? Or call someone?"

He cocked one dark, golden brow. "I walked up after you'd already taken him down, petite. After that, I jus' enjoyed the show."

"Excuses, excuses." Kaeli grunted. "Wouldn't want to hurt that purty hide of yours, eh?" And it was a purty one, but not girlish in any way. She couldn't stop looking at him. *Trouble. Keep telling yourself that. Trouble.*

"I couldn't chance you gettin' hurt if I came up and distracted you."

"Very heroic of you." She was being an asshole but couldn't help herself. Hell, the guy said he hadn't been there from the start. She was always like this around hunks. No damn wonder she hadn't been laid in forty forevers. Prickly bitches just didn't seem to hold much appeal for men for some unfathomable reason. It spoiled her mood just thinking about it.

"Not all women want to be rescued, petite. Besides, I didn' know but what you weren't some militant feminist. I don' like bein' chewed on," he paused, grinning, then continued, "not like that...."

She couldn't help smiling at his innuendo. She definitely had a craving for big meat right now. And she couldn't blame his reasoning for holding back when he'd come. Where she was from, men had been blasted for one thing or another until they'd lost all shred of their manhood. They'd been bitched at so much you couldn't even expect to have a guy come up to you anymore and ask for a dance or buy you a drink. It was hell being a woman these days.

"You forgive me, petite? I'll be your shinin' knight next time you're attacked."

"Sure." She shrugged. She could take care of herself--she was used to it.

As snippety as she'd been, he still offered to see her into the club. Once they passed through the blackened glass doors at the entrance and the music blasted their eardrums, he left her to go to his friend.

It was a shame really. She'd always liked those charming bad boys. He was almost enough to make her forget how the night started. After going to the bar and phoning in a tip and leaving the kid's wallet, she ordered a white russian and set out to find her friends. She spotted them almost immediately, getting off the dance floor.

Shawnda and Mina waved, and she followed them back to their table. It was a little quieter in the corner away from the dance floor. Only minimal yelling was needed to communicate.

"Girl, what took you so long?" Shawnda asked after hugging Kaeli and sitting down.

"Ya, I'd done give up on you coming. Called the hotel five times and got no answer," Mina said, settling into her chair.

"Sorry. I got mugged just outside the club." Kaeli took a sip of her drink and grimaced at the alcohol stealing her breath.

"Omigod!" they screamed in unison and passed hugs all around. "What happened? Are you okay?"

Kaeli smiled at them. "I'm all right. Just some damn kid looking for kicks. That ain't the half of it though. Some guy came up right after."

Mina perked up, instantly recognizing Kaeli's interest. "Oh?"

"Spill it, Kaeli. Was he hot?"

"Take a look for yourself, Shawnda. He's right over there." Kaeli hooked a thumb over her shoulder toward the opposite corner of the bar where she'd seen him sit down.

They both stood and gaped. "Jesus! Kaeli, which one is it? They're both gorgeous," Shawnda said.

"The blond one. His name's Navarre."

"On a first name basis now?" Mina asked as she sat. "Why didn't you jump him when you had the chance? We came here tonight for dick, and girl, you need it worst of all."

Kaeli nodded. They'd all been single so long, she was sure she was growing cobwebs.

"I'd eat him up. You don't pass up a good thing like that when it comes along." Shawnda finished off her fuzzy navel and leaned back in her chair, narrowing her dark eyes at Kaeli in mock severity.

Kaeli shrugged. "He's not my type." At their guffaws, she grinned. "All right. Lies, all lies. I want him so bad I can practically taste it." Glancing over her shoulder through the smoky interior, she saw him stand up and walk toward the exit.

"Damn. He's leaving."

"Well, go after him," Shawnda prodded.

Torn, Kaeli sat there. She talked big, but when it came down to doing the deed with a virtual stranger--no matter how hot--she was all talk and no action.

Shawnda and Mina both stood and grabbed her arms, hauling her up.

"Get the lead out of your ass and go after him before he gets away," Mina said.

They were right. You only live once. "Just bitch slap me for the coward I am if I come home early tonight." She pulled free. "You sure y'all will be all right?"

"Hell, we were having a great time until that guy bit Mina."

"Huh?" What the hell kind of city was this? Muggings, guys biting girls in clubs--wait, that sounded like home. Mental forehead smack.

"On the dance floor. We were grinding and then he just up and bit me. I smacked him good. You know I don't allow that without dinner first." Mina grinned. "Now, quit stalling and go."

Kaeli nodded and hugged her friends, then headed to the front entrance. She knew he'd come through the alley. There was a good chance he'd leave that way too. Liquid courage surging through her veins and ears ringing, she walked as fast as she dared. It was as she neared the corner of the building that the sounds of a fight finally registered in her brain.

Someone was getting the shit kicked out of them. She rounded the edge and froze, heart suddenly pounding. "Jesus H. Christ!"

Chapter Two

Navarre thought Raoul was a fool for risking his heart and his life for a human mate, be they ever so tempting. A fling perhaps, but he would not chain himself to a woman who could never be his equal. As arrogant as that made him sound, he couldn't help the thought. They were too fragile. And to risk war for a woman not their kind was suicide ... and worse. Not that the shaky truce between vamps and Lycans held when pressed. Each stayed on their own ground. Crossing over almost always meant a fight once the vamps had risen from their slumber.

He'd risked attack coming here to talk his friend out of this foolishness, but Raoul would not be swayed. He'd chosen the course of his life and Navarre could not stop him.

Of course, he would not have met the brazen Kaeli had he not come.... Navarre put the tempting vixen out of his mind. He could not chance embroiling more humans in their affairs--it always ended in their death.

To think of her caramel skin bleached and lifeless, the sassy glint of her hazel eyes snuffed, fouled his mood.

Navarre took a deep, cleansing breath as he exited the club. His ears rang with residual beat, and he shook his head as though that would clear it. The stench of sweat, smoke, and liquor clung to his nostrils, near overpowering him but lessening in potency as he walked past the club's facade. Rounding the block, he strode into the alley, ears perked for danger. He'd parked his car on the other end of the building as a precaution from thieves and alerting vamps of his presence. Not that it mattered this early.

He slowed his steps as a hush settled. The wind whistling through the confines halted in anticipation, as though sucked into greedy lungs.

He wasn't alone.

Navarre crouched, muscles tensing, scanning the edges of the roof for attack. The trace scent of blood drifted to him-- a scent of vampire--permeating the air just as the vampires struck.

A dark shape whipped past him, seemingly from nowhere, though he knew it a trick of the mind--*flashing*. Navarre extended his claws in an instant, slashing as it rammed his side just as a second slammed into him from behind.

Navarre whirled with the hit, striking flesh, felt the stinging rain of blood shower upon him--his own and that stolen from an innocent victim.

The vamps stopped in the alley, and his gaze shifted back and forth, keeping them in sight, his muscles fluid, ready to attack, yet he waited to see what they would do next. Long had it been since he'd killed a vamp, and he would not do so now if he could help it. If they continued their attack, however....

"It's hardly fair two of you attackin', *mon ennemi*," he said, leveling his stare on the dark one but continually glancing at the heavy blond.

The dark haired one glared at Navarre, hissing as he clutched his side, stemming the flow of blood. "You don't belong here," he spat out. He examined the shredded jacket and slowly closing wound on his side. "I just finished feeding. You'll pay for the meal you stole."

Navarre grinned, lengthening his claws to daggers. "Gladly."

They rushed him as one, right and left. Navarre spun from the slash of their nails and teeth. He couldn't allow them to bite and inject their venom. Running along the alley, one vamp breathing down his neck, he ran at one of the walls and jumped, hitting high and bounding off it. Chunks of brick shattered under the grip of his hands and the strike of his feet, scattering like pebbles. He slammed into the thick middle of the blond vampire just as he launched at Navarre.

Navarre straightened his arms like swords, tearing into the vamp's soft belly. Hot blood gushed over his arms, showering the pavement in a widening slick. The blond screamed and hit the pavement with a meaty thud, slipping in his meal as he struggled to hold his belly together.

Navarre shook the tainted blood from his hands, landing on his feet, staggering as his boot heels struck scattered brick, rolling beneath him.

The lead vamp grabbed him from behind as he recovered his balance. Navarre twisted in the vamp's grip, baring his neck as he punched his right hand back across his chest, driving into the vamp's side, reaching for the heart. The grip tightened. He heard the pop of his shoulder as it slipped out of the socket. Navarre continued driving his claws into the dark haired vamp, faster and faster, but his hold didn't loosen. He growled in wolfen fury, barely noticing the pain as the fangs sank in and savaged his throat and shoulder, shredding his skin.

The vampire's poison flooded his veins, paralyzing him. His arms dropped as the paralytic drug consumed him. The blood pulled from his body, sucked away like the remains of a thick shake. Sluggishly, his wolfen powers worked to heal him, but he could do nothing so long as the vampire fed off him.

Navarre sank to his knees, barely feeling the pavement dig into his flesh through the thin leather pants.

Heat singed his hair with a whining zip--a bullet buzzed by his head, slamming into the vamp holding him in thrall. He was released abruptly, and then he heard the scream of a woman echoing through the alley.

* * * *

Some *thing* was eating Navarre. Kaeli looked at it in horror, the blood frozen in her veins, her stomach convulsing in an agonizing clench to empty its contents. Even at this distance, she could see wildness in its--the man's eyes. Thick red coated his blinding white skin, long ivory nails dug into Navarre's bronze flesh. His mouth latched on to Navarre's neck, shaking him like a dog with a chunk of meat.

Kaeli choked back the sickness threatening to overwhelm her and pulled her gun out of her purse without conscious volition. She aimed and pulled the trigger, feeling sluggish, as though she moved under water.

The gun popped with a small crack like a roman candle, kicked back, waking her from her stupor. She blinked rapidly at the muzzle flash, watching with morbid fascination as the man thing fell back from Navarre, dazed. A hole blossomed on his cheek like a crimson rose. Navarre dropped to his hands, freed at last, shaking his head in confusion, his blond hair matted with blood.

The world returned to full throttle in an instant.

"Get the fuck away him!" she screamed. The man looked up at her, a killing look wiping the stunned surprise off his face. With amazing speed, he gained his feet and rushed her.

He should be dead. Not running. Not attacking.

Kaeli didn't hesitate, fired straight into him. The gun popped rapidly, smoke filling the air. He didn't pause a second, as if the slugs were no more a nuisance than mosquitoes pelting his hide.

He reached her and she fired again, heard the tell-tale click of the empty chamber. *How could she have emptied the gun so fast?* He snatched her gun from her steely grip with breathtaking speed, slashed at her. She dropped to the ground and his nails glanced through her braids trailing in the air as she ducked. He ran past, and she whirled in her crouch, kicking her leg out, saw he was gone--as though he'd flown away or something.

Kaeli straightened and shuddered, then turned and ran to Navarre as he gained his feet. He moved his arm, and it crunched with a sickening pop.

He gave her a wry smile then slumped against her. "My thanks," he murmured against her shoulder.

She wrapped her arms around him for support. He was wet, sticky. His shirt squished as she hugged him.

"Oh, Jesus!" she gasped. His back was soaked through with blood she found as she pulled her hands away, the thick liquid black in the shadows. She swallowed against the nausea, felt around, but she couldn't find a wound, no bullet hole telling she'd missed his attacker and hit him. There was only a small tear on his neck. She wiped at the blood with her palm, trying to see the wound, but after a few seconds, even that didn't seem so bad. But the head area bled the worst. That could account for his drenching, and not all of it could be from him.

He could barely stand though and moved like he was drunk, his limbs too heavy to lift.

"We have to get you to a hospital. I'll get someone to call inside." No one could have heard that commotion over the music pounding inside--her suspicions confirmed when no one rushed outside to see what had happened. She had to go back and get help. She didn't even consider calling the cops because, frankly, she despised them. And they'd probably haul *her* in for having had a gun.

"No," he said and pushed off her, his strength returning. "No hospital. I'm goin' home."

"You stupid son of a bitch. You're hurt. Bad. You're going if I have to carry you myself."

He smiled, and some of the color seemed to come back to his face, though it was hard to tell with the shadows. Moonlight and security lights could only reveal so much.

He started walking down the alley.

"You're gonna fight me, huh?" she asked, jogging up beside him, glancing back to make sure the thug wasn't sneaking up behind them.

He spared her a backward glance over his shoulder. "But of course, petite. Don' worry, they're both gone."

Two? Two had jumped him? She hadn't even seen the other. It was no damned wonder he was hurt. She didn't even want to think about how she'd emptied her clip into one of the bastards. She wasn't ready to question that just yet. Navarre knew something, and as soon as she made sure he was all right, she'd get the truth from him. Besides which, that *thing* had stolen her gun and she wanted it back.

"You got a car?" she asked, feeling doubtful. She didn't relish the idea of walking him home, in the dark, without protection. Plus, she was wearing heels and they weren't conducive to long nature walks.

"Jus' ahead."

"Good. I'll take you home since you're so damn hard headed."

She ducked under his arm, ignoring the fluttering in her stomach at being pressed against him. He was hurt. You can't lust after a half dead man. Hell, she was as bad as a damn dog panting after a bitch in heat.

"You know it's illegal to bring a gun into a bar, chere?" It was more of a riling statement than any question.

"Huh," she grunted. "Saved your ass, didn't it?"

"I 'spose it did."

She grinned and they continued on until a sleek silver viper appeared in sight, parked under a flickering light pole. Without a touch of concern, he tiredly fished the keys out of his pocket and handed them to her.

She accepted them and helped him to the passenger side, disengaging the alarm before opening the door. He dropped into the low ride, and she watched in dismay as he bloodied the black leather interior. It was his car, his blood ... maybe--what did she care?

Kaeli sunk into the driver's seat and adjusted it for her height, giving him a once over before she fixed the mirrors to her line of sight. Unfortunately, she had no clue how to get to the hospital, or she would have abducted him and gone straight there. Instead, she followed his directions to the old industrial district. The traffic was light and it didn't take long to reach their destination. She'd worry about getting to the hotel when that time rolled around.

He slept as she drove to his address and pulled along the end of the block. He woke as she slowed the car and directed her to the entrance. A warehouse rigged with motion sensitive cameras attached to a keypad allowed them inside, and she parked the car in the cavernous sub-level. She got out and shut the door, jumping as the slamming thud echoed in the large interior. She was breathing heavily and sweating by the time she walked him to the elevator, knowing she'd never make it up the stairwell with him slumped over her shoulders.

The elevator groaned as it took them up, and she supported him as it made its shaky way to the second floor. She couldn't help but notice how hot he was, compared to her own body temperature. Could fever be setting in so quickly? They reached the level, and she halted the elevator, freeing herself from him to open the heavy gate.

"Welcome to my humble home," he said, nudging her inside.

Her eyes widened as she took in his place. "Humble my ass."

He grinned in response.

It was big enough she could yell and get back an echo. Raw iron beams extended overhead, light flooding down from huge fluorescent fixtures, revealing a sumptuous living space that encompassed the entire second floor. Blackened glass closed in the walls on all sides.

She couldn't understand why someone would want to live with so much space. It creeped her out having a thirty foot ceiling, and she couldn't help but keep looking up at the dark space above the lighted beams. It made her feel naked, watched. Anything could be hiding up there. No way could she live here. Not that he was asking.

"All right. Let's get your pale ass into the bathroom so I can get you cleaned up. I want to make sure this isn't all your blood."

"I had no idea you cared."

Kaeli grunted and followed him to the bathroom. He seemed better now, could walk on his own, but she had a suspicion he was acting more hurt than he was just so she'd stay near. There was some hint in his body language--something she couldn't quite put her finger on. Or maybe she just had a nasty suspicious mind.

The bathroom stood near one wall, and beyond she could see the edge of a bed. The area had been closed in, almost like a wrought iron arbor hung over the space, keeping the ceiling to a normal low. Inside, the bathroom was as obscenely large as the rest of his place. A whirlpool took up one wall--large enough for a small orgy. A shower stood off center, encased with etched glass doors sparkling clean. Everything gleamed with polish and care. A beveled mirror took up the space above a dual, marble sink, and recessed lighting edged the ceiling with a mellow glow.

Men, they always denied loving the bathroom. She could tell this one spent a lot of time in here primping. He had to with all that gorgeous blond hair.

"Who gets the job of cleaning this place?"

"I do."

She was impressed and it showed. The man cleaned. Most bachelors lived like they were in frat houses. His mama raised him right. "All righty. Take off your shirt."

"So soon? We hardly know each other."

Ha! As if any straight man wouldn't jump at the chance. "Boy, there ain't a shy bone in your body and you know it. You've been plastered to me almost the whole way here."

He dropped down on the lip of the whirlpool, smiling slightly, his feet propped on the marble steps. She narrowed her eyes. "You ain't acting like you're much hurt." That wasn't entirely true. She could see his mouth tighten as he pulled his shirt off.

His chest and neck were smeared with dried blood, obscuring her appreciation for his beautiful muscles. At least there wasn't any gushing like a fountain. She wasn't so sure she could handle that right now.

Kaeli picked up a washcloth from the sink, wet it, and began wiping the grime from his neck and chest. Beyond a red welt, she couldn't find any sign of a wound. Nothing on his back or chest either. Only old scars. She ran her fingers along his scalp, feeling for lacerations. Nothing.

The hairs rose on the back of her neck. There'd been a tear on the crook of his neck before. She'd seen it with her own eyes. Felt it. She hadn't imagined what had happened--no one had spiked her drink. She was as lucid now and then as she ever had been in her life.

Kaeli stepped away from him, noticed a slight shiver of his skin. He watched her steadily, his eyes glittered with interest and something more ... something primal.

"What the hell is going on here?" she demanded.

"What do *you* think is goin' on?"

"Don't start playin'. I saw what happened. I saved your ass. You owe me an explanation. Who was that guy?"

He sighed and bent, removing his boots and dropping them to the floor. He peeled the black socks off his feet, tossing them at a hamper.

"Vampires," he said after letting her stew in silence several minutes.

He was joking. Had to be. This whole damn night was one big joke. Only he wasn't laughing, and the dead serious expression on his face confirmed he was nuts--or telling the truth. And she was just crazy enough to almost believe him. "You mean like the Goth kind, right?"

He smiled as though humoring her. "I mean the undead, humans-are-food kind."

Kaeli leaned against the wall for support. "Why'd they attack you?"

The look he slanted her chilled her bones. She could almost forget he was "injured."

"I'm a werewolf," he said with a little growl that danced along her nerves.

Jesus! She had to get out of here. Her feet wouldn't budge. "That doesn't explain much."

"My friend angered the vamps by taking a human mate marked and favored by one of their own. He's been at it for days. I only went to Inferno to stop him, for all the good it did."

Mates. It sounded so ... barbaric. "Don't y'all have your own? Mates?"

If this was a joke, she didn't like it. Her humor tended toward the dry and sarcastic. Practical jokes were beyond her.

"Lycan women are rare," he said, his eyes darkening.

That didn't make any sense. Who'd have the puppies? She almost laughed, but she didn't think he'd appreciate it. "Why don't you make some? In the movies, all it takes is a bite or scratch--"

"No. Human women almost never survive the transformation."

"Downer. So you take human mates?" she said, not really asking. The whole idea was preposterous.

"Some of us do ... to ease the loneliness." His jaw hardened, and his hands clenched into fists.

"I get the feeling you don't agree. What about me? Would I make a good mate?"

He relaxed fractionally. "Ah, chere, you could tempt a priest to forsake his vows." His gaze lingered on her breasts and the wide curve of her hips.

Unfamiliar heat crept up her neck. She was suddenly very aware of how close she stood to him, how much bigger he was than her--injured or not. It wasn't a fear of being hurt that had her awareness jumping, but a fear of having too good a time and getting addicted. It wasn't like men were beating down her door or anything. She pushed off the wall with her shoulder. "I have to go. You make a good argument, but you're nuts."

"No one ever believes until it bites them on the ass." He stood, matching her stance.

"Are you coming on to me, or are you just teasing?" She narrowed her eyes. Maybe there was some truth here, unless she'd completely mistook what she'd seen. It wouldn't be the first time some acid head had run through a barrage of .22 slugs.

He grinned as if to say he was, then unbuttoned the fly of his pants. "Do you like being chewed on, petite?"

Kaeli swallowed, propping a hand on her hip to look relaxed. She glanced down at his relatively clean chest and the sunburst tattoo. Hadn't she promised herself a good time on this trip? Gorgeous, crazy men deserved nookie too. She watched the black leather fly fold open with eager eyes. "Depends on what you're chewin' on."

He slumped against the door, halting the unveiling of his girl toy. *Dammit*. "Something the matter?"

He rubbed his eyes tiredly, pushing his long hair out of his face. "Venom. From the vamp. They release it when feeding or killing. I should be dead now, but it's hard even for Lycans to come down from an attack. If I get into the shower, I'll feel better." He looked at her, an elusive quality in his gaze. "Care to help?"

"Ha ha ha." Did he have to keep reminding her about that? She'd just started getting into the fantasy ... now he'd spoiled it. Like it or not, he genuinely seemed like *something* was wrong with him, and she couldn't very well jump his bones now. She doubted she'd have a very good time if he was too tired to even stand.

"Sure, I'll help," she grumbled, slipping her feet out of her shoes and opening the glass door. There was enough room inside she could run the water and not get wet, and still have him behind her without touching. Steam clouded the glass almost instantly, and she could see the blurred image of him removing his pants. She quickly glanced away as the door opened and he stepped inside, turning her mind to getting the water temperature and jet stream force right so she could leave.

The door clicked shut and a weight fell against her back, pushing her into the hot, streaming water. "Shit!" she yelped, blowing the water out of her eyes and turning as the weight slipped down her back and legs.

Navarre sprawled on the shower floor, arms thrown out carelessly, faint red water swirling around him as it washed the residual blood away. He was also buck ass naked, and his cock stood nearly straight up, hard as a rock. Kaeli couldn't decide which emotion reigned: humor, horror, or concern.

She decided irritation was her friend.

She'd already discovered he was quite the story teller ... might he also be an actor? She was tempted to leave him there to drown. "Asshole. You got me wet. Get up. The game's over." Kaeli nudged him with her toe. He didn't budge.

Steam billowed, making the remaining dry patches of her clothes cling to her body. She picked at her shirt uncomfortably, irritated, looking down at him. He was playing a trick, she knew. Everyone always played tricks on her. "Navarre! Get up!"

No response. She nudged him again, but he didn't even flinch. Panic made her heart race. Maybe he'd overdosed on viagra or something.

"Fuck!" She *knew* she should've taken him to a hospital. Kaeli dropped to the floor, cupping his face, splashing water on him. "Fuck, shit, hell, damn! Don't be dead. Fuck!"

She gave him a shake, and his eyes opened just as he wrapped his arms around her, hauling her close. Kaeli's knees slipped out from under her and she fell against his chest with a grunt and enough force to stun her for several long seconds.

His lips curled into a slow smile, and his amber eyes crinkled with amusement.

"You bastard! You damn faker--you tricked me!" She planted her palms against his chest and pushed away, to no avail. His grip tightened, flattening her breasts against him. She could feel every detail of his body through her saturated silk blouse, the hardness of his chest and belly. And she remembered with horror that he was naked--and erect as a damn tower.

She squirmed, felt her skirt ride up her splayed thighs, exposing her to the rough hair of his legs.

"You got a dirty mouth, ma petite," he murmured, smelling her skin, his lids bedroom heavy with lust.

"You think you got something to clean it out?" Jesus, he hadn't looked so big when she was standing above him-- something about perspective.... His cock seemed to swell against her hip. She felt weak just thinking about him burying it inside her.

"Maybe. What would it take?" he asked. His husky voice stroked her senses, and she had a hard time concentrating just listening to his drawling, mesmerizing accent. The man's voice was enough to wipe out coherent thought, igniting a proliferation of carnal images.

With an effort, she looked away from his mouth and blinked back visions of him dragging it over her skin. He was close enough his breath tickled her lips, and she could smell the faint scent of scotch on his breath. "Damn." She was dying to be kissed. *Jesus*!

He frowned, arched a brow. "Petite," he said in a warning voice.

"What you have in mind ain't gonna clean me out," she said, frowning back at him. Though she was certain she'd feel like she'd been reamed if he poked it into any of her orifices. Her legs might not close for days.

"I like a challenge. We can always ... try. There's no harm in that, is there?"

He trailed a hand down her back, massaging the base of her spine, just above her ass. She desperately wished she could ignore how good it felt. "I thought you were hurt."

Hell or high water--nothing short of cutting it off could stop a man from a piece of ass if it was willing.

"I got better."

"Right. Werewolf."

"I jus' playin', petite."

Playing? About everything, or being hurt? She didn't want to ask.

"I like how dirty your mouth is." He slipped a hand around the back of her neck, pulling her down.

Kaeli turned her face at the last moment, not sure why she was suddenly afraid. He released her at her gentle push, and she backed off onto her knees, looking down at him, breathing heavily like she'd run a race.

Something slipped behind his eyes, making them darken. The look he gave her scorched. "You should go. While you still can...."

CHAPTER THREE

Kaeli snatched a shirt that lay carelessly on the floor of his bedroom and slipped off her own soaked blouse before putting his on. She'd return it another time. His scent enveloped her, stifling rational thought, and she could barely punch out the numbers on the phone to the taxi company she found in the phone book.

Navarre didn't leave the bathroom, for which she was thankful. There'd been something inherently dangerous in his eyes that had scared her, and in that moment, the facade of the laid back Cajun had stripped away, revealing a wildness that thrilled and terrified her all at once.

She ran out of there as fast as she could, braving the empty street and the whipping wind rather than stay. Goosebumps spread over her chilled, damp skin, and she scarcely noticed when the taxi arrived and took off with her mumbled directions to the hotel. His scent engulfed her, faint as it was, reminding her of how close she'd come to ...

to what? To having sex with a stranger? With a lunatic? Whatever else he was, he wasn't crazy. But he was dangerous. And his looks with that provided a lethal combination for her sense of preservation.

It wasn't until she was safe in her room that she realized she'd even gone through the motions of getting back. She'd moved like an automaton. Shock. That was what affected her. It was no damn wonder. She'd gone through two attacks tonight. It was almost like being home.

The suite was empty, proving it wasn't as late as she thought it was. Which meant her girlfriends may or may not be coming in tonight. Which meant she had only her chaotic thoughts and the nagging ache between her legs to keep her company.

Fat lot of good it did her to get out.

* * * *

Navarre turned the hot water off, his skin jumping in shock as the cold water pummeled his hide like hail, barely stemming the flow of blood to his cock.

He could practically taste her fragile scent, a musky mix of arousal and Obsession, and his fingertips throbbed with the sense of her skin and the supple strength of her muscles.

He'd been hard ever since he'd seen her in action at the mugging, and it had only worsened when she'd pressed against him in the alley offering help. He'd not been nearly so injured as he'd led her to believe, and despite his better judgment, he'd allowed her to see him home. Strong women had always been a weakness for him.

He should have known it wouldn't be enough. It was never enough to only touch--it was pure torture that had him salivating to lick her all over. He wanted to ram into her, spew his cum across her naked body and mark her with his scent so that no other man would dare touch her. Could she handle being fucked by a Lycan? He'd like to think so, but he couldn't chance it. His control was too shaky around her, and he could hurt her irreparably if he tried. What a damn fool he was.

His possessiveness toward her, the need to mark, appalled him, but not enough to deny his feelings. It had taken every ounce of his control to release her and allow her to go. He knew she wanted him. That in itself would be his downfall. Never in his life had a human woman blind-sided him this way. He could not even remember a time when his emotions ran to the coolness of a human male, so long ago had it been since he'd turned wolfen.

Promises to stay away from humans seemed like so much ash in his mouth. Despite her hard ass attitude, he sensed her vulnerability and knew he'd frightened her when his wolf flashed in his eyes. He doubted she realized what she'd beheld, for he knew she hadn't believed him about the vampires.

All the more reason to stay away from her. Humans could not comprehend that their presence on the top of the food chain was precarious at best, held aloft only by their numbers. And that scale could tip at any time.

Eventually the cold water washed away the blood and cooled his head--both of them.

Navarre damned the creature that had made him this monster. For he could never have what he most wanted and never realized could be snatched away ... the chance to love and be loved. There would be no mate for him, human or Lycan.

* * * *

Shawnda and Mina didn't come back that night, but they were considerate enough to call and say they were spending the next few days up at Lake Ponchatrain with some hot guys they barely knew and had plans to behave as immorally as possible. Kaeli didn't like it, but it wasn't like she could stop them. They were big girls, and if anything, Shawnda was meaner and tougher than she was.

Kaeli spent the morning lounging in bed, fingering his shirt--which she still wore--and enjoying the smell of him on her skin. It was almost like he'd rubbed on her and left his mark, even though he technically hadn't loaned her the shirt.

Despite all her inner warnings, she wanted to see him again. She couldn't let it rest. It was like an itch in the middle of her back that she couldn't quite reach, and it was driving her crazy not knowing what it'd be like to fuck him.

She could admit it. He'd filled her dreams last night, and she'd woken up wet with arousal. It was a natural, earthy response to a man she was attracted to--no matter how off-balance he was.

Kaeli ordered room service and flipped through the channels on TV, trying to take her mind off him. Finally she flipped to a music channel, but a metal band from the 80s was on, and all those tight leather pants brought her immediately back to Navarre. She turned off the TV, frustrated.

She needed to return his shirt anyway. And while she was there ... she'd just see what would happen. She didn't think it would take too much effort on her part to drive him over the edge. Afterwards, she could analyze her disgraceful behavior all she wanted--right now, she aimed to have some fun. Hell or high water.

She chuckled and spiffed up, shampooing her black braids and making sure none had raveled loose. She took her time shaving her legs and under her arms, even her bikini area ... not that she should expect anything to happen, but it never hurt to be prepared.

Getting out of the shower, Kaeli dried off and buffed her skin and nails, and smoothed unscented lotion on her skin until it was velvet soft and glowing with health. She left the bathroom and pulled her underthings out of her suitcase, sitting on the bed as she rolled her hose up her legs. She stood and slipped a garter belt on and, with great difficulty, snapped the garters on her thigh high hose. Her legs were short enough the hose rode up nearly to her crotch, but she thought it was still a sexy look.

The bra she fastened pushed her breasts together, creating an illusion of deep cleavage--the small breasted girl's best friend. Kaeli donned a skin tight, black mini dress that barely covered the lacy edge her hose and the tops of her breasts. She couldn't take a deep breath, but she was as sexed as she could get.

She picked up his discarded shirt, folding it as she headed out. It was still early enough in the year that the days were short. The sun was fast dwindling as night approached, and she wondered how she could have spent so much time getting prepared, but then, she'd had a lot to do.

The doorman hailed a taxi for her and she directed the driver to Navarre's. Within half an hour she was there, standing at a blank metal door and an intercom unit. A camera watched with its unblinking, glass eye. She'd left the cab driver a big tip to wait until she was inside.

Kaeli pushed her thumb on the buzzer, then awaited a response.

"Why you back, chere?" his voice came through the speaker, sounding distant and slightly irritated.

"I just came by to drop your shirt off." She waved it in front of the camera as proof.

"Keep it. Or leave it outside. I don' care."

It was a button down Dolce and Gabbana stretch silk shirt--easily six large ones. He'd want it back, no matter how much damn money he had, and the thrifty shrew in her couldn't stand to just leave it on the street for anyone to pick up. "Let me in, Navarre! I'm not leaving until I return this to you."

There was a long pause, and then the door buzzed. Kaeli turned the handle and pushed the door open, and she waved the taxi on. She could always call another one ... later.

Her confidence started dwindling as she walked through the lower floor to the elevator, listening to the hollow echo of her heels on the concrete. By the time she reached the elevator, she'd determined she'd only return his shirt and go back to the hotel. Maybe if she kept this up, at this rate in a week or two she'd be ready to make the first move. She never had a problem unless she was attracted to a man, and then her tongue got tied and her belly clenched with nervousness.

He was out of her league anyway. She didn't know why she thought he'd be interested in her. Her ass was too big, and her breasts were too small. And she was a few inches shy of average height--short.

Hell. It was no damned wonder she hadn't had a man in so long, the way she down-rated herself. Kaeli squared her shoulders on the ride, determined to show him what a good thing he was missing out on.

His apartment came into view, and Navarre faced the elevator as it groaned to a halt. He was half naked, and all thought of confidence and nobility and whatever other crap she'd fed herself incinerated as her libido kicked into overdrive. Her throat went dry looking at the bulge of his muscles, the flex of them as he bent and lifted the gate and stepped inside. The elevator shifted slightly with his weight, balancing. Any other time she might be unnerved. Now, her mind was blank.

Kaeli dumbly held the shirt out to him, not really aware of what she was doing.

The irritated look he'd assumed vanished as his gaze stroked slowly down her body and back up to her face. All that time she'd spent preparing suddenly seemed worth it. The smoldering eyes that met hers burned away the last of her reservations in a flash of heat.

He was upon her in an instant. His hard male body crushed hers against the elevator wall, his fingers dug into her hair. She moaned at the near bruising pressure, the feel of her body melding to his.

"Damn you," he mumbled, a harsh breath against her lips. He kissed her, unyielding, forcing her open to his invasion. His tongue thrust inside her mouth, and hot need welled instantly between her legs. She could taste the anger in his kiss, reveled in the rough thorough slide of his tongue as he explored the moist crevice of her mouth. Her scalp burned under the grip that tilted her face up as he kissed her greedily.

She felt wet arousal trickle down her thighs, and then he ground his erection into her apex, sparking a primal reaction deep in her core.

Kaeli dug her nails into his biceps as he thrust against her, her hem riding up her thighs until only a thin scrap of panties and his own jeans kept him from ramming inside her. Her clit felt like it would explode under his pleasurable abrasion. She closed her legs around him convulsively, moaning into his mouth.

With one hand, he peeled back the neckline of her dress, exposing a wanting nipple from the cage of her bra. He broke from her mouth, breathing heavily as he cupped her breast and flicked a thumb across her nipple. It hardened beneath his callused pad, and piercing ecstasy lanced her breast. He made a rough noise of excitement, deep in his chest, scored her throat with his teeth as he bent and took her nipple into his mouth.

He cupped her ass cheeks, kneading them, grinding her into his cock as he tugged her nipple with his lips. A strangled moan tore from her throat. So long ... it had been so long since any man had *wanted* to touch her this way. She raked her nails up the taut line of his shoulders, holding him closer. He sucked her flesh until the bud was harder than she ever thought possible, and then dragged the covering fabric away from her other breast with his teeth.

Kaeli lifted her body from the wall with a moan, arching her back as he suckled her breast, tightening the inner cord that pulled at the nerves of her pussy. He shuddered, breaking from her nipple to cover her chest with small, sucking kisses, traveling up her throat. He scored the fine tendon of her shoulder and neck, nipping her earlobe. His teeth were exquisitely sharp, his lips and tongue like brands. Her blood raged, making her dizzy and mindless with need.

"Please," she begged, unable to stand this torment any more. Her legs felt like they would give out at any moment, and only the press of his body kept her from falling.

He freed one cheek of her ass, pushing back from her enough to free his cock from its confinement.

With one tug, he ripped her panties away, stinging her hips, but she didn't care. All she cared about was getting him inside her to soothe the savage ache. He grabbed her ass roughly, his fingers digging into her muscles, hauling her legs wide apart as he lifted her against the wall, shoving her towards the corner.

Cool air tickled the thin line of hair on her pussy, brisk on her saturated labia and the tops of her thighs. The musky scent of her arousal drifted to her nostrils, spurring her desire. He buried his face against her neck, breathing deeply. He halted suddenly--his muscles jumped. Kaeli squirmed, wondering at the interruption. Navarre made an anguished sound deep in his throat, muffled against her shoulder, his arms shaking as though he waged war himself.

"What is it? What are you doing?" she breathed hoarsely, tightening her legs around his hips, needing him so badly.

"Making ... a ... mistake."

He jerked as a shudder ran through him, and his cock pressed against her pussy, so close to where she wanted it. Kaeli wiggled, trying to raise herself so he could impale her, biting her lip with the pain of need.

"Oh god. Oh god ... oh god. Don't move, petite," he ground out, shaking hard, panting with the effort. His breath came harsh and fast against her neck, fanning the flames that threatened to burn her alive.

Her pussy throbbed with his teasing nearness. She groaned in frustration, arching against him.

He growled suddenly, sinking his teeth into her neck as he ground against her swollen lips, sliding through her juices past her clit. Pleasure sliced through her, her throat closed on a soft sound of excitement, whimpering as he drove up past that bright center of exquisite torture.

He sucked in a sharp breath, chest heaving, fingers bruising her ass as he pulled back and thrust again. He rocked his hips, stroking the hard underside of his cock against her clit, building her toward release with excruciating slowness.

"I want you inside me," she gasped, digging her nails into his back, urging him to take her.

He shook his head against her, breathing raggedly, faster and faster. "No ... god ... no ... oh Jesus...." He kept repeating it again and again, driving against her, harder and harder, moving in a rough frantic motion.

He drew little twitches from her, sliding in her wetness, not giving enough ... too much. Kaeli panted, her heart racing in her chest, climbing to that high that was so addictive, fighting for release. His scent engulfed her, his breath, his sweat dampened hair. Kaeli tightened her thighs around him, rolling her body with his, getting so close. And then the orgasm burst upon her with a shocking suddenness. Ecstasy rolled over her like a tidal wave, obliterating everything but the sweet agony traveling through her limbs.

Kaeli cried out, feeling as though her entire body whirled apart. His breathing came faster, and he convulsed against her like he was dying, jerking his hips in a maddening rhythm that kept the orgasm flooding her. He made a hoarse, anguished cry as he shuddered, and a burst of hot liquid struck her pelvis as he came.

His chest pressed tight to her breast as he released her ass and her feet dropped to the floor. She could feel the rapid flutter of his heart on her chest, his shaky, hot breath on her neck.

He'd only managed to contain the fire a brief moment. Already she felt like she could go again--her body wasn't nearly sated enough for him. She wanted all of him.

Navarre pulled away from her, his hair falling over his face. Kaeli itched to push it back, to run her fingers through it, but she restrained herself, sensing he was torn.

He faced away from her and left the elevator, his hand on the gate. He did not look at her, as though he was ashamed of losing control, of what they'd done.

"Leave. Leave, ma petite, or you will die."

Chapter Four

The hairs stood up on the back of her neck. She ignored the warning. "This attack of conscience is nice, and correct me if I'm wrong, but you enjoyed that as much as I did."

He faced her, his features impassive, but his gaze was blistering ... and agonized. "You cannot stay. Now go." He pulled the heavy gate down, watching her through the metal slats. "I don' want you hurt."

Hell, what had she expected? He wasn't as interested as she'd thought, or maybe he just thought her a skank and not worthy of poking his cock into. Most guys would have. She didn't understand him at all. Why the hell did he think he had to save her? Why was he being so *noble*?

Kaeli glared at him. "Fine, but the next time you think you're going to *save* me, don't."

"I'm sorry you don' understand, petite." He hit the button and the elevator started down. "I'll call you a cab."

"Thanks," she mumbled, and then he disappeared as the elevator lowered beyond the floor level. Kaeli straightened her dress, trying to ignore the sticky residue of their *almost* fucking between her legs. Of course, she'd never felt so thoroughly fucked in all her life, and it had nothing to do with pleasure and everything to do with betrayal.

It was unreasonable to expect anything from him, after all, she didn't know him. What was the world coming to when you couldn't expect a guy to oblige when he so obviously wanted it too? Worst of all, she felt cheap, and she couldn't quite figure out why. Maybe it had been the begging....

Kaeli cringed, remembering every little detail as she exited through the dim lower level to the outer door. She might as well resign herself to the fact that she couldn't have what she wanted. The knowledge stung, just as it always did when she reached this conclusion.

There was a taxi waiting for her at the curb, and she startled to see it sitting there, the engine running exhaust out of the tailpipe. She hadn't expected one to get here so soon, but they may have been in the area when the call was received. There could be no other explanation.

She shivered and hugged herself as she stepped up to the taxi, then opened the door, wanting to get back to the hotel as soon as possible. Light flooded the interior as the door swung open, and she leaned forward to get inside. A blond man grinned from the back seat, and the driver turned to look at her, snatching her arm when she would have pulled away.

It was the man who'd attacked Navarre in the alley. She gasped as he smiled and flashed wickedly long canines at her. Thick red stained the sides of his mouth--blood.

"Fuck!" she screamed and snatched at her arm, pulling back with all her weight. The blond lunged for her, catching her braids in his hands, dragging her into the taxi.

She grasped the edge of the door, trying to get free, screaming as she slashed at the hands holding her, biting at anything that neared her mouth.

The men laughed, their strength unbelievable. She realized they wanted her to struggle and scream--they were enjoying it.

"Navarre!" she screamed, "Get the fuck down here! God dammit!"

Her nails snapped as the blond pulled her fully inside. The driver reached past her flailing limbs to pull the door shut.

The blond pressed her into the seat, his elbow in her throat. She gagged, trying to breathe, clawing at his throat. Her nails punctured and slashed his skin, but he didn't flinch. Her eyes closed as the air choked from her lungs. He eased the pressure on her throat, giving her a shake, forcing her eyelids to flutter open.

He grinned, flashing his predatory teeth, the wicked ivory nearly glowing in the dark. "I smell his cum on your skin. Did he mark you? I always wanted to know what a human tastes like after a wolf marks her."

He lowered his face toward her, fangs extended, and Kaeli knew she was a dead woman.

* * * *

Her scream pierced his ears like needles, sending pain shooting through his head and heart. Without hesitating, he raced down the stairs, through the empty lower level, cursing himself for his stupidity. He should have known one attack would never satisfy the blood thirsty bastards. He'd tried to keep her away. But he hadn't tried hard enough.

He heard the torrent of her profanity, the laughter of the vampires who'd attacked. Blood scented the air as he neared. He reached the door, threw it open just as the taxi's wheels spun, rubber burning in the night as he ran outside.

The driver stuck his arm out the window, giving Navarre the finger like in some bizarre satire of a horror movie. But this was his life--and he was one of the monsters.

He saw red--a haze of blood. He raced back inside to his viper, jumping inside and slamming the key into the ignition. His worst fears had just been realized. The vamps ... they'd taken her ... because of him.

They were dead anyway, but if they hurt her ... he'd torture them for each drop of blood she shed ... for each bruise on her flesh....

The viper barely scraped under the opening garage door, and it shot out into the night like a silver bullet.

The streets were deserted on this end, empty as a ghost town. Within seconds, he caught sight of the red glowing tail lights, disappearing around the corner onto a side street.

They were headed out of town. Navarre increased his speed, pressing the narrow pedal to the floor. The sleek viper easily caught up to the old taxi. He pulled alongside it, glancing in the dark windows, trying to see her.

Streetlight glanced off the glass, revealing nothing inside, but the car shook on the road as if she struggled with her captors. His ears perked to the faint sound of her voice, but he couldn't make out her words, couldn't reach with his senses. His inner beast raged, pumping the tempo of his blood to a furious pitch.

His hands tightened on the steering wheel, knuckles gone white as he raced ahead of the taxi, pulling in front of them, forcing them to slow down. The taxi whipped around him in a sudden, maniacal swerve that caught him by surprise, and he heard the howling, mocking laughter of the driver through the window as he dragged ahead.

Navarre tensed, unwilling to ram them here, with the road narrowing to a single lane. The dwindling street lamps disappeared entirely, going dark as they continued on their suicidal course. Trees rose up from the night like dark sentinels, obliterating the sky, closing around them like the ranks of an ancient army. He could not see the moon, but knew its full shape would soon be rising--and that light would only help him.

The taxi fishtailed in front of him, taunting, forcing him back when he tried to pass. He gritted his teeth, having no choice but to follow, watching as the speedometer climbed past 60, higher, inching past 70. Killing speeds. Gravel spewed beneath the wheels in front of him, striking the windshield with a barrage, cracking the glass.

The headlights bobbed as the taxi jumped a dip in the road. Navarre followed, saw the deer dart out in front of the cab a split second before them. He slammed on the brakes, watching in horror as they struck the startled doe.

Blood flashed in the headlights, spilling over the car like rain, throwing the animal away into the dark. The cab whirled on the gravel, flying at the shallow ditch. Mud sloshed as the wheels slammed through the soggy earth. The car flipped as the ground gave beneath it, rolling with a shatter of screaming metal and glass.

The hood peeled back, crushed into the ground as it continued to roll and crash into an ancient oak before stopping, up-ended on the ground like an overturned beetle.

Navarre hydroplaned, his brakes locking as the car spun in a wide circle as though the road were saturated with water. He gritted his teeth, compensating for the spin. The viper skidded to a halt, the high beams flooding the crash site. Navarre leapt from the car just as the dark haired driver emerged from the broken car--unhurt.

Navarre stopped in the middle of the road, his chest heaving as he stared the vamp down. Movement caught his eye as the blond crawled through the windshield and stood beside his partner, facing him. He licked something off his fingers as he smiled. "Delicious," he said loud enough his voice carried over the distance.

The headlights lit the night with broken light. He could not see her stir in the car, smelled her blood in the air, and knew the vamp tasted her blood. Something broke inside him.

"Tonight, you die," Navarre growled, extending his claws as he lunged with death in his eyes.

* * * *

It was the hoarse cry that woke Kaeli from her stupor. She opened her eyes and groaned in pain at even so little movement. Kaeli moved her hands, felt the smooth lining of the car's roof.

Her ears rang as she sat up, nausea washing over her until she dropped back down. Her ribs hurt, she could barely breathe, could hardly move, and couldn't see anything.

Outside, the sounds of a fight finally registered in her tired brain. She could hear his voice, knew Navarre had somehow come for her.

But he was in trouble. They were going to kill him. He couldn't fight two vampires--for she now knew that's exactly what they were, that he'd been telling her the truth all along.

She had to help him ... somehow.

The car door was stuck, and trying to open it left her panting for air. The windshield was gone though, and the only escape route she could see. Breathing through her teeth, Kaeli dragged herself along the car roof, grimacing as the car shuddered from her movement, afraid at any moment it would just collapse on top of her.

It didn't, and she managed to pull herself out onto the wet, muddy grass.

Heavy boots stomped in front of her, and Kaeli tried to roll away, but she wasn't fast enough. The man grabbed her hair, nearly snatching it out of her head as he pulled her to her feet.

He jerked her hair, wrenching her head back. With her last strength, she kicked him, gasping at the movement. He laughed and squeezed an arm around her middle until she screamed and black light danced before her eyes.

Kaeli knew in that moment, she was going to be the death of Navarre. And there was nothing she could do about it.

* * * *

The dark haired vamp vanished from his view as he reached the blond--*flashing* ... mind tricks. Navarre kept his eyes on the second, weaker vamp, kicked off the ground, lunging at the blond before he could react.

He hit him square in the chest, knocking him to the ground. The vamp hissed, kicking, shredding Navarre's arms as his extended claws struck the vamp's belly, digging in.

There were only a few ways to kill a vampire--and Navarre knew the most proficient. The vamp screamed in agony as Navarre's hand reached like a scalpel through his body, bucked, trying to free himself. Blood flooded the air, pooling around Navarre's arm.

The muscle pumped against his fingertips as he reached the heart, wrapping his clawed hand around it. Biting back his disgust, he crushed it, and the vampire went still, his screams suddenly silenced. His body crumbled instantly around Navarre's arm ... crumbling to dust that mingled with the mud.

It was kill or be killed. He should not have been disturbed--but he had been. It had taken mere seconds to kill the vampire. Seconds more to stand and face his remaining foe.

He wondered that the dark haired vamp hadn't attacked him from behind, but saw he had better quarry.

He held Kaeli.

Navarre hardly recognized her. Her face was a mask of blood. It matted her hair, and the headlights made her eyes shine with wild pain.

Navarre tensed, dropping his arms for a killing stance. He moved forward, halting only when the vamp twisted her head back, threatening to snap her neck. She grimaced, digging her nails into her captor's arm around her chest--to no avail.

"Don't come any closer," he said, smiling with a confidence that boiled Navarre's blood.

Navarre's fingers curled with the urge to take his heart.

He licked the blood from her neck with one long swipe, drawing a strangled gasp from her throat. "Mmmm. She tastes almost as sweet as Lycans. Maybe it's because she fucked one."

"Why are you ... doing this?" she gasped out, her hands falling limp to her sides.

He gave Navarre a look. "Why not?"

"Did Danior send you?" Navarre said between his clenched teeth. Was this some twisted method of revenge on the Lycans? He would kill Danior if it were true. If he lived through this night.

He laughed, a mocking, snickering sound that grated Navarre's strained nerves. "Danior has gone. Disappeared. He told us not to touch the Lycans, but he is nowhere to be found, so we do not obey his commands. Perhaps I will be the new master."

"Perhaps not, mon ennemi. Perhaps we all die this night." Navarre tensed imperceptibly, waiting for the moment of inattention that would be her salvation.

"I think you are right. Let's start with this bitch." He slammed her head to the side and sank his teeth into her neck, shredding her throat.

Kaeli's scream cut off almost before it began, her body going limp as the poison paralyzed her body. Blood bubbled from her lips.

It was his only chance. Navarre jumped, shifting in an instant, ignoring the pain of transformation. His pants fell away as his body melded from man to wolf, sailing through the air, propelled by inhuman strength. He hit them both with his heavy forepaws, knocking her to the side, out of the vamp's grip.

A fountain of red liquid streamed from her neck as the suction of his mouth broke away. The vamp's eyes had gone red with his glut, her precious blood flowing down his chin.

Navarre landed on the ground, his veins singing with his beast. He twisted, tearing at the vamp's belly, forcing him back. The vampire slid on blood slickened grass, his feet flying beneath him as Navarre pressed forward, going down.

Navarre was on him before he could *flash* and use his own mind against him. He landed on the vamp's chest, teeth sinking into his throat. He shook him like a rag doll, the taste of blood fueling his rage, taking over his human half, drowning out his reason.

There was nothing but the taste of the kill, the flutter of his heartbeat, hands ripping at him, feet flailing ... and then nothing. The head rolled away. He'd severed it without realizing it, so fogged with bloodlust had he become.

Seconds only had passed, an eternity for the last moments of life. Navarre released the vampire, padding to Kaeli as the vamp crumbled to dust.

She lay in a crumpled heap, her eyes closed with the pain. Blood and saliva frothed her lips, thick red pumping from her jugular.

In a moment more she would be dead. He had but one choice to save her. If it failed, she would suffer a more horrible death than he could imagine.

Chapter Five

Kaeli was mercifully unconscious as he knelt over her and pressed his snout against the wound on her neck. One bite, one scratch in this form was all it took to infect her. The full moon had risen above them, dappled light shining down through the edges of the trees. The change would be almost instantaneous ... if she survived.

May god have mercy on his soul.

Navarre sank his wolf's teeth into her neck. She moaned softly, whimpering as he released her. He shuddered, shaking off his shift as he changed into his human form. He crouched next to her, naked, touching her body as the first spasm wracked through her.

Her eyes flew open, looking up at him but not seeing, filled with pain. She screamed, grasping his wrist with a strength that would break a mortal man. A ripple flowed over her skin like water. The blood from her wounds ceased its flow abruptly. Fire flashed beneath his palm, her skin going feverish hot, and he felt the movement of bone, heard the sharp crack as it shifted, collapsing upon itself.

She screamed again and again, arching her back, releasing him as her body seized. Bile rose in his throat, and he choked it back, his gut clenching with her pain. He wanted to halt her torment, but he was as powerless to kill her as he was to let her die. She rolled onto her side, convulsing, curling into a ball. Her limbs drew up, shortening with agonizing slowness as she became wolf.

Fragile hope spread through him as he watched, unable to look away. She was going to make it. Never had he met a human woman who'd survived so much.

She gasped, hassling as fur sprang from her skin, growing like some bizarre plant in time release video.

He blinked, unable to believe his eyes. The wolf lay on the ground, panting, then slowly stood and shook its fur as if wet, throwing off the remnants of her gown. Glowing, golden eyes met his as the wolf regarded him. He reached for her, slowly, and ran his fingers through her silky hair.

She tilted her head, watching him as he petted her, marveling that the change had completed. He smiled wryly, allowing his racing heart to slow to normal. He should have known better than to misjudge her strength and tenacity to survive. No woman had ever fought so hard. No woman had ever captured him so completely.

"Are you ready to change back?" he asked softly, rubbing her fur in soothing circles.

He sensed her acceptance, her eagerness to return to human form with the slight tensing of her body. "All you have to do is wish it. The first change always comes with the moon. Once you survive it, you can change back and forth at will. It gets easier with time." Until then, each shift would be painful, but never like the first time. The body acclimated with the cellular change, able to heal and recover faster as it took hold, until shifting could come as easily as a thought.

And with experience, the rising full moon would not shift her immediately to wolf, though it was hard for even an old hand as himself to resist the seductive lunar call.

"Concentrate," he whispered. "See your human self and it will come."

Long moments passed and nothing happened. She whined, and he knew what was wrong. The moon was as yet too strong, still in the sky. Once it set, she could shift back. He'd forgotten something so elementary.

"Soon," he promised. He scooped up his jeans and led her to his car for a night that promised to be long.

She hopped into the passenger side and curled in the seat, watching him as he settled inside and cranked the car, heading back to his apartment.

One step more and she would be his ... if she didn't kill him first. And he rather hoped she wouldn't since she hadn't yet ripped his throat out.

* * * *

Kaeli awoke with a startled gasp, clutching her neck. She'd dreamt of being savaged, having her blood drained, her body crushed. Had it been real? Or was it just a nightmare? Her questing fingers brushed down her throat, felt tender ridges that had not been there before.

Slowly, she opened her eyes and discovered she was in his apartment, in his bed. Silk sheets clung to her naked curves, rasping across her skin as she sat up and clutched the top edge to her breasts. Her skin tingled, responding to the caress of silk.

She shivered, looking around the dark room. The door was closed, only the barest sliver of light escaping beneath its lowest edge. And yet every shape in the room appeared clearly to her. She could see her hand touching the bed, the edges of a night stand at one side. Further, her gown lay crumpled on the floor, and she could see the tears in it, smell the blood that stained it.

Her heart quickened with fear ... and excitement. She swung her legs out from the bed, wrapping the sheet around her. No weakness assailed her as she walked lithely to the door. She breathed deeply, smelled the aroma of brewed coffee, the cooking fat of bacon.

It was real. Somehow, she'd become more than human. And she was suddenly ravenous for the man responsible.

Kaeli opened the door and padded lightly through the apartment to the kitchen area. He stood with his back to her, turning the bacon. She tiptoed closer, grinning inside.

"If you mean to frighten me, it won' work, petite," he said with a teasing note to his voice.

Kaeli nearly jumped out of her skin. Her heart flopped in her chest. He took the pan off the burner and turned the stovetop off. He faced her with a smile, heat gleaming in his eyes as his gaze roamed down her body.

Kaeli's flesh warmed at his look, at the scent of him and her own arousal. Already she was wet and wanting. He'd put her off before. She wouldn't allow it now. Not with everything that had happened. But first she had to know if her suspicions were true.

"What did you do to me?" she asked quietly, stopping mere feet away from him.

His eyes darkened, pain flashing across his sultry features. "You were going to die. I made you Lycan to save you."

"Why?"

He took a step closer, then another, stopping only when their bodies nearly touched, when all it would take was a deep breath to feel him brush against her nipples.

"I did it because I couldn' stand the thought of you not being in this world. Perhaps we suffer from misguided honor and old superstition. It is not every woman who is willing to sacrifice so much ... nor any Lycan who would risk losing his love."

Kaeli felt breathless, dizzy. "How can this happen so quickly?"

"Love cannot be measured in time, ma chere. It consumes in an instant. I've known you mere days, and yet it seems a lifetime I have longed to be with you and make you my mate. I love you, petite, and now I am going to make you mine."

His sulky mouth curved in a smile full of wicked promise as he wrapped his arms around her. She'd heard once that extreme circumstances forged unbreakable emotional bonds like those between comrades at war. Whatever the reason, her heart swelled with indefinable emotion, a joy to hear his words, feel his touch.

The silk sheet dropped to the floor as he scooped her into his arms. Kaeli let out a small gasp of surprise. "Put me down! You'll hurt yourself!" She was no lightweight, and she didn't want him to get a hernia. She probably weighed more than he did, knowing her luck.

His smile widened. "Afraid I'll drop you?"

It was silly. He was a werewolf. They could do anything. "No."

"I sense you doubt me." It became a test of manhood after that.

She laughed as he strode into the bedroom, demonstrating his strength as he carried her with one arm. Kaeli shrieked and giggled, terrified he'd drop her, but knowing he'd never dare.

Light spilled across the bed from the open doorway, and he deposited her on her feet before it. All mirth disappeared from his eyes as she slid down his naked chest, her nipples rasping against his smooth muscles.

Each touch felt electrified, powerful, sizzling over her skin.

For what seemed an eternity she had dreamed of his kiss, of feeling him inside her. Everything vanished except the need to be as one with him.

She closed her palms around his back as his arms came around her, feeling the heat of his skin, the corded strength of his back. It excited her immeasurably, his hard dangerousness. She was now a part of his world, a part of him.

With a soft growl, Navarre lowered his head. Kaeli whimpered as his lips closed over hers, only the strength of his arms keeping her from falling. His tongue plunged into her mouth, slightly rough, overwhelming her senses with the spicy taste of him. He groaned and moved against her as she responded, his thick erection rubbing between her thighs and her bare clit with debilitating roughness.

Wet heat surged through her body, pooling between her legs. His tongue stroked hers, savoring and voracious all at once, as though he couldn't taste her enough.

Kaeli needed more. She couldn't take his slow pace or she would go mad. Frantic, she tugged at the waist band of his jeans, forcing her hands between them to his fly. He tore away from her mouth, his callused hands pushed hers away, opening the fly, pushing them down his hips.

Small, frustrated moans escaped her throat as she helped him, unaware of herself. His cock sprang from its prison, and Navarre groaned as she wrapped her hand around his thick length.

He shook his head, pushing her back on the bed, pulling off his jeans completely before dropping down to the floor. Kaeli scooted to the edge, trying to reach him, but he held her still with two palms planted on her thighs. Her body screamed for him, frustrated, her nipples engorged and sensitized, her clit throbbing for his touch.

She groaned and fell back as his rough hands slid up her thighs, his grip tightening, forcing her legs wide apart.

Her body burned for him, weeping creamy juices in anticipation. She couldn't move, couldn't breathe. Could only wait, gasping for his caress.

The first touch of his tongue on her swollen folds had her jerking her hips up from the bed. He growled in warning, holding her down, fingers parting her folds as he burrowed into her. His hard tongue thrust into her core and she screamed, clutching the sheet, ripping it from the bed, trying to find some hand hold that would keep her from flying apart.

Her pussy contracted hard, grasping his tongue as he pushed into her spasming, clenching muscles. He made a rough noise of excitement, his chest rumbling as she shuddered with pleasure.

His nose rubbed against her aching clit as he licked her pussy, tongue fucking her, harder and harder. Her hips jerked against him, and a moan strangled from her throat.

She tossed her head, arching, needing more, feeling the edges of climax coming. He pulled back as if sensing her nearness, and she would have screamed if she'd been able. She gasped with near pain at the loss of his mouth on her.

He slid up her body, crushing her into the mattress, his body unyielding. He rubbed his thigh against her pussy, teasing her. She nearly cried at the torture. He nuzzled her breasts, his breath hot against her chest, teeth grazing over one nipple.

Kaeli arched as he took it into his mouth, sucking hard, pulling at her distended flesh until she thought she would cum just from the feel of him suckling her nipple. He moved to her other breast, repeating his action, closing his callused palm over one breast to knead her flesh and tug at her wet nipple with his fingers.

"You're killing me, Navarre," she breathed, raking her nails against his back.

He broke away from her breast, looking up at her from below, his mouth curved in a wicked smile. "Truly, chere?" he asked, a rough hue to his voice, husky with need.

Kaeli growled and pulled his shoulders. He moved up her body with one long, rough slide, heightening the pleasure of her skin. Goosebumps rippled over her flesh, making her hair stand on end. The strength left her muscles as he settled between her thighs. The flared head of his cock parted her folds, nudging at the entrance of her pussy.

Her muscles clenched with surprise at his girth, her thick juice barely easing his way. She gasped in pleasurable shock as he plunged into her, her flesh stretching to near pain around him.

She burned with the feel of him stroking deep inside her, growing wetter, more excited.

"Kaeli," he ground out against her neck, his lips pulling at her skin. He sucked behind her ear, hard, leaving his mark. She arched her neck, wrapping her legs around his hips as he drove into her. She clenched with each rough withdrawal, each ramming invasion. Her hips lifted from the bed.

She panted for breath, her blood sizzling like lava, her heart pounding in her chest. He crushed her, groaned hoarsely against her neck, moving faster and faster in a hard driving motion until she thought she would die.

His pubic bone ground against her engorged clit with each thrust, throbbing like an extra heart beat. Pleasure shot through her body with breathtaking suddenness. She screamed as it enveloped her, engulfing her senses with a riot of bliss. Gasping and arching, she dug her nails into his shoulders. Her pussy clutched at his cock driving into her, forcing the orgasm higher.

He groaned, his shoulders flexing, his breath ragged and hot by her ear. His pace quickened, hips jerking against hers, his cock head moving deep into her core with blinding force.

He threw his head back, breaking her holding on his shoulders, crying out hoarsely as his body convulsed with his orgasm. A jet of liquid heat shot from his pulsing shaft, and her body milked him, sucking greedily at his member.

He collapsed on top of her, panting, their breaths mingling, hearts beating in time to one another.

Navarre lifted up after several long moments, looking in her eyes, his own gleaming.

Kaeli fought to catch her breath, the climax still trembling through her. She ran her fingers through his hair, looking up at him. "Will it always be like this?" she asked, panting with exhaustion, feeling as though she would melt into the bed.

"It gets better, ma petite. I've barely scratched the surface."

Already he hardened inside her. Kaeli groaned. "I ... can't ... take any more...."

His eyes darkened with mirth, and he moved his hips, causing her to squirm with pleasure. Kaeli gasped softly in surprise. Already she responded to him, her body hassling for more despite twinges of orgasm still twitching through her body.

"Petite, you have no idea how much lovin' a wolf can give you. Didn' I tell you I love a challenge?"

Her mouth fell open as he thrust his hips against hers with sensual promise. Kaeli arched, looking at him with heavy lids. She wouldn't allow him to wear her out so quickly. How arrogant he was--and hers in every delicious way. She'd show him how much loving a woman could give him.

"I think I have an inkling," she said with a smile, pulling him down for a kiss.

The End

CARNAL THIRST

Dedication:
To my best friend, who lost her own dream but gained so
much more.

Chapter One

The computer disconnected itself, and Maggie O'Roarke knew it was the last time she'd get online. She couldn't pay the bill, and anyway, what was the point? The whole reason she'd had it to start with was for her company. Now it was gone.

At long last, after years of sinking every dime back into it, working two and three jobs to keep it afloat, all the while ignoring everyone who told her she was just being hard-headed and it would never succeed--her company was finally dead. She supposed she should've conceded defeat a long time ago, but she'd begun operating out of the red. Unfortunately, the declining economy had decimated her last shred of hope.

What was she going to do now? She'd spent her most of her youth trying to get out of the poorhouse, and still had nothing to show for all the sacrifice but a huge ass and a worn down computer. She didn't even have anyone she could call and talk to about it.

Maggie stared at the dark screen with the star field

screensaver spinning by, wondering how she should feel, besides sorry for herself. Of course, she knew how she should feel--she should be bawling her eyes out, raging against her competitors and the government, anything but being consumed by this utter emptiness.

She *was* feeling sorry for herself, and as good as it would feel to wallow in self-pity, it wasn't going to do her a damn bit of good right now.

Maggie popped her neck and rolled her shoulders, feeling another tension headache trying to set in. Pushing away from her desk, she rose and walked to the kitchen, grabbing her Excedrin from the table. Pouring out two pills, she looked in the refrigerator for her water, found it, and took the medicine.

Hell, why was she even drinking water? She needed to get drunk. Or better yet, get off this damn diet that wasn't doing her any good anyway. She couldn't remember the last time she'd lost even a pound.

She needed some comfort food, like her mama's ribs and pork rice. Her eyes stung at the reminder that her mom was gone, forever.

"Just in a *wonderful* mood tonight, aren't we?" Maggie muttered to herself, wiping at her eyes with a knuckle. "I might as well go for the death by calorie intake. At least it'll make me happy."

The fridge was empty though. Her '86 Bonneville had finally died two weeks ago, and she hadn't had the money to fix it. The repairs would've cost at least ten times as much as the car was worth.

It was an eyesore anyway.

Besides, she still had the problem of no food. Of course, there was some, but none of it appealed to her mood. There was flour and sugar; mayonnaise; something in a bowl that might've been tuna salad; a jug of water; one cracked, frozen egg; and a bag of green slime that used to be salad fixings. Maggie closed the door with a distasteful shudder. In a depression, you had to have something decadent to make it all better, like chips or chocolate or....

"Ice cream. Chocolate chip," she said on a reverent

whisper. She practically orgasmed at the thought. Cold weather and depression always put her in the mood for it.

Grabbing her purse, Maggie counted out her cash--twice to be sure she had it right. Not that it was hard to count six dollars in bills and change. She could've sworn she'd had more than that. There was her other change, a huge stash, but that was in her car ... at the tow truck place.

Six dollars wasn't enough to pay for a cab to the store, even one way--not and still get something to satisfy her craving. There was a market close enough she could walk it, just a few miles. She might even burn up enough calories not to have a heart attack when she dug in to the treat.

It was late though, and the neighborhood wasn't exactly one of the best. She shrugged dismissively. She wouldn't have to worry about being a target for a serial killer, Typically, they targeted tiny women who were easy to subdue quickly-- in the five foot, one hundred pound range. Seeing as how she was damn near twice that weight and almost a foot taller she couldn't imagine running into anyone who thought they could just toss her over their shoulder and haul her off. If she got mugged, they'd probably only take her purse and the credit cards that had been canceled long ago.

"Screw it," she said, tucking her money in her Jean's pocket rather than carrying a purse, which might tempt muggers--and might tempt her to commit murder if they tried to make off with her ice cream money. Determined now, she marched out the door into the brisk night, not bothering with a jacket or sweater since she figured the walk would keep her warm enough.

The hour was later than she'd thought it was. There wasn't a soul to be seen on the sidewalks, and precious few cars, or traffic to be heard even in the distance.

Uneasiness touched her briefly, but she dismissed it. She felt invigorated by the outdoors, excited to be going somewhere after two weeks of being locked up in the house--even if it was only to the store.

She really needed to get out more. She couldn't remember the last time she'd gone for a walk or stuck her head out while the sun was still shining. The moon was perfect though--her sun--since she was a night owl.

Feeling a giddiness brought on by too little sleep and possibly mild hysteria, she put a skip in her step and enjoyed herself. An hour later, with the market in sight, her feet were killing her and her nose and toes felt like they were going to freeze off. She knew she should've put on shoes instead of using her sandals.

Maggie dreaded the trip back, but the ice cream called to her. Sugar made anything better.

A lone car sat in front of the store--probably the clerk's. A wash of neon from beer signs and fluorescent lighting blazed from the storefront onto the darkened street, running over the pavement like shining blood.

Wind ruffled in her hair, sending a chill up her spine. She shrugged her shoulders, shivering slightly at the eerie feeling that descended upon her, increasing her pace.

When the blow came, she was too stunned from the force of it to do anything but throw her hands out to brace for a fall.

A hard object slammed into her right flank, pummeling into her shoulder blade and sending her sprawling to the pavement. The skin peeled away from her palms as she skidded onto the ground, gasping for breath. Fire seared her palms and knees, but it was nothing compared to the pain in her back.

She whipped her head around, dazed, unable to comprehend what had happened. She felt someone near but couldn't see them, couldn't hear them. Her heart pounded unaccustomedly hard, the beat so rapid she thought it would explode. Her lungs felt frozen, achy from too much breathing, but she couldn't get enough air.

Planting a palm on one alley wall, she struggled to her feet, screaming for help in the direction of the store. The alley she'd been thrown into funneled her voice, but the wind seemed to snatch it away. The air around her vibrated with the sound of a gasp just before another blow struck her back and knocked her fully to the ground.

Legs locked around her waist, pinning her in place. She

bucked against the weight, trying to free herself. Her attacker wasn't heavy. He had to be at least twenty five pounds lighter than her, but she couldn't budge him, couldn't turn to scratch his eyes out.

She was trapped.

She dug her hands against the pavement, seeking purchase, her legs flailing as she tried to get a knee under her for leverage. A male laugh reverberated against the walls, echoing against her ear drums, mocking as fingernails scraped over the back of her neck to wrench her hair aside.

Maggie screamed again, unable to believe no one could hear her, that no one had seen her being attacked.

What did he want? To rape her? Mug her? Kill her?

"Get the fuck off me, you bastard!" she screamed in fury, ineffectually slapping her hands back at his knees.

He pressed her face into the pavement with inhuman strength. Grit and broken rock ground against her cheek, tearing at the corner of her mouth and eye. She gritted her teeth, growling in pain.

Air fanned over her neck, stirring the fine hairs there, sending chills down her spine. A tongue laved her and pulled back, leaving a cooling swath of flesh in its wake.

"What a tender little pig you are," he said above her, chuckling. His grip in her hair tightened to pain, stretching her scalp until she expected to feel the sharp sting of separation.

Maggie clawed at the hand gripping her head, felt her short nails break the skin. She dug into him, desperate to pry his hand loose. He grunted and tugged her hair harder, ignoring the pain she knew she inflicted. Wrenching her head at an angle, grinding her face across the pavement, he pulled her so hard her neck bone cracked and she felt the tendons in her neck stretch painfully taut.

She ground her teeth, sucking in a sharp breath as twin blades pierced her throat. Dimly, she heard the soft pop of her skin being punctured, felt the hot rush of blood well to the surface to puddle on the pavement beneath her. A slurping, sucking sound pushed past the fog clouding her mind. Lips latched onto her. A tongue pressed into the wound, working the blood out faster.

Oh god, oh god, oh god. Teeth. Teeth ripped into her neck like some animal.

He was eating her.

It was a nightmare she'd had ever since she'd been a child. A nightmare of cannibalism, of blood drinkers, of the undead converging on the living to devour them ... ever since watching Romero's Dawn of the Dead.

This couldn't be real. She'd been drugged somehow. She felt chemicals traveling through her system, shutting down her body. But her sight and hearing was intact. She could hear him sucking at her neck as though he were eating melting ice cream.

She'd heard of attacks with men and women having their veins slit open and blood drained, with no memory of how it had happened. She hadn't believed it. She hadn't *wanted* to believe it. She'd thought it some new vogue movement, like vampiric goths--not something real, something deadly. The attacks had happened near the highest trafficked areas, the clubs and tourist spots irresistible at any hour of the day.

Not here. Not so close to her home.

Not to her.

Maggie slowly blinked, watching the growing pool of blood her attacker let slip from his lips. It looked black in the darkness, an ooze too distasteful to believe gave her life. She reached for it weakly, as if she could scoop it back into her body.

She felt the man above her stiffen. He stopped suckling at her neck and pulled away, as if studying his kill.

Maggie tried to buck him off, but she could only shrug one shoulder. She felt drugged and knew it had to be loss of blood that had her so weak. It was too much to hope she was only having a nightmare. The pain and horror were too intense to be anything other than real.

Teeth pierced her neck again, sinking deeply, blotting out the fleeting pain coursing through her neck with each heart beat.

Her vision dimmed to a pinprick, no further than her

fingertips. She smelled ozone, and then her sight snapped away into nothingness.

* * * *

Freshly spilt blood wafted on the air like the scent of a sumptuous feast. In his weakened state, its allure was irresistible.

Danior Blake dropped to the ground, his leather duster whipped out in the residual energy blasting around him like the wind.

The vampire feeding looked up at his approach, wiping the blood trailing down his chin with the back of his hand.

"My lord," he said, bowing his head before standing.

"Zane." Danior nodded, coming to stand over the body. His fangs lengthened at the spicy, sweet scent, resisting his efforts at control. The battle with the lycan, Raoul, had left him weaker than he'd supposed. His body still bore the brunt of the fight, for his wounds would not heal completely until he'd fed.

"You have the smell of wolf on you," Zane said.

"I've been hunting Lycan," Danior said, meeting his gaze coolly. "You know the council has forbidden the killing of humans in the city. We don't need the attention right now."

Zane's face did not betray his emotions, but Danior felt the fear in him. "She is different, my lord. I--"

The woman moaned, so softly it was barely a whisper of sound. Danior knelt beside her, frowning. Humans had no immunity to vampire venom. "Did you not bite her?" he asked, touching her wound.

"I did, twice in fact. It did not paralyze her. I think if not for her blood loss, she would be fighting even now. She will not succumb to mind tricks, my lord. There would be no disguising this attack."

Danior nodded. It was true. Only through telepathy had they controlled what humans knew of them so far. It was how they'd escaped destruction for hundreds of years.

"Her blood is strong, sweeter than any I've tasted before. She can't be allowed to turn. Will you finish her or should I?"

The council had forbidden the creation of more vampires,

as well. The city was overrun with them, and no vampire would leave for fear of showing weakness. Weakness was deadly in these strained times. "Leave. I'll take care of this mess."

"Yes, my lord." Zane bowed and took to the sky, leaving Danior alone with the woman.

Without the anti-coagulant of vampire saliva, the blood flow from the wound at her shoulder and neck slowed to a dribble.

She was a large woman, heavy and sturdily built. He puzzled over why she could resist the venom and why two bites along with the blood drain had not killed her almost immediately.

Her eyelids fluttered as he brushed her hair back, the corner of her mouth twitching as if she would speak. She seemed caught in some unspeakable nightmare, as horrific as reality, he surmised.

If the blood loss did not kill her, the venom coursing through her vitals could possibly turn her. She had an equal chance of either, perhaps better than most, for he'd never once seen a human resist the paralyzing effects of a vampire bite.

It was rare to turn a human. A small bite for normal feeding would result in no more than the feeling of a hangover afterward. Three bites over three days could chain a human to a vampire, leaving them addicted to the bite like a drug, but with some of the benefits of vampirism and none of the worst side effects.

Anything more than small increments was almost inevitably fatal. Those that managed to survive were forever infected with the virus that humankind knew as vampirism.

Some indefinable emotion swarmed Danior. He searched his memory but could not recall its name. Lust and hunger he knew. Anger. Rage. Desire. But this?

He shook his head and scooped the woman effortlessly into his arms.

He was curious to see the limits of her resiliency. The others would tear her apart in this state, though, so he could not take her beneath his club, nor to any other haunt of his kind.

There was only one place they feared to go--a place even he hesitated to go.

Chapter Two

Maggie woke from deep sleep completely disoriented. Her face pressed into the pillow, and she turned her head, wincing at the stiffness in her shoulders and neck. Something had awakened her--she'd heard a sound, something alien and unfamiliar. She held her breath, listening for the noise that had roused her, lying still as she tried to remember where she was.

This pillow wasn't hers. It smelled old, musty with age.

Of course, that wasn't much different from her own ancient pillows, but these were made of feathers instead of polyfiber filling. This definitely wasn't her house, which meant she definitely wasn't alone.

She rolled onto her back, biting her lip as her sore back connected with the bed. She touched the crook of her neck and found a small, square bandage.

It was all real. It had really happened. Had the bastard kidnapped her? Since she wasn't home, it was as good an assumption as any.

After listening for several minutes, she decided she was alone in the room. She felt like if she hadn't been there would have been a reaction anyway when she rolled over. Still, she thought it was better to err on the side of caution, and she scanned the room as far as she could see before she finally sat up.

To her relief, she saw that she really was alone.

The room was devoid of furniture save for the wrought iron bed. Directly opposite it stood two windows with heavy brocaded drapes. On the wall that housed the headboard of the bed were two doors. The right bedroom wall held another door, and on the wall opposite to that was a fireplace with a built-in mantel. The fire within it was the only light in the room.

It was an old room, evidenced by the hardwood floors and authentic plaster walls and ceiling. She had to be inside a Victorian era house, perhaps one even older.

From the twelve foot ceiling, a bare bulb hung from a chain in the center of the room, dangling a pull cord.

Old wiring too.

Maggie got up and pulled the cord. Light spilled down, weak, leaving the edges of the room still dim.

Seeing that her assessment of the room was accurate, Maggie decided to check the door closest to her. It wasn't locked. She wasn't certain whether that was a good thing or a bad thing. It might mean nothing threatening at all. It could mean that whoever had brought her had only done so to help her.

On the other hand, it seemed to her that most anyone who might have found her would've taken her to a hospital. But how likely was it that her attacker would have taken her anywhere, much less patched her up?

After several minutes of indecision, she finally decided to err once again on the side of caution. Turning away from the door, she moved as quietly as possible to the first window. When she pulled the drapes back, she discovered that the window had been boarded over tighter than a nun's butt. Light squeezed through the minute cracks where putty had separated from the wood.

Maggie squinted painfully at the bright pinpricks, her heart skipping several beats as she let the curtains fall back in place. As much as she would've liked to believe that there was an unthreatening explanation for it, it seemed that she had to accept that she'd been imprisoned in the room. Unwilling to accept that assessment when she had already tested the door and found it unlocked, she decided to check the other window. It too was boarded up.

The unlocked door was either a trap, or the person who had left it unlocked had made certain that the rest of the building was secure. Regardless, she wasn't about to just sit and wait for whoever had taken her prisoner to come in and do whatever he wanted to her.

Maggie searched the room for anything she could use as a weapon. To her surprise, she found several objects that would make surprisingly good weapons. There were a pair of brass candlesticks on top of the mantel and near the fire, a poker leaned against the wall. Deciding she liked the looks of the poker best, because she really didn't want to have to get close enough to hit him with the candlestick, she took the poker and moved toward the door again.

Pressing her ear against the panel, she held her rasping breath, trying to listen above the rampaging rhythm of her heart. After listening intently for some time, she finally decided to open the door and have a look.

Turning the knob very slowly, she peered into the room--- and discovered it was a bathroom.

"Shit! Shit, shit, shit!" she whispered. She looked around the bedroom. There were two other doors. She was betting one of them was a god damned closet.

The narrow one *had* to be the closet.

Tiptoeing across the room, she pressed her ear to the other door. Still tremendously unsettled by her first wrong guess, Maggie only listened at that door for a few moments. Slowly, she turned the knob.

It was locked.

"Shit!"

"If you'll tell me what you're looking for, perhaps I can help."

The deep male voice directly behind her nearly gave Maggie heart failure. Acting purely on instinct, she whirled, swinging the poker for all she was worth--and buried it into the wall on her other side. Plaster burst from the impact like snow.

Stunned, she merely stared at the poker for several moments, wondering how she could have possibly missed him. That thought made her look around quickly.

He was lounging very casually against the bedpost.

Maggie gaped at him.

Even if she'd been blind, she would've sensed the danger

surrounding him. Lethal practically oozed from his pores. It was hard to explain with certainty why she felt it, but he looked like the last person in the world to play good Samaritan.

He wore a black, peasant-style shirt open to the middle of his chest--the opening revealing a pale olive expanse of sculpted pectorals free of hair except for the thin beginnings of a happy trail that disappeared beneath the fabric before she could follow it. Leather pants hugged every inch of his legs and groin, showing off his package like prime rib in the meat department. He wore ass kicking boots, laced up to the knee with overlay buckles meant for tearing the hide off anyone dumb enough to brush against them.

He had an odd ensemble going on. Part tortured poet, part bad ass biker--all succulent man.

Leather tended to lend itself to a "bad" image, but this guy went way beyond that. Inky black hair framed his face, falling around his shoulders in thick tendrils almost indistinguishable from his clothing. His face was the most arresting part of him, however, and what set her heart to pounding uncontrollably.

It wasn't the square jaw or high cheekbones that were testament to high testosterone. It wasn't the wickedly black eyebrows arched sardonically as she continued to stare at him. It was his eyes. They were the eyes of a predator--so dark a gray they could easily be mistaken for black, and with the smallest tilt to them, making them appear as exotic as an Egyptian painting. They were intensely scrutinizing without seeming to be, lazy and hooded, like a cat just before striking.

Calling him dangerous would be an understatement.

"How did you do that?" she gasped when her brain finally seized on the warning and began functioning again.

"Which 'that' are you referring to?" he asked, throwing her off balance. He didn't act in the least threatened by her weapon.

She stared at him. She'd been thinking about the fact that he'd managed to move so quickly out of the way when she'd swung at his head. The remark, however, reminded her that she'd thoroughly checked the room.

"How did you get in the room?"

"I walked."

Maggie gritted her teeth and jerked the poker out of the wall. "Look, I don't know who you are, and I don't know *what* you had in mind when you brought me here, but I'd like to leave now."

He shrugged. "Unfortunately, I can't allow that. You've been bitten."

Her eyes widened. "You son of a bitch! You're the one that attacked me, aren't you?"

He smiled faintly. "Not I."

She wanted to wipe that smug look off his face with the poker, but she didn't want to get that close to him. If he was the one who had attacked her, he had thrown her around as if she was some shrimpy ninety pound weakling. "Why is it that I don't believe you?"

Again, he shrugged, as if it was a matter of indifference to him one way or the other.

She studied him for several moments when he didn't respond. "You can't keep me a prisoner here."

He looked at her with interest. "Why not?"

She gaped at him. What the hell kind of conversation was this to be having with a maybe/maybe not killer? "What do you mean, why not? Because you can't, that's why not! People will be looking for me. I have friends! They'll have the cops down on your ass so fast you won't know what hit you."

He looked at her intently for several moments. "You have no close friends and no relatives. Even if you did, it would be of no consequence to me. Nor, might I add, does the thought of having cops on my ass particularly distress me."

"How do you know I don't have any friends or family?" she demanded indignantly.

He pushed away from the bed abruptly. Before she could even blink, he was standing practically nose to nose with her. She felt her jaw sag in disbelief. He lifted a hand and very lightly traced it along her temple.

"Because it is here."

Maggie swallowed with an effort. "What are you, a fucking mind reader or something?"

"No, I'm a fucking vampire," he said, smiling thinly.

* * * *

He wasn't sure why he'd brought her here. It was not physical attraction that had drawn his attention, though after he'd cleaned her, he saw that she was very appealing and womanly--reminiscent of women born in his own day. Physically, she was not what his "type" had become over the long years. He preferred small, slender women, but then, it seemed modern society had shifted to that preference decades ago and he along with it.

He'd tended to her for three days while she struggled to stay alive. Bathed the feverish sweat from her brow, changed the dressing on her wound, and cleaned the blood from her skin. He'd seen every inch of her body in repose.

It had almost been like tending a child, except she resembled no youth, and her appearance was such that he had no trouble distinguishing her from one so unsuitable for his carnal appetites.

She was buxom and tall, leggy. Her bare legs had entranced him while she writhed in bed. He'd had to sponge bathe her, touching every inch of skin, and he was surprised at how smooth she was, how hairless and fine her flesh. She was strong and muscled, but the hard edges of an average weighted woman did not exist on her. Softness appealed to him immensely. Women should be soft, malleable to a man's rough body.

It had taken a supreme effort of will not to explore her body as she lay helpless, but he found it distasteful to take advantage of a woman recovering from death and going through the change.

It amused him to know that he was not so much a monster as he'd supposed he was. Had he been, he could have fucked her as much as he pleased and left her to die when he was through. He'd known of others who had, and the act disgusted him more so now than it had before.

She was awake now. And the set of her jaw and stance,

the fire in her eyes and her threat to take his head off both amused him and made his groin tighten uncomfortably.

This was no fleeting desire. She promised full, lasting passion, if only he could unleash it. Now he could press her and release the lust that had built inside him. He'd been long without a woman of any kind. The vampiresses could not move him as short lived humans could, vibrant with life and passion. He'd expected to have a human of his own by now, but the woman he'd found most appealing had been taken from him before he could complete binding her. He'd come upon Maggie after his fight with Raoul over that woman. How odd that losing her had led him to such a welcome surprise.

The resistance of her mind to his probing fascinated him. He marveled at her strength of will, perhaps more so because she could resist him even near death. Once he'd broken through, the memories that lay inside allowed him to explore the facets of her personality, to know the depression she'd sunk in to after her mother's death and the loss of her business.

Strangely, it moved him.

He'd not been moved emotionally in far too long, nor challenged in centuries, and he found himself eagerly anticipating it.

Arching a brow, he smiled as her eyes widened. She seemed caught between watching his face and staring at the bulge in his pants. She found him as appealing as he found her.

That was good. It would make the journey so much more pleasurable.

He could touch her any number of ways by bending her mind to control her sight, allowing him to move unseen around her. While parlor tricks were amusing among the inexperienced and unwary, he craved making her respond to him in a wholly new way.

She was shocked by his words, disbelief etched on her face. No one believed in vampires until they were bit on the neck....

His smile deepened as he brought his hand up to touch

her face. In that moment, she tried to kill him.

* * * *

Maggie had lost all desire to leave the room. She couldn't contain the shock on her face. She had thought the man was a serial killer or something. Then he had claimed to be a vampire, and she decided he was just plain insane. The problem with that comforting theory--and she would never have believed that would be a comforting theory before-- was that the words were no sooner out of his mouth, than she swung the poker at him again for all she was worth.

Once again, she didn't manage to do anything except dig another whole in the wall. While she was trying to pry it loose, he skated a cool finger over one cheek that sent chills down her back.

"Such fire," he murmured huskily. "I believe I'm going to enjoy this far more than I had anticipated. You will join me downstairs to dine, chere?"

He promptly vanished. Just vanished.

One moment he was there, and the next … he was gone.

She'd never come as close to fainting in her entire life. She didn't even want to check the door anymore. She scurried back to the bed and pulled the covers over her head.

Lying flat, she squeezed her eyes shut. *I'm going to wake up. I'm going to wake up.* She repeated the mantra until she calmed down enough so that her heart wouldn't beat her to death.

Idly, she wondered if fear induced pulse racing would burn as many calories as an elliptical machine. She'd never felt more fatigued in all her life. This had to be good for something more than shaving years off her life.

When she finally nerved herself and pulled the covers down, she discovered she was in the same room and hadn't magically transported to her bedroom. The only difference was the door was now standing open.

Did he seriously think she'd eat with him? He'd attacked her, hadn't he? Maybe not. It didn't make much sense that he would reign himself in now, after she'd tried to brain him twice. She'd certainly provoked him enough if he was going to be violent. Then again, he *had* abducted her and wouldn't let her leave.

Maggie looked down at herself. Her clothes looked bad enough she wouldn't want *her* at the dinner table. Her jeans were torn at the knee, probably from when she'd fallen to the pavement. There were also brown patches along one hip. Her black knit shirt was ripped at the neck, making the neckline drape almost to her cleavage. They were clean though. That realization put her in a cold sweat. She felt sick to her stomach. Surely he hadn't undressed her and done her laundry? The thought was just too horrible--and unbelievable--to contemplate.

Maggie looked around the room for her sandals, but her shoes were nowhere to be found, and she mourned their loss. It would be impossible to get replacements at this time of the year.

She finally decided she'd stalled long enough. There was nothing for it. She had to leave here somehow.

Retrieving her poker--not that she thought it would do her much good since she'd only managed to hit the wall so far--Maggie exited the room, padding down the hallway on the dusty floor. Her skin crawled at that dirty feeling between her toes, but she ignored it. Almost immediately she spotted the grand, curved staircase leading to the lowest floor.

The front door stood at the bottom of the stairs like a beacon.

Maggie sailed down the stairs. She was halfway down them when she saw the man step into the foyer. Escape was practically in her grasp, however. She tensed all over, envisioning the scenario in her mind. Of leaping over the banister, landing sure-footedly on the floor below, and dashing for the door--all while he merely gaped at her in stunned amazement at her agility, too surprised by her speed to block her path.

Unfortunately, she'd never been terribly coordinated. She thought it was much more likely that she'd hang her foot in the banister and land on her face. And even if she managed to scramble to her feet and he was laughing too hard to move as quickly as he did before, she thought her limp would probably slow her down too much for her to make her getaway.

It was probably locked anyway, she thought glumly.

After her brief hesitation, while she tested the scenario in her mind, she continued down the stairs, pretending it hadn't occurred to her to make a break for the door.

A knowledgeable smile curled his lips. *Asshole*. He knew what had been running through her mind. She had to learn better control over her expressions and her bad habit of letting every thought show on it.

"Leave the poker by the stairs," he said. He crossed his arms over his chest and gestured at her with one forefinger, pointing to where she should leave it.

Maggie thought about clobbering him with it, but she wasn't certain he'd stand still this time anymore than he had the last. Heaving a reluctant sigh, she leaned her weapon against the wall and stepped off the last step, moving toward him.

He bowed when she reached him, lifting her hand and kissing the back in the sort of quaint, old-fashioned chivalry that might have seemed ridiculous if anyone else had done it--or made her feel ridiculous. Instead, it made him appear indescribably suave, and it sent a delicious quiver through her belly.

Resolutely, she ignored it as he turned and walked her down the hallway toward an arched opening at the other end.

It was a formal dining room. And although, like the rest of the house, she knew that it was sadly aged, the tapers burning in the center of the table lent a mellow, golden glow that softened the harshness of the room's aging.

The tablecloth was pristine and set with elegant china and crystal. It seemed so incongruous, given the setting and situation. Nevertheless, she took her seat without comment when he pulled her chair out for her.

The entire situation took on a sort of bizarre, surrealistic edge as he removed the covers from the dishes on the table, displaying food that was as elegantly beautiful as the table setting. Try though she might to imagine him slaving over a hot stove, the image simply did not fit the man sitting across from her.

She didn't know why, but she'd assumed the two of them were alone in the house. Now she wondered if there was an army of servants lurking in the dark. That made no sense either, however. Surely if he had kidnapped her, he wouldn't have that many people that he could trust to aid him in his abduction?

She didn't bother to question him about it. She knew she couldn't trust anything he told her anyway. Instead, she forced a smile. "The food looks delicious."

He nodded at the compliment and served her plate. She wasn't actually hungry. She was way too terrified to be hungry, but she thought that the best way to get him to let down his guard long enough for her to have a chance to escape would be to behave as if she accepted the situation.

When he'd served her plate, therefore, she smiled up at him again and thanked him. The first bite she took brought tears to her eyes. Not because the food was inedible, but because she immediately sank her teeth into her tongue. Her tongue went numb at the wound and throbbed in her mouth like a live thing. The taste of blood filled her mouth.

With an effort, she chewed the food and swallowed anyway, feeling a little sick. It was her blood, of course, and she shouldn't have found it disgusting. She'd always had an aversion to blood though. She wanted desperately to spit the food out, but good manners precluded it, and even in her current situation, especially with that very elegant gentleman sitting across from her--kidnapper or not--she just couldn't bring herself to do anything that crude. Wouldn't her mama be proud to know that she *could* act like a lady?

"Is there a problem with the meat, chere?" he asked, arching a brow.

She blinked the tears from her eyes and looked at him. "Actually," she said, blushing, "I bit my tongue."

"That would be the fangs, chere. They can be inconvenient. And it does take some time to grow accustomed to them."

She stared at him, but he didn't appear to be making a joke. "I don't have fangs," she said.

"Didn't," he corrected.

"Don't," she said, feeling a little childish. "I'm not a dog."

"Certainly not. You're a vampire."

Chapter Three

While they dined, he talked about the history of New Orleans. Despite everything, it soothed her. The sound of his voice stroked along her nerve endings like the caress of a hand. She was surprised to discover that she ate most of the servings that he'd placed on her plate. She'd drank the wine as well, more wine than she'd intended, and certainly more than was wise. Her weight and height usually allowed her to drink more than the average person, however, so she wasn't worried about it. She couldn't remember ever even having a buzz from alcohol.

She didn't comment on his suggestion that she was a vampire. If he thought she'd believe that, he was crazy. Besides being ridiculous, she didn't feel remotely different than any other day of the week, and they'd both eaten the food he'd served--which canceled out all credibility of either of them being a vampire. Vampires could only drink blood. Everyone knew that.

He didn't seem insane, but on the other hand, sane people didn't usually brutally attack women on the street. She remembered hearing once that insane people were incredibly strong. That might explain how he had managed to attack her when she felt that she should have been fully capable of going toe to toe with pretty much any man.

The wine calmed even her fear of his mental stability. She found herself smiling at some of the anecdotes that he told.

"How old were you then," she asked impulsively at something he'd said.

"Six hundred and fifty nine years."

She burst out laughing. "No, really."

"Ah, chere, would you have me whisper sweet little lies in your ear instead?" he said on a husky note that made her insides quiver.

"I'm not sure I'd want you getting that close."

"Wouldn't you?"

Smiling devilishly, he reached across the table, and with his index finger, began swirling a little pattern on the back of her hand. "Perhaps I'm not close enough," he whispered.

Warmth flowed up her arm, lifting the fine hairs on her arm and the back of her neck. A delicious little shiver skated down her spine as she looked into his dark eyes. There was a smoldering look in his gaze that she immediately identified, despite the fact that she'd never had a look like that directed at her in her memory. It sent heat surging through her. Her belly clenched as a sweet, sharp spasm reverberated from the core of her sex straight up to her heart.

A warning voice niggled in the back of her mind. He was a kidnapper and insane besides. She was convenient and his captive, otherwise, she was sure a man that looked like him would never be interested in even looking at her, much less touching her. She was used to people swearing to go on a diet after one look at her size eighteen frame--not with any kind of desire.

That more than anything else was the clincher. She forced a slight smile. "You're not trying to seduce me, are you?"

He smiled wryly. "Not very successfully," he murmured, "if you can ask."

It occurred to her that she was probably a little bit tipsy, but she knew that she was still clear-minded enough to take advantage of the fact that he obviously believed her judgment was impaired by the alcohol she'd consumed.

She gave him her most sultry look, propping her arm on the table and dropping her chin onto her hand. "Now you're teasing me."

Something flickered in his eyes. "I can, if you like."

The breath rushed from her lungs as her heart lurched in

her chest. Despite her wayward libido and her natural reluctance to encourage this sort of conversation under ordinary circumstances, she reminded herself that she was trying to catch him off guard.

"What did you have in mind?" she said in a throaty voice, smiling at him faintly.

He studied her for several moments and finally rose from his chair, took her hand, and led her from the dining room. "I'm much better at showing than telling."

A wave of dizziness washed over her. She struggled to throw it off, refusing to admit even to herself, that it was as much or more pure carnal lust than the wine she had drank. Blushing, she smiled at him in what she hoped was a combination of interest and shyness as he placed her hand on his arm and escorted her from the dining room. In the doorway, she turned slightly toward him, lifting her hand and placing it on his chest.

"I hardly know you. I don't even know your name," she whispered, grasping two handfuls of his jacket.

"Danior," he said, leaning close, his eyelids heavy over his dark eyes.

Even as he leaned his head toward her, she brought her knee up between his legs as hard as she could and gave him a shove backwards.

Whirling, she made a mad dash for the front door. She was on it so fast she slammed into the door and nearly knocked the breath out of herself. She twisted the knob but the door wouldn't open. Through the glass medallion in the center she could see it was also boarded over. How the hell had they even gotten into the house? There must be another door, but she didn't think she had time to look for it.

Turning, she scooped the poker up from the stairs, smashing through the glass. The poker bit into the wood with a thud. She hammered at it with gusto but failed to do more than break off splinters of wood. What the hell had he closed this with? Four by sixes?

"You can't leave that way," he said directly behind her, scaring the life out of her.

Maggie whirled around, gasping, swinging the poker. He

caught the poker mid-air, halting her strike. Frowning, he jerked it free and sent it sailing across the foyer with a metallic clatter as it hit the floor.

Maggie gaped at him as his fingers locked around her wrists. She brought her knee up. He smiled grimly as he blocked her ball busting move with his thigh, grunting at the impact.

"That was a nasty thing to do, chere," he said, tightening his hold on her wrists, pulling her back toward the stairs.

"I don't know why you expected anything different. You kidnapped me!" she gritted out, digging her heels in. She felt slivers of glass cut her bare feet and winced at the pain that shot through them.

He pulled her inexorably toward the stairs. Visions of torture swamped her mind. She couldn't let him take her up there.

She went limp, forcing him to release her as she dropped to the floor. Ignoring the bruise to her hip as she landed, she rolled onto her stomach to get to her feet.

"Merde," he cursed and landed on top of her, pinning her to the floor.

Maggie gasped as his weight locked over her, his knees around her waist, his hands on her shoulders. It was just like the attack. Panic gripped her, sending her heart racing, her lungs burning for air, her mind in a mad whirl of chaotic thought. She reached out for anything, any kind of weapon.

Glass sliced a finger open, drawing her attention. She grasped it, ignoring the pain as it laid open her right palm. She reached across and stabbed at his hand on her left shoulder.

He hissed in pain and broke her slick grip on the glass, flinging it away. Lifting off her struggling form the briefest moment, he flipped her over and straddled her hips, pinning her hands to the floor.

"You little fool. I should let you open that door and kill yourself, if only to make you believe."

"You're crazy!" she gritted out, struggling against his grip. Jesus! He was stronger than she would have ever imagined. Her fingers were going tingly, numb from the pressure.

He sighed wearily and pulled her arms down, shifting his weight until he could pin her hands down with his knees.

Once his hands were free, he straightened and looked down at her, his hands resting on his splayed thighs. Her chest rose and fell drastically with each breath as she continued to struggle to free herself. She couldn't move her arms more than to flap her elbows. Her legs were useless, not because she couldn't move them, but because no matter how hard she strained to buck him, he couldn't be budged.

"Hold still if you don't want me doing something you'll regret," he warned in a voice rough with arousal. She looked up at him and caught him staring at the movement of her breasts. More than the sight of his eyes devouring her, the erection straining the fly of his leather pants snared her attention.

He caught her startled gaze as it flew back up to his eyes. She immediately went limp, a lethargy spreading over her at the feel of his power spreading through her body. She thought the wine had gotten to her but knew that was wrong, that this was different. She could feel him *inside* her, holding her mind in thrall, trying to bend her to his will.

It was working. He kept her thoughts churning, unable to focus on anything so simple as commanding her body to move, to fight him.

He slid his hands down his thighs, bending as he spread his palms over her ribcage just beneath her breasts. Her bra was gone, and in her supine position, her breasts had spread, leaving her cleavage wide enough he could press his lips there if he so chose.

She imagined him tugging her neckline down to scrape his teeth and tongue over her flesh, to nip and lave her breasts until they were ripe and achy from the grip of his large hands.

Maggie slowly blinked as the images changed and he thrust his hand down the front of her jeans, cupping her mound to dip his fingers in the top of her slit and flick the hidden bud there. Her mouth parted on a sigh, the waking dream so intense, her body reacted as if it was real. Her slit moistened, her clit pulsed with a rush of blood and arousal.

Maggie blinked once more, recognizing her descent into the forbidden. She felt drugged--no--mesmerized. These weren't her thoughts. She felt his suggestion, recognized the imagery as his own.

He smiled knowingly, eliciting a quiver inside her vagina that had her clenching the muscles tight.

He slid a hand up, stroking the valley between her breasts, spreading his fingers until they grazed the rounded edges of her breasts. Maggie mentally flinched from him.

He stopped just shy of touching her where she shamelessly wanted to be touched, watching her. "You don't want me to touch you? Is it because you are repulsed by me, or is it something else?" His strange accent flowed over her like deep, mellow music. She wanted to cave into it. Needed to in the worst kind of way.

You crave to relinquish control to a man, he said in her mind.

No, I don't, she responded, clenching her jaw. *Even if I did, I wouldn't want to with you.* But she did want to lose control. Something was wrong with her. She'd always wanted to be dominated by a man. She'd never found one strong enough to command her in the bedroom. Men were intimidated by her, and even if they hadn't been, most were shorter and lighter than she was and couldn't dominate an ant if their life depended on it. She couldn't imagine some weakling taking sexual command of her. She was too much of a realist, her will too strong to tame.

More than that, her body repulsed her in a way that she could never truly let loose and enjoy herself. She'd never found a man capable of making her forget what she was.

He gave her a pleased look after a moment, his heavy brows arching with amusement. *You are shielding your thoughts from me.*

Good. Now let me go. She didn't want him prying into her mind.

"I've never found anyone so young capable of shielding,"

he said thoughtfully, removing his hands from her body to prop on his thighs once more. "Do you believe I am what I say?" he said aloud.

He released her from thrall, allowing her to speak. "No," she gritted out defiantly, shaken by how close she'd come to giving in to him. Her body ached in that oh-so-familiar way of unrequited lust. She could feel the dampness in her sex, the throb of her clit begging for surcease from the strain of unfulfillment. He hadn't done a damn thing to her and she was practically panting for him to fuck her brains out.

It had been so long since she'd been touched by a man that she couldn't even remember the last time. Well, she didn't want to remember the last time. Abstinence seemed to have made her weaker, not more resistant to the lure of sexual impulse.

He sighed and reached for a shard of glass on the floor. Maggie winced, thinking he was going to hurt her, instead, he touched one edge to his palm. "If touching your mind cannot convince you, then perhaps this will. Here's your proof of what we both are," he said, slicing his hand open without hesitation.

"No," she whispered, unable to stop him. Maggie felt sick watching the blood flow. She wanted to look away but couldn't stop watching the well of bright red flow down his arm. It dripped onto her chest and stomach, soaking her with a warmth like hot water.

"Watch," he said softly. The blood slowed to the barest trickle and then stopped. He wiped the blood away with his thumb, clearing the wound.

Maggie watched in disbelief as the wound closed to a scratch and then faded to a thin, red line.

"Your own wounds are gone, if you care to look."

He freed her hands, standing above her as she checked her fingers and hands for cuts. Only dried blood remained. No wound of any kind.

"How is this possible?" she asked, coming to her feet with his help. She winced as her weight landed on heels and the glass embedded there.

"You have the healing ability of the vampire now. It's part of what allows us to live so long. Come, we have to get that glass out of your feet before it heals inside you and has to be cut out."

Without another word, he bent and scooped her into his arms, carrying her up the stairs.

* * * *

Maggie expected to hear the snap of arm bones breaking or the pop of his shoulder joints as they dislocated. Miraculously, nothing like that happened. She never dreamed she'd meet anything short of a crane capable of lifting her off her feet, let alone a man who could carry her up an entire flight of stairs and down a hall.

Secretly, despite the discomfort of the position, she found it thrilling and terrifying that he was strong enough to bear her. There was something so incredibly masculine about it, that it gave her the illusion of being small and feminine. She could feel the power in his shoulders beneath her arm she'd draped around his neck, and as she watched his face, she felt like he had more yet to reveal, as if he was restraining himself from unintentionally hurting her.

He wasn't even winded when he kicked open the bedroom door and took her into the bathroom she'd found earlier. He sat her on the closed lid of the toilet, moving away to the medicine cabinet before coming back with a pair of tweezers. Sitting on the edge of the claw-footed tub, he looked at her expectantly.

"Give me your foot," he said. His tone sounded like he expected her to fight him, but that he would win anyway.

Feeling weird and unsure of herself, she gave him her foot, wincing as he carefully removed the tiny shards of glass imbedded in her skin. He frowned in concentration, his brows drawing close together. His hair fell across his forehead, and he kept having to push it behind his ears.

As he finished, he brushed his thumb over the pads of her toes and ball of her foot to check for anything he'd missed, tickling her.

Maggie yelped and tried to jerk her foot free, but he held her still, tightening his knees around her calf. The position was extremely intimate, with her leg trapped between his thighs and his hands probing her. Again, she felt small next to him. His hands looked large on her feet, making them seem almost dainty. The image of him nibbling down her toes and up her leg flashed in her mind, leaving her warm beneath her clothes.

The heat of his erection pressed near her heel, adding to her discomfort and awareness of him as a desirable man. It embarrassed her to see it and be so close to grazing it, but it embarrassed her more to realize she *wanted* to touch it. If she moved just a little and he let go, she could rub her toes upon it. Press down and massage with her toes to give him pleasure.

He tickled her foot one last time, deliberately provoking her and snapping her back to the present. Giving her a wicked smile, he finished his inspection and demanded her other foot--the one with most of the glass.

She couldn't quite comprehend her attraction to him, not when he had to be the person who had hurt her before.

It was strange watching him do something so tender. Despite how large his hands were, his fingers weren't thick and chunky. They were tapered and elegant, like the fingers of an aristocrat. He didn't fumble with the painstaking work, and she knew, implicitly, that he would not be inept with more delicate tasks.

She could hardly reconcile him with the attacker in the alley. He'd tended her wounds, fed her with elaborate dishes equal to fine cuisine in expensive restaurants … tried to seduce her. And now she knew that he was a vampire-- that she was, if he was to be believed.

It had to be true. Nothing else could explain the rapid healing. And yet….

"I don't feel any different," she finally said, almost to herself.

He looked up briefly from his task. "You won't until your first thirst. Your fangs will swell with your first venom, and only fresh blood can override the imbalance in your body's hormonal system. It will drive your thoughts until you appease it. It will kill you if you deny it. Too much venom kills even us."

Blood. It made her sick even thinking about it. "Why did you attack me in the alley? Is it because you were thirsty?" she asked impulsively.

He frowned, his eyes shuttered. "I didn't attack you."

Somehow, she knew it was the truth. Perhaps deep inside, she'd known it all along. Had her subconscious allowed her to become attracted? Or was it something that couldn't be controlled, even if a man was a bastard and a killer? So many women seemed trapped unto death by men she deemed real life monsters. She liked to believe her own judgment was not so impaired. "If you didn't, who did?"

"Another vampire. Before you ask, yes, he was hungry. Would you like to know his name so that you can hunt him down and stake him? I confess, I would not have his actions any different. Had he not bitten you," he said, his voice dropping an octave, "I would not have you now."

For some absurd reason, that statement sent a flurry of pleasure inside her. Gawd, she was such an idiot. She ignored it. "Did I die then? Am I ... undead?"

He chuckled, brushing his fingers over her foot, searching for glass. She shivered. "You are breathing, are you not? Vampirism is a disease, nothing more."

"What about your special powers? What else can you do?"

He tucked the tweezers away in his pocket and massaged her foot, sending pleasure up her calf. The pain was already gone. She couldn't doubt her body's reaction--her rapid healing.

And she couldn't ignore how she responded to him.

"If you live as long as I have, you will learn as much and more. I have nothing but time on my side. When I was turned, I was vulnerable, as you are now. It is the main reason that a fledgling vampire must have a master--you need the protection."

"How long will that take?" she asked, feeling warm and drowsy.

"Your mind is strong. Perhaps in ten years you will be ready to go out on your own." He massaged her calf, bending over her leg.

"Hmm." She wiggled her toes and stretched them, brushing against his erection. It was as hard as she imagined, thick and huge. She grew damp just thinking about wrapping herself around it.

He stopped and looked at her. She smiled lazily and leisurely stroked up his length. It throbbed beneath her, hot, aching for feminine wetness.

He stood abruptly, releasing her. She dropped her foot to the floor.

"You should bathe the blood from your body and rest while it is still light out."

Disappointed, she watched him leave and sighed. She wasn't sure if it was the 'vampirism' or going too long without male companionship, but she was horny as hell. Frustrated by his lack of responsiveness--which she should have expected--she closed the bathroom door and took off her bloody, torn clothes, dropping them in a pile on top of the hamper. As bad as they looked, she should've just put them in the trash, but then she'd have to walk around naked.

If she was skinny, she might be tempted, if only to get a real rise out of Danior and see what would happen. As it was, she rather thought strolling around naked in front of him would be a hindrance to any amorous designs she might have. She hadn't looked at herself naked in a long, *long* time, since it always seemed to put her in a funk and in the mood for ice cream, but she knew without looking that she wasn't in the least desirable.

He'd had an erection, but that didn't mean a damn thing. Men *stayed* aroused. They'd screw a fat girl in a heartbeat just for a warm, wet hole, but they'd never tell anyone about it. It was one of the reasons she hated men.

It was one of the reasons why she hadn't had sex in almost eight years--not since her first time, when she'd found out it had all been a really bad joke and the fat girl's virginity had been the punch line.

Ignoring the hurt at that memory, Maggie turned on the water, adjusting the temperature, then turned on the shower head and climbed into the tub. Water rained down on her head, washing the dried blood away as she pulled the curtain around the tub. It fluttered with the billowing steam at the back, and she bent to tuck the curtain in and put a bar of soap on top to hold it in place.

As she did so, she noticed movement out of the corner of her eye. Pushing wet strands of hair off her forehead, she poked at a fold in the curtain, freezing when she saw a spider the length of her thumb.

Maggie stifled a scream and pinched up the curtain, trying to smash the gray striped monstrosity. It scrambled up the curtain.

She gulped down another scream, fighting to keep calm, releasing the curtain as she took the shower head and tried to point it at the spider to drown it. It wouldn't reach. Putting her hand in the water stream, she tried to angle the water at the curtain, splashing at it. When that failed, she took in a mouthful of water and spit a stream at it.

Water hit the spider. It fell into the tub and instantly crumpled. Maggie jumped out of the shower, dripping all over the floor as she looked into the tub. The spider floated around the two inches of water, heading in the opposite direction of the drain.

"I hate spiders," she muttered, shivering in revulsion and with the cool air brushing over her wet skin. No way was she getting back in there with that spider's carcass.

Looking around for something to scoop it out, she spied an empty toilet paper roll poking out of the trash can. Grabbing it, she leaned over the tub and tried to scoop the spider out.

Like a flower, the spider's legs bloomed out from its body as it clambered up the toilet roll. Maggie screamed and thrust the soggy roll in the water, trying to smash the spider. She lifted it carefully and the spider popped up and ran up the tube. Screaming again, Maggie smashed the tube on the side of the tub, smearing and pounding with the soggy cardboard until she was sure it was dead.

With a sense of dread, she carefully peeled it up and peered on the other side, feeling satisfaction to see its crumpled, flat body pasted onto the brown paper.

Shuddering, she dropped the roll into the trash can.

Behind her, the door burst open and slammed against the wall.

Chapter Four

Danior was sweeping up the glass when the first scream pierced his senses. His heart halted one brief moment and set into a gallop as adrenaline pumped into his system.

Fearing that their hiding place had been discovered, he dropped the broom and raced up the stairs, taking them two at a time. Another scream rent the air, louder this time, fueling his sense of dread. She could be dead before he ever reached her.

Danior rushed into her bedroom. It was empty. He heard water in the bathroom, the sounds of a struggle, the pounding tempo of her heart.

He burst through the door, letting it rebound noisily off the wall as he stopped stock still in the door frame at the sight that greeted him.

She whirled and jerked her head up, shrieking and covering her nakedness.

A fog of lust overwhelmed him, making him sway and take a step back. It curled through his body to tauten his nerves with desire. His blood flow redirected, leaving him light headed as it aimed for his cock, bringing it to throbbing life with the resounding beat of his heart. He took a step inside, barely able to break his gaze away from the soft, ample curves of her body to inspect the room for danger.

"What has happened," he demanded, wrenching his mind away from the ripe, woman shapeliness in the corner just begging for him to give her a roll. Concentrating, he looked around the small room, seeing nothing amiss. Without his gaze locked on her form, he was able to think clearly. He could sense no other presence, now that he had calmed enough to reach out with his mind. Her screams had made his mind betray him, set him into a near panic. He could not allow her to weaken him in such a way.

He looked back at her when he confirmed they were alone. Desire swelled again, abetting his descent into pure, carnal, mindless need. God above, she would be the death of him.

"Get out!" she screamed, "Get out, get out, get out!" She backed up, pulling the nearly clear curtain over her body as if it would shield her from his gaze.

He closed his eyes a moment, willing himself to leave the room. His lids opened once more, defying his waning willpower.

She obviously didn't realize just how much the curtain revealed. He could see the shadow of blonde hair at the apex of her thighs, see the turn of her waist up to her ribcage. Her small, pink nipples flattened against the vinyl, breasts bulging against the fabric like they were contained in a corset, urging him to rip the covering away and suck them into his mouth.

His salivary glands tightened, a sharp pain jarring his jaw muscles. His mouth watered as hunger overtook him, hunger that could only be appeased by a warm, willing woman.

Without conscious volition, he stepped toward her, closing the distance between them until he had backed her up nearly to the wall. Steam wafted in the air, making her skin damp. Her hair clung to her forehead and throat in an array that drew his attention to her veins as effectively as an arrow shot.

They shown pale blue, a tracery over her chest and throat like a fall of delicate lace about her neck. His fangs ached to see the life blood flow in her veins, to see the translucent skin unmarred and pink from the heat of the nearby shower and her own response to his nearness.

"Why were you screaming?" he asked with an attempt at feigning a calm he didn't feel, yet his voice was still thick and rough with arousal despite his effort.

Celeste Anwar

She swallowed, her throat working to put moisture into her mouth. He clenched his jaw, tightening his hands into fists as her muscles moved sensually slow. "A spider tried to get me," she said huskily, watching with a wary eye caught between him and a route of escape.

He smiled despite himself. He hadn't met a woman yet who didn't hate spiders. "You're nearly immortal now. It wouldn't have hurt you."

She tightened her grip on the curtain, shifting on her feet. "Phobias are an irrational fear. I can't help myself."

"Hmm." He couldn't either, and he was weary of playing by the rules of society, the rules of the council ... and her rules. Perhaps that's why he'd broken one of the oldest dictates of the New Orleans underworld--to allow a human to be turned vampiric. It was a death sentence to defy the council, one that he'd welcomed with relish before. But now....

He watched her without speaking a long moment. Tension built in the air around them. Expectancy made her breath rush between her lips. She breathed hard, as if she couldn't get enough air. He felt suddenly as breathless as she, his heart pounding in time to her own.

Such moments were rare for him, this sense of urgency to sate his appetite mingling with the near hidden fear of rejection. The uncertainty sharpened his yearning, awakened a new hunger, stronger than any other before it, more ravenous.

Scarcely aware of himself, he lifted his hands and ripped the curtain away. Her gasp spurred the rapacious, overwhelming need to take and conquer, devour her cries and consume her passion. She wrapped her arms around her breasts and pubic mound, trying to hide. His belly clenched with the impact of her defenselessness. He smiled in anticipation, eager to see her and kiss her until her shyness dissolved under his tongue. Already her cunt wept for his possession. Its subtle scent perfumed the air, driving his need to unbearable heights.

"You draw attention to yourself, chere," he said, slowly locking his hands around her wrists, forcing her to free her body for his greedy gaze.

"I don't do it on purpose," she gasped, jerking at the tether of his hands, fighting, but not fighting hard enough. "I don't want you looking at me. I don't want anyone to look at me."

"Don't you?"

She tried to pull free, to turn away, but he wouldn't allow it. No, not this time. He'd seen her before, when he'd cleansed her body and laid her to recuperate in the bedroom, but her limp form was nothing as it was now, vibrantly alive, aching for fulfillment and freedom.

When she couldn't escape, she closed her eyes, as if that would hide her somehow, as if it could disguise her embarrassment.

She hated herself, her body--that he knew, but the driving need to change was something he'd never understood about women. His cock swelled at the sight of her pale flesh. She was all rounded curves and no hard edges. She would be soft to touch, soft and welcoming to the pounding of his body into hers. He ached to sink inside her, drum into her pussy until the world dissolved around them.

Her breasts were smaller than he'd supposed, and if she'd been a smaller size, she would probably be nearly flat-chested. As it was, they were a modest handful, tipped with virginal nipples no larger than the tip of her pinkie finger. He could tell just from looking at her and her response, that she'd never allowed a man to look at her naked. Had she allowed a man to suckle her breast?

He thought not. It pleased him to think he would be the first to taste her, to see her.

"Stop looking at me," she gritted out, twisting in his hold, ashamed of herself.

Her shame made him ache, long to erase whatever held her repressed to her own natural beauty. He was angry that she'd loosed his hold over himself, that she denied him and herself. He was ravenous, and he saw no need to deny the hunger what it willed.

"You're right. I've looked for long enough," he ground out, wrapping his arms around her and trapping her hands behind her back, forcing her to arch against him.

Her breasts flattened against his chest, her soft stomach melded to the muscles of his flat belly. He groaned as his cock met her naked mound, only his leather pants between him and the sweet heat between her thighs. He held her there a moment, soaking in the feel of her pressed so intimately against him.

Her heart fluttered against his chest. Each rapid breath made her tighten to him, increased the furious tempo of his own desire.

Biting back another groan, he bent his head and closed his lips over hers. She gasped against his lips, indignant, surprised, angry. He tasted her sweet breath before plunging his tongue inside her mouth, sweeping past her short fangs to tangle with her tongue.

She was hot and wet, vulnerable against him. Her hands twisted at her back, fighting him. Aggression surged in his veins at her defenselessness. Toying with her tongue, he nibbled her lips, urging her to taste him back.

Her tongue was limp in her mouth, resistant to his teasing, leaving him disappointed.

He released her hands, cupping her buttocks as he crushed her back against the wall, bringing her up hard against the ridge of his cock.

She moaned into his mouth, gripping his forearms as if she would thrust him away. He plunged his tongue in and out of her mouth, mimicking the grind of his hips as he rocked against her mound.

She whimpered, deep in her throat, sucking on his tongue at last, sending his will careening out of control. He kissed her harder, coaxed her tongue into his mouth so that he could suckle her as he massaged her buttocks. The weight felt good in his hands. He spread them, unbalancing her until she was opening for him, spreading her thighs around his hips as he pushed her up the wall and took her weight into his hands.

His groin nestled in the apex of her thighs. He knew her cleft wrapped around him, bared to his cock, wet and burning for the hammer of his body. He tore his mouth from hers, dragging it over her jaw line. Her small gasps urged him on, fired his blood in a way he hadn't felt in years. His body had felt dead before, lifeless to emotion. Now he was alive and starving for the taste of her, of this woman that hated him and what he was.

He opened his mouth on her neck, dragging his teeth over her throat. She shuddered, her pulse quickening beneath his lips as if she knew what he wanted ... and feared and welcomed it.

He had yet to taste her blood, but he craved it, craved the ecstasy that could only be wrought by the intimacy of blood bonding.

The thought brought him up short, quenching the fire in his loins like a dash of ice water.

"Oh ... god," he groaned against her neck, his breath fanning off her skin against his own lips. His fangs lengthened, anticipating the pleasure of piercing her flesh, to become one with her. His salivary glands spasmed again, making him hiss in pain.

He laved her neck, tasting the salt of her skin, the fear and desire trembling beneath the surface, pulsing in her lifeblood. It called him like a drug, promising a high unlike any other, an addiction he wished to embrace again.

To want it was the ultimate weakness.

He thrust against her cleft, her liquid heat near burning him through his pants. He groaned and closed his eyes, driving against her, trying to draw the anguishing, needful thirst to his throbbing cock.

She moaned, panting and whimpering. He grazed her neck, calling the blood to its surface.

With a growl of fury, he tore himself away from her, breathing heavily, resisting the lure of her eyes, glazed with passion and fear and disappointment. Her mouth and throat were reddened from his kisses. Her lips were parted and wet, pouty, begging to be tugged into his mouth and sucked. And a line was drawn across her throat, from his teeth, testament to how close he'd come to breaking his vow to himself.

He stalked out of the room before he could make such a

drastic mistake as blood bonding with another woman. The last time he had, she'd nearly killed him.

* * * *

Maggie watched him leave, unsure if she wanted to scream at him for touching her, or run after him. She knew it was stupid, but she couldn't help feeling like he was disgusted with her for some reason. She didn't want to embarrass herself if that was the case and ask him to stay.

Had he felt some cellulite on her ass and been turned off? She didn't know, and not knowing what had happened made her sick to her stomach.

She felt as dumb as a teenager. She didn't have enough sexual experience with men to know how to deal with their mood swings, to know what every nuance of an expression or rejection could mean.

Maggie felt herself descending into a depression. Strangely, she didn't long for a stomach full of something sweet. That was a bright note, but she was still ashamed to admit that a man made her feel this way. It was weak, and she hated being weak or dependent on another person.

Strange as it was, she could barely remember how she'd felt the night she'd been attacked--the same day her world had changed because she was out of a job, car-less, and practically on the street with no money for necessities like a home and ice cream. Instead, her thoughts centered around a man she didn't even know, who'd taken her in for some unfathomable reason. He was a vampire. She should hate him, be scared of him, not feel this insane attraction.

But she did, and she couldn't stop herself.

Maggie finished her shower, washing the scent of him off her skin, the taste of him out of her mouth. Try as she might though, she couldn't erase how it had felt to be touched. God, it had been so long. She'd forgotten what it could feel like, how exhilarating it was to feel arousal and have that same feeling reciprocated.

But it wasn't. No more than it had been the first time.

Miserable, she left the bathroom and found that he'd laid out a new set of clothes as well as a pajama shorts set. She checked the sizes and was mortified to see that he had them exactly right. There was no pretending that she was something she wasn't. She hated the idea that he knew she was a size eighteen--hated that he'd seen her naked when she'd been so careful all of her life not to allow it.

She dropped her towel and changed into the pajama set. Miserable, and not knowing what else to do, she climbed into bed and was asleep only a few moments later.

The nausea woke her. She broke out in a cold sweat as her gut clenched. Hoping the feeling would pass, she lay perfectly still until she knew that it wouldn't. Unable to fight it any longer, she threw herself out of bed and rushed to the bathroom before it was too late.

She barely made it to the toilet in time. The elegant dinner she'd enjoyed went straight into the toilet, scouring her throat and mouth with fire. Tears streamed down her face, making her eyes blur. Her stomach convulsed again and again until she had nothing left inside her, and even then the disgust continued to make her dry heave.

Finally, she was able to stop and flushed the toilet, crawling to the tub and running water to rinse her mouth out and wash her face.

She heard the door open and knew he'd come in.

If things weren't bad enough, they always got worse. Maggie kept her back to him, bathing her face in cold water.

He touched her shoulder gently, pulling her hair back from her face.

Maggie shrugged him off, going stiff all over. If it wasn't bad enough that he'd rejected her, to have him see her this way should have killed her dead on the spot from mortification. Someone up above liked to torture her for fun too much. "Stay the fuck away from me, you bastard!"

He dropped his hand, but she could still feel him right behind her, watching.

Maggie tried to ignore him. The pain helped. Her head felt like it was going to split open. Even her teeth hurt, ached as though someone had tried to pry them apart. Pain gnawed at her belly now that it was empty, but she'd be damned if she'd experience that again for something to fill it and take the ache away.

"You have to feed. I thought having some food in your stomach would slow the process, but I see it hasn't."

Pain lanced her gums. She tasted blood and knew they'd split. She gulped a mouthful of water and spit it out, seeing small threads of blood run down the drain.

"Your fangs have come fully in. It's the overabundance of venom that sickens you and drives the hunger," he said softly, as if he knew what she was experiencing.

She half wondered hysterically if a dentist could pull them and fix her little problem. She cried into the tub, pressing her palm into it to keep from falling inside as she spat more blood out. Bile rose in her throat. She'd always had a problem looking at blood, much less tasting it. The coppery taste repulsed her. How could she ever stand drinking it willingly?

"What's wrong with me?" she whispered, sobbing against her arm.

"You need blood. If you don't hunt tonight, you'll die."

Chapter Five

He helped her stand, steadying her as she wavered against him. He closed his arms around her, comforting her in a way she hadn't been since before her mom died. He rubbed his hands on her back in soothing circles.

"Do I have to kill someone?" she asked, horrified by the implication of feeding off of another human being. She was in so much pain though, she thought that maybe she could off a bad guy if this went on long enough. Prolonged torture could make a person do anything to make it stop. She had a horrible aversion to pain and suffering.

"We're forbidden to kill humans. But that's not what we will hunt tonight. I dare not take you into the city, regardless. There is wildlife nearby, and it will be easier for you for your first time."

So far, there was nothing remotely romantic about being a vampire. Someone, somewhere had screwed up on the glamorous parts.

Not speaking further, he led her into the room and she saw he'd brought her another outfit. She appreciated him shopping for her--even if she didn't know when he could have done it--but his taste just didn't fit her body style. Spread on the bed was a fire engine red, leather bustier; black lambskin pants, boot cut; twenty eye, Doc Marten boots with red flames stitched on the sides; and a leather duster. If she was about forty pounds lighter, she'd love his taste in clothing. As it was, she didn't need any help looking bigger.

Despite her pain, there were some things she couldn't let rest without saying something. "Haven't you heard leather makes fat people look fatter?"

He sighed and ran a hand through his long hair in irritation. "It's easier to clean the blood off of leather and vinyl. I'll wait for you downstairs."

She was just delaying and she knew it. Killing something and drinking its blood was inevitable. Swallowing hard, she changed from her soaked pajamas into the leather clothing. Unfortunately, the lining clung to her damp skin and made getting into it extremely difficult. She felt like a fatty piece of meat shimmying into a sausage skin. When she was dressed, panting from exertion, she took a quick trip into the bathroom to check herself out. The mirror wasn't full length, but it gave her a good idea of what she looked like.

She actually didn't look that bad, considering. The leather, tight as it was, held her stomach in, shaped and lifted her butt, and the bustier made her breasts look huge. The man was seriously kinky with this whole leather fetish.

A wave of dizziness made her close her eyes, and Maggie knew she'd delayed long enough. The sleep she'd gotten only seemed to have made her groggy rather than rested, and she wasn't sure how many of the symptoms she was feeling could be attributed to this 'thirst for blood'.

She dragged herself downstairs where he waited in the foyer, lounging against the banister, dressed in unrelieved black like it was some vampire uniform. The glass and blood streaking the floor from earlier had been cleaned up.

Maggie felt her breath catch as he looked up at her. He really was beautiful, in a completely male sort of way. She couldn't remember ever seeing another man that affected her the way he did. Her desire for other men seemed pathetic now, as weak as dishwater compared to the blinding force of his sexual attraction.

Potently masculine, he oozed carnality. Just looking at his face sent her thoughts whirling away from her own hurts to imagine sensual aches that would hurt so good in all the right places. She craved it with a hunger equal to that to ease her pain. If she could think about sex while feeling like she'd expire at any moment, she felt her chances were pretty good that she'd live.

She wasn't sure how long she could stand to be around him, knowing that he'd found something repulsive about her. She preferred not knowing exactly what it was and just picking at it with her brain rather than know that it was something she'd *never* be able to change about herself.

He held his arm out expectantly, and she wrapped her hand around it, surprised when he led her away from the front door down the hall that went beneath the stairs. In the back, past the kitchen and other rooms sealed off from her view, there stood the back door. It was boarded up from the inside, but as he unlocked the knob, she found it was only an illusion. That, or he'd come in here while she was upstairs and pried all the nails loose.

She was surprised to see the moon high in the sky. It was later than she'd thought it was.

Here at the back of the house, parked under an oak tree sat a car covered with a tarp. She couldn't make out the model, but whatever it was, by the curves, she could see it was sporty.

Instead of leading her to it, he took her into the woods. Close to the house, the land seemed to have only recently been taken over by nature. Scrub cluttered the ground chest high, and fresh saplings grew with trunks no thicker than her forearm, but the ground was perfectly flat, which led her to believe it had only grown over perhaps five years or so ago. Surprisingly, despite the dappled light making it darker than it should have been, she could see well enough not to fall on her face.

Her night vision seemed stronger than it had been before, but she couldn't know if that was an overactive imagination or not. She hadn't displayed any other 'super' powers.

They didn't talk as they worked through the woods.

She breathed shallowly, creeping behind him as he moved silently to the leaner wood, thicker and dark, with a covering of leaves thick enough to stifle the growth of underbrush. She sensed he was tense, watchful. He looked up suddenly, as if he'd heard something, startling her with his abrupt reaction. Without warning, he took off at a run.

Maggie trailed after him, but dressed all in black, he blended into the dark so completely she lost him within seconds. She stopped, holding her breath as she listened for him. In the distance, snapping sounded, echoing through the trees like a rifle shot.

She jumped at the sudden noise and ran in that direction. In seconds, another wave of dizziness washed over her, leaving her weak. She stopped, leaning against a tree as she waited for it to pass. Each heartbeat accentuated the feeling, until her entire body throbbed with acute pain. She dropped to her knees as her stomach spasmed on a hard knot. Gasping, she clutched her belly, closing her eyes tightly as she tried to meditate and convince herself it didn't hurt so bad. Over and over, she repeated the mantra, a cold sweat drying on her brow, giving her chills.

Behind her, something fell to the ground. The scent of blood assaulted her nose, making her want to retch.

She swallowed with difficulty, huddling on the ground, trying to control her shivering.

"It's worse than I thought," Danior said from behind, moving around before her. In his arms he held a young deer. It was still alive, but its eyes were glazed as if it had been tranquilized.

Just by looking at it, she knew that he held it enthralled.

He knelt before her and produced a butterfly knife,

flipping it open with one hand as he lay the deer on the ground. He sliced its throat open without preamble, without struggle or pain to the animal. It lay there as it's life bled out of its throat.

Blood scented the air, sharp and pungent.

"Drink," he whispered.

Maggie shook her head, closing her eyes against the sight. Her teeth seemed to pulse. Her gums swelled. Saliva pooled in her mouth, making her feel like she'd drown.

Danior moved until he caught her by the back of the neck, pushing her inexorably toward the deer. Her lips touched its neck, warm liquid wetting the sensitive skin.

"Drink if you want to live," he commanded.

Fighting nausea, she opened her mouth against it, letting her teeth sink in to the bare flesh. Her gums convulsed as her teeth connected, she felt something ejaculate from her teeth--like a stinger releasing poison ... or fangs. The pain in her head ceased immediately, as if a fluid had been built up, causing unbearable pressure that had now been released. Fresh blood welled into her mouth in that instant, making her gag. She choked on it, tried to pull back to spit it out, but he wouldn't ease the pressure on the back of her neck, forced her to drink.

She swallowed. Warmth spread into her belly, quieting its painful uproar. She felt the same as if she'd gulped a draught of wine.

"More," he said, urging her to drink. She did, drinking more as he commanded her, until her body prickled with sensation.

Apparently satisfied she had had enough, he released her.

Maggie turned away from the dead creature, standing as she wiped blood off her mouth with the back of her hand. She bit a knuckle, choking back tears. She continued to taste it and feel the pulse beating, growing weaker beneath her tongue. Worse than drinking it's life, as her belly had filled and the warmth spread into her arms and legs--she'd enjoyed it. The pleasure was akin to orgasm, not the peak, but the afterglow. Waves of energy traveled inside her, like a sigh of endorphins radiating through her body.

He closed his arms around her, wrapping her in his heat and scent, obliterating any chance of seeing her kill as she recovered.

She was repulsed by what she'd done, the way she felt. How could she enjoy something so horrible? Would her humanity drain away each time she fed, until she was nothing but a monster? "How often will I have to do this?" she said brokenly, sobbing against his chest. "I'd rather die than do this every night."

He rubbed her back, rocking her in his arms. "Each vampire is different. Some require constant feeding. Others do so perhaps once a month, or a few times during a year. We won't know how often you will have to feed until the next time it happens."

"I can't stand it. I can't be here, Danior. Take me back to the house, please."

* * * *

Though she'd been sleeping most of the time since her attack, Maggie was exhausted. She felt emotionally drained by everything that had happened. Her nerves were raw, easily rubbed to the point where the smallest, inconsequential detail would hurt her, memories an agony. She was so tired, so ill at the turn of her life, that all she wanted to do was sleep.

Danior seemed to sense her weariness and bade her return to her room to sleep until she felt better. She did so gladly.

In her sleep though, she was tortured by images of dead things. They were all around her, demanding her life in return for theirs, claiming she was their murderer. Maggie screamed and ran away from them, but always she was hungry, looking for a new victim, looking for blood. She had to go through them to ease the unquenchable thirst. They clawed at her legs, nails painful, poisonous. Her legs were deteriorating beneath her, leaving her prey to them, unable to run away.

Maggie cried out in her sleep, struggling to wake herself. She knew she dreamed, but she couldn't fight the hold of her slumber, could only repeat the horrors again and again.

Cool hands touched her forehead before grasping her bare

shoulders. They shook her, gently, and she came awake at last with a gasp. Danior stood above her, his face inscrutable in the dark.

Seeing him brought her a sense of relief so profound, it brought tears to her eyes. She wanted to ask him to hold her, but she wasn't brave enough to risk rejection--wasn't sure enough of how he would respond.

"You were having a nightmare," he said softly, brushing the tears from her cheeks with a thumb.

Maggie shivered. It had been years since she'd suffered night terrors. Stress and uncertainty caused them, and she had this unwelcome feeling that they would only continue and grow worse. "I know, but it didn't feel that way to me. It felt real. Horrible."

"It happens to many of us," he said. Without asking, but as if he knew she sought his embrace, he climbed into the bed, facing her beneath the covers. He pulled her against his bare chest, wrapping an arm around her back for support.

He was all muscle, hard and unyielding, but his gentleness with her made her feel indescribably tender, achy and needy for him.

The rhythm of his heart lulled her fears. She almost felt like she could trust him to keep the nightmares at bay, that she'd found a knight in shining armor instead of a creature of the dark ... a living nightmare.

It couldn't fight the hopelessness welling inside her, the despair--rational or irrational--that she would become a monster surrounded by other monsters more terrifying than anything she could imagine. She was a realist. This was an abandoned house, not a place where he lived. In the back of her mind, she knew they were hiding, that something bad hovered on the horizon, waiting to attack. She couldn't bring herself to ask him and confirm her suspicions, and she suspected he would lie about it anyway to spare her. Something bad was going to happen. Something worse than anything she'd experienced thus far. She felt it in her bones. "You should have let me die," she whispered, turning her face into his chest as sleep overcame her.

* * * *

Danior flinched at her words, tightening his arm at the small of her back. How often had he wished much the same thing? Eternity paled when there was no hope for a better existence, no hope for the common dreams of man. Immortality seemed to suck the life out even as it granted forever.

He felt her thoughts, felt the horror and despair, her uncertainty. She sensed a malevolence approaching just as he did. Her gift of clairvoyance was fledgling but promising.

He could tell her the truth, but he was reluctant to. She was strong, her will great, but she'd been hit by too much, and she hadn't yet fully recovered from the first stages of her disease. She would not come into her powers until the virus had time to spread through her body like a cancer, mutating cells instead of devouring them.

The council had likely discovered by now that Zane had left a changing human at Danior's mercy. In the week since, he had not returned to dispel surfacing rumors. They would know what he'd done, and they would kill him for it. He wondered idly who they would send to do the deed.

The only way for the council to maintain control was to issue death to any who broke their rules. Among the long lived, death was the only thing they feared. Ostracism had never worked, for most were loners by nature. The new world orders had forgone the torture of the old world in favor of dealing swift, lethal justice. There were too many vampires to hide. If their numbers increased, they would be discovered. As advanced as this age was, they would still be destroyed for their way of life, for feeding from the living--or taken for secret experiments.

Danior had understood the rule, had agreed with it for as long as he'd lived here, since the signing of the Louisiana Purchase.

It would have been better to let her die. She wanted it, but he simply couldn't bring himself to destroy her, no matter how hard the devils of reason spurred him to.

It was too late now to make a difference one way or

another.

This place of massacre would not shelter them long. Only reluctance and fear of the past had kept them away for this long. Time was not on his side. He had to get her out of the states, to the old world and their old traditions.

That meant negotiating passage to the old world, so that they were not killed on sight. He had his cell phone in his back pants pocket. He could make the arrangements tomorrow. There was bound to be a ship they could take from port.

It meant leaving all she knew behind, but he'd read enough of her thoughts to know that no family held her here. Fortunate enough, since she would have had to sever all life ties anyway.

Danior stroked her hair, enjoying the silk of it between his fingers. Though he couldn't see its color in the dark, he knew it was a burnt amber, threaded with gold. It would turn dark as she spent her years in the night, as it did for most of their kind. The fair-haired were rare.

He nuzzled her temple, breathing in the unique scent that was all her own. She was helpless, in need of his protection. For the first time in his life, he felt needed, whether she wished it or not. He'd selfishly indulged his whim, but he wouldn't change his decision. His rule of the city as vampire lord had been meaningless. He was not needed for control--because the council were the keepers of the law. The vampires in the region were aged, fully capable of defending themselves, and fully willing to start wars with rival factions and their natural enemies, the Lycans.

Danior felt more like a politician shuffling for favor rather than able to bring about change and prosperity for his kind.

They did not need him. Life would go on as it always had. But for Maggie....

How long had it been since he'd comforted a woman, comforted anyone for that matter? He'd only ever thought of his needs before. Women were to be used only for carnal pleasures. Hadn't he been taught that lesson over and over again? Love was a weakness, a dangerous emotion--one that would get him killed.

He felt strangely calm holding her, soothed by the motions of soothing her as she slept to keep her terrors at bay.

He hadn't slept during the night in centuries, not since his turning, but he found that just this once, he wanted to engage in it, if only to imagine he was human for just a little while.

Chapter Six

The dream changed. There had been something in the darkness around her that terrified her. Like most nightmares, she wasn't certain of what it was, only that it was dark and evil and it would hurt her if she didn't escape. When she'd tried to run, though, she'd found she couldn't. She struggled as hard as she could, but it was all she could do to move at all. Her heart was pounding, suffocating her. She fought to drag a decent breath of air into her lungs even as she labored uselessly to run.

She had reached a point of despair, knowing that whatever it was that pursued her, it was going to catch her and something horrible would happen. And then, she wasn't alone anymore. She felt safety in the presence beside her.

His hands soothed her, easing the painful pounding of her heart. For many moments, peace settled over her. And then the dream changed once more. This time, she lay in a man's arms and, as with the dream before, she knew with certainty that he was her lover. Warmth flowed over her like mulled wine as he caressed her and her heart began to beat rapidly again, this time with desire as his caresses became more intimate.

She sighed in delicious anticipation as she felt him pull her thighs apart. Blood flooded into her labia, making them pulse with fevered longing. Moisture gathered there, as well, as he dragged his tongue slowly along her cleft from the mouth of her sex to her clit. A shiver skated through her. Her breath caught in her throat. She tensed, waiting, hoping to feel his touch again. And as he stroked her once more and the heat and tension built inside her, she felt a strange rise and fall of her senses as she moved slowly upwards through the layers of sleep into a hazy, almost drugged consciousness.

There was no abrupt awakening, jerking her away from arousing fulfillment. She surfaced to the certainty that her dream lover was, in fact, entirely real, but she was beyond caring about anything except the feel of his tongue as he stroked her.

Her cunt sizzled as his hot breath whispered over her wet nether lips, cooling and warming all at once. He massaged the insides of her thighs, coaxing as he nudged them further apart. She moved them eagerly, moaning as he settled more deeply against her, opening his mouth and flicking his tongue across her clit. The heat swelled, roiled. The muscles in her belly tightened.

Her vaginal walls clenched on a spasm of pleasure, quivering at the rapid response of her body. She thought it couldn't feel better, but then his mouth closed over her clit and sucked it hard into his mouth, nibbling the tender flesh.

Maggie gasped, discovered she could no longer be still. She moved mindlessly, her senses drugged, her mind reeling with the exquisite torture of his mouth and tongue as he teased her on and on.

Abruptly he stopped, rolling from between her thighs, pulling her with him with unimaginable strength. She rose over him, felt the power of his body between her legs as she straddled his chest. He looked up at her, barely discernible in the dark, and cupped each ass cheek in his hands, pulling her toward his face.

She trembled inside, afraid she'd crush him, but her pussy wept for the feel of his mouth again. Helpless to her raging arousal, she shifted higher on him, crying out as he swathed her cleft with his tongue.

She grasped the headboard for support, unconsciously

tightening her thighs. His lips moved against her labia, feeling almost like a smile, and then his hands pulled at her cheeks, spreading her lips as he thrust his tongue deep inside her cunt.

Her womb convulsed on the blunt, liquid stab, jerking as if wounded, but with exquisite pain that made her ache for more. Her vaginal muscles tightened around him, as if gasping, drawing hard on a breath that wouldn't come. He tongue fucked her, wringing broken cries from her throat, devouring her. She ground herself against his face, biting her lip as he nibbled up to her clit.

Her heart pounded. Her blood sang through her veins, moving like an endorphin rush throughout her system. Her skin prickled with life, making her aware of the flex of his shoulders beneath her, the brush of his breath, his hair tickling the insides of her thighs. She couldn't hear past the roar in her ears, of her own harsh breathing. Nuances assaulted her, leaving her raggedly vulnerable.

His lips plucked her nub, his tongue toying with it's base, plumping it up in his mouth. It throbbed with the gentle touch, making her crave more.

From behind, he thrust a finger inside her soaked channel, pumping into her vagina as he flicked a rapid staccato across her swollen nub.

He'd suckled her reservations away, at least for a little while. Now all she wanted was to enjoy him, revel in the moment that might not come again.

He groaned into her mound, lapping up her juices as if dying of thirst. She whimpered, her arousal growing each second. Her knuckles ached from her grip on the headboard. Her thighs burned from the effort not to tighten around his face when every muscle in her body wanted to curl, curl around the pleasure and keep it deep inside.

He forced another finger inside her, stretching her to the point of pain, unrelenting, working her toward that bright bliss that she so longed for.

She felt herself hovering near release. She closed her mind to it, holding it at bay so that she could enjoy the feel of his mouth only a little longer, just a little longer.

Abruptly, it burst inside of her blindingly, wracking her body with spasms of pleasure and wringing helpless cries of ecstasy from her throat. Her muscles contracted on the plunge of his fingers, gripping him as if she would float away without the anchor of his hand and mouth clinging to her.

On and on it rolled, sizzling along her nerves, zipping like lightning in her veins. She shuddered, trembling from the impact, pressing her forehead to the wall as she succumbed to her orgasm and rode it as he wrung pleasure from every twitching nerve.

Weak, she fell off of him, rolling onto her back as her heart rhythm and breathing returned to normal.

He moved over her then, dropping down to kiss her belly. Normally, she would never allow it, but tonight she felt freer, eager for him to explore her, and eager to explore him.

He kissed a trail up her stomach, his hand cupping her mound, toying in the damp thatch of hair there. He elicited fresh tremors from her sated body, and as his mouth moved over her, higher and higher, she felt the beginnings of renewed need.

To her surprise and dismay, he stopped abruptly. Pulling away, he sat up and withdrew something from his pants. She heard a small buzz, recognized it as a beeper or phone.

She wasn't in doubt long.

"Blake here," Danior said into the phone, clearing his throat of its huskiness as he paused to listen. He knew who'd called him. He'd only given his cell number to one person, Raheem, his second in command.

"The Nesani are coming for you. They've already dealt with Zane."

Danior's gut clenched at the news Raheem delivered. He glanced at the windows in the room, as if he could see through the curtains and boards to find the hunters coming for them. They only had an hour before dawn. They were safe at the moment, but he had no doubt that once night fell, the Nesani would come for them full force.

He had no one he could ask to back him up. Anyone

aiding him would be killed.

He had only today to make arrangements to leave the country, and getting to a ship before the Nesani caught their tails would be a close feat.

"You risk your life warning me, Raheem," he said finally.

Raheem grunted. "Just returning one last favor. Take care man. And good-bye."

Maggie had turned on her side and was watching him worriedly when he put the phone away. He studied her for several moments and finally sighed. She wasn't going to like it, but there was no choice. They would die if they stayed.

He would not leave her.

"We must go, and do so quickly."

Her eyes widened in confusion. "I don't understand. Isn't this supposed to be a safe place?"

He lay down beside her, stroking the soft skin of her cheek, and then her shoulder. "There are laws. I have broken them--the punishment is death. Raheem called to warn me. Even now the Nesani hunt."

Fear filled her eyes then. "What have you done that is so terrible?"

He skated his hand down her arm and took her hand in his, lifting it to his lips and kissing her fingers. "I have … taken something for myself that was forbidden."

"What?" Maggie asked breathlessly, as much from the fear as the heated currents traveling from his lips and up her arm.

He sucked one of her fingers into his mouth, curled his tongue around. She was so sweet, it filled him with indescribable yearnings. He could live a thousand years more and never find another half so sweet as his Maggie. "You, chere."

He felt an incredible sense of urgency now, to find peace in her arms before it was too late. He couldn't die not knowing what it would be like to make love to her. She wasn't ready for him. Her feelings were in turmoil. Danior knew it was too soon to press her, but he couldn't contain his desires any longer.

Her lids grew heavy, giving her a half-lidded, seductive look as she watched him suck her fingers and kiss the sensitive pads. He kissed her palm, brushing his lips over the inside of her wrist, tasting the rapid pulse there with his tongue. "I want to make love to you," he whispered, holding her steady when she flinched.

He looked up at her then, away from the delicacy of her skin.

Her eyes shimmered with unshed tears. Her pain made him ache. "I ... I don't know you, Danior. I know nothing about you except that you're willing to risk your life for a stranger."

"Isn't that enough?" He rubbed his thumb in her curled palm, watching her steadily, holding her gaze with his own. "Do you think explaining myself would make you understand?"

"It would go a long way," she said as she pulled her hand free and twisted the covers in her lap. The flickering flames from the fireplace caused shadows to dance across her worried face. She looked down at her lap. He found her shyness unbelievably enticing.

He had to tear his mind away from mentally disrobing her, to her words. How could he explain when he didn't understand it himself? For the first time in longer than he could remember, he was uncertain of himself. He'd never felt so awkward. He'd never had a seduction go so foully, but then, this meeting had never been a game. It had always been about life and death.

Precious few hours remained for them, hours of safety. When night fell, he didn't know what would happen to them.

"I know I'm not the kind of person a man like you would be interested in under ordinary circumstances."

She was being serious. Without mental probing, he knew she referred to her weight. "There is nothing ordinary about this, nor about my attraction to you." He lowered his voice, saying softly, "I want you as you are now, Maggie. I wouldn't change you."

She looked up at him in surprise, but her eyes turned

wary. "It's hard for me to trust men."

He watched her a long moment. She was shielding something, some secret. He knew it lay at the root of her problems. "Tell me why."

She looked away, her face blushing with shame. "I don't know. It happened a long time ago. I … I don't remember all of it."

She was lying. Slowly, as if trying to capture a wild creature, he lifted his hand and cupped her cheek, meeting her eyes steadily. "Will you let me inside? I want to understand," he said softly.

A tear slid from the corner of one eye. She shuddered, taking a deep breath. "You'll hate me. Everyone does…."

"No," he said, rubbing a thumb against her cheek. "I won't. Give me your trust. I want to understand."

"Yes," she whispered, closing her eyes.

He touched her temple, strengthening his connection to her as he poured himself into her mind past the walls blocking her innermost memories.

* * * *

"I want to make love to you," Danny said softly, cupping her jaw, rubbing his thumb across her bottom lip.

Maggie fought the urge to turn her face away from his grasp. She shivered, unbidden pleasure coursing over her skin. She wasn't used to dating. No one had ever been interested in her before. She still couldn't believe Danny had asked her over to his house. Having the most popular boy in school want to seduce her was the last thing she'd ever expected.

"I don't think--"

"Don't think," he said just as he covered her mouth with his lips.

A thrill raced through her at the connection. She draped her arms around his shoulders and slanted her head, nibbling his lips back. Maggie gasped when his tongue pushed through her lips and touched her own. She'd never been frenched before. The experience made heat flash between her thighs.

He curled his tongue around the inside of her mouth,

running his hands up and down her back, each time getting closer and closer to her ass until he finally cupped it and plunged his tongue deep inside her mouth.

She moaned, getting wet as he crushed her against his erection.

He lifted his head, looking at her with a smile. "Will you?"

Yes! Oh god, yes. She wanted to make love to him so badly. She'd fantasized about him since she'd been a freshman. For three years she'd watched him and lusted, dreamed of being his girlfriend. He was a senior now. He'd be leaving soon, going to college. She couldn't fool herself into thinking anything more could come of this. They ran in different circles, and everyone knew long distance relationships were tough. This was her last chance to have one good memory from high school.

"Yes," she said softly.

His smile widened, and he pulled away from her. He walked across his room to his bed, sitting. Picking up the remote to his CD player, he turned on Boyz II Men's "I'll Make Love to You", then looked at her expectantly.

"I want to see your body. Naked."

Maggie stiffened, shifting on her feet uncertainly. "Are you sure we should do this here?" she asked, looking around his room at all the electronic gadgets he had-- anywhere but at him.

"My parents are gone for the weekend, don't worry. No one will see you but me."

"I don't know," she said, tugging at her clothes uncomfortably. She'd never gotten naked in front of anyone. Not since she'd been a little girl.

"If you'd rather go home--"

"No," she said, screwing up her courage. "I can do it."

"Take off your clothes," he said, smiling.

Feeling awkward and uncomfortable, but at the same time both excited and happy, she peeled her clothing off, trying to hide her discomfort, trying to make herself seductive for him. When she'd finished, she had to quell the urge to cover herself as he studied her with a look in his eyes she found difficult to interpret. Triumph? Excitement?

Swallowing with an effort, she moved toward him. He held his hand out to her when she reached the bed. Pulling her down, he kissed her until she was weak with wanting, until her discomfort had been replaced with the tension of rising desire.

She was confused when he rolled her over. She looked up at him through half closed eyes and he leaned down, kissing her, stroking a hand over her back. "I love to do it doggy. That's my favorite position. It's makes your pussy so tight."

Uneasiness threaded through her. She'd never done it at all, much less 'doggy' but it wasn't a difficult concept to grasp.

She didn't want him to think she didn't know about these things.

Obediently, she got up on her hands and knees, feeling the drugging effects of her desire lift slightly, enough to allow the uneasiness to creep back inside her … enough to still the flow of lubricating juices within her vagina.

She looked back at him as he positioned himself behind her, realizing that he hadn't undressed. Her discomfort increased, but the avid look on his face as he caressed her ass reassured her that he was as turned on as she'd hoped.

She heard the sound of his zipper and then he nudged her with the head of his cock, seeking her opening. She held her breath, partly from nerves, partly from excitement--she would be giving her virginity to the most popular guy on campus, the guy she'd been dying for for years.

As she felt him wedging his cock into her opening, he slapped the cheek of her ass. "Fuck me, bitch! Tell me how much you want it! You want my cock in your pussy?"

Maggie gulped, feeling a strange sense of unreality descend over her.

He pushed a little ways into her, stretching her painfully. "Say it! Tell me you want my cock inside you bitch!"

Swallowing, Maggie nodded.

He slapped her ass again. "Beg for it!"

"I want it," she said uncertainly.

"You want my big cock in your tight little pussy, don't you bitch?"

Maggie licked her lips and repeated what he'd said.

He began humping against her, slowly working the little juices that remained into her by thrusting and retreating. Maggie squeezed her eyes shut. She hadn't expected it to hurt. She'd thought it would feel good.

"It hurts."

"Of course it hurts, bitch. 'Cause I've got the biggest cock you've ever had. Say it."

She swallowed when he slapped her on the ass again, harder this time. The stinging distracted her as he thrust into her again, but not enough to dull the pain as he breached her hymen. She choked out a cry, trying to pull away from him, but he had an arm locked around her hips. The blood from her burst hymen collected with the natural lubricants, easing his passage, allowing him to pump into her harder and harder.

She dropped to her elbows, trying to keep from crying, covering her face, just wanting it to be over. It seemed to take forever before he uttered a strangled cry and stopped pounding into her. Finally, it was over however. She winced when he withdrew his flaccid member. Gasping for breath, he collapsed beside her.

"Hey! You OK?" he asked after a moment.

Maggie regained control with an effort. "It hurt. I didn't know it would hurt."

He caught her face in his hands, forcing her to look at him. "Hey, kid, I didn't realize it was hurting. I'm sorry, baby. I was just too far gone to stop. You've got such a sweet, tight little pussy it just blew my mind."

He looked so regretful, Maggie immediately felt better. The pain had subsided to a dull throbbing. She snuggled next to him, soothed by his stroking hands.

She'd only begun to relax, however, when he slapped her on the ass. "Hey! You need to get out of here. I've got a friend coming over and I don't think you'll want to run into him. He might figure out what we've been up to, huh?"

It was enough to galvanize her instantly. The one thing

she didn't want was to have everything ruined by running into one of the assholes he hung around with. Climbing from the bed, she jerked her clothing on nervously. He lay still, watching her, a half smile on his face. When she'd finished dressing, he held up his hand, summoning her, and she moved toward the bed again.

He sat up, kissing her. "Tomorrow?"

Surprise touched her briefly, and then a stirring of happiness, mixed with a healthy dose of doubt and dread at the idea of doing 'that' again. Summoning a smile with an effort, Maggie nodded. "Yeah … I guess … sure."

She met up with his buddy, Todd, on her way out. Todd looked her over with a superior grin, sniffing at her as if he was a dog. "Do I smell bitch?"

She glared at him, pushing him away and stalking out the house.

"Why is it, I wonder, that red heads are such fucking bitches?" he wondered loudly as she stomped down the stairs.

She shot him a bird over her shoulder, but a sense of satisfaction filled her. Danny liked her and he wanted to see her again!

He didn't call, though, even though he'd said he would, even though it had been his idea to invite her over again, not something she'd asked. She was tempted to call him, but she restrained herself, reminding herself that he'd invited her. Something must have come up, otherwise he would have called, surely? And she didn't feel comfortable with the idea of calling him.

When Sunday rolled around and she still didn't hear from him, she began to feel doubts crowding into her mind. She kept telling herself that his parents must have come back early and that was why he hadn't called to invite her over, but that didn't explain why he hadn't called to tell her.

She knew the moment she arrived at school Monday morning that she'd been the butt of yet another hateful joke. Ordinarily, she walked among her classmates like a ghost, invisible unless they were feeling particularly nasty and mooed when she walked by.

Today, that had changed. They began to smirk and whisper at her approach, giggling. Sickness welled in her stomach, but she kept her expression carefully blank and pretended not to notice. It was the only thing that had ever worked at all--not that it worked all that well, but, mostly, so long as she pretended to be unaffected, they lost interest pretty quickly and moved on to someone else to torment.

Except for a handful of people, who either looked at her with pity, revulsion or the sort of horrified fascination freaks evoked, everyone in the school that she passed looked as if they would burst out laughing.

She found out why when she got to her third class.

Emily, who'd always clung to her, more Maggie suspected because she thought Maggie might protect her than from any real sense of friendship, had given her the same horrified look of fascination that she'd seen on so many other faces. So sick with dread now that she felt like she would throw up, Maggie finally felt a surge of something she could deal with--anger. "What?"

Emily gulped. "It's just … was that really you in the video?"

The bile that she'd been holding at bay rose to the base of her throat. Maggie swallowed convulsively several times. "What video?" she asked hoarsely.

"The one Danny put on the internet."

It had taken every ounce of courage and fortitude that she possessed, more than she'd known she possessed, to make it through the rest of the day. By the time she'd gotten home, she was seriously considering suicide. She couldn't face that again. She just couldn't. Not only had he hurt and humiliated her in bed, but he'd made it a public spectacle, shared it with everyone. The boys had barked at her as she'd trudged through the halls heading home.

It was only in the wee hours of the night, when she'd wracked her brain for some method of killing herself that she could actually contemplate that she'd finally realized that they'd win if she did. They would have beaten her. They would be gloating and giggling over the fact that they had the power to so destroy her that she'd taken her life.

She hated them all. She wasn't going to give them the satisfaction.

Chapter Seven

Maggie's crying pulled Danior back to the present. He curled his hand around the back of her neck and pulled her against his chest, holding her while she sobbed against his chest.

It took all his strength to withstand the rage tearing inside him at what they'd done. The insane urge to leave the safe house and hunt them down gripped him. His arms shook with the effort to control himself. Her shudders brought him down from lunacy.

That was why she'd hidden herself away all these years. Why she didn't date. Why she hated men and resisted her attraction to him.

They'd scarred her and made her hate herself, and she'd turned to food for comfort while shielding herself from the outside world.

He wanted to kill them for what they'd done. Again, the urge surfaced to hunt them down and make them beg for the mercy and compassion they'd failed to give her. They would not find him so forgiving.

Merde, she drove him to a madness he could scarce believe. The intensity of his response alarmed him. He had to force his heart to calm its galloping, force his hands to remain tender at her back, when all they wanted to do was tighten into fists to strike down those who'd hurt her.

"Shh," he soothed, rubbing her back as he calmed her and himself. "I'm sorry, so sorry…."

"It's … it's not your … fault," she said haltingly, sniffling as she tightened her arms around his chest. The shudders wracking her had eased to the smallest tremor.

"I know it's not, chere," he said, brushing kisses over the top of her head. He almost imagined he could taste the berry scent in her strawberry locks. "I'm sorry for your pain."

She pulled away from him, rubbing her eyes and the wetness from her cheeks. "Don't be. I'm over it. I was over it a long time ago. It was just some stupid high school prank. I don't even know why I cried about it. It must be that time of the month."

He regarded her a long moment while she composed herself. "You're not." He stroked a forefinger down the hollow of one cheek. "It's not always like that. Some men can be trusted."

"I haven't found one yet," she said, looking away. She got up and moved to the fire, stoking it with the poker.

He stood and came up behind her as she straightened, hugging her from behind. She shivered in his embrace, rubbing her hands on her arms for warmth.

Slowly, he brushed her gilded locks away from her neck, pressing his lips there in a tender kiss. She stiffened, her breathing quickening.

"Don't pull away from me," he breathed into her ear, smoothing her chill bumps away from her arms to close his hands around her wrists.

"No one wants me. You don't. It's all a mistake," she said, her voice breaking.

"I want you, Maggie. More than I should ever want a woman. I don't deserve you. I never did."

She turned slightly in his arms, craning her head, looking up at him with doubt, with hope. He held her gaze one heart stopping moment, letting her see the truth in his eyes, then he brought his lips down on hers.

How could he say something like that? He was so beautiful, he made her hurt just to look at him. But something in his eyes spoke to her, more than his words did.

Maggie gasped as his warm lips closed over hers in a kiss as hungry as his eyes. His tongue pushed past her lips, sweeping into her mouth voraciously, igniting instant, painful need deep in her womb. He freed one wrist, cupping the corner of her jaw as if afraid she would escape him.

She could no more leave him now, deny herself this kiss, than she could cease breathing.

She turned, pressing her chest against his, molding herself to him to soak in his heat. Warmth radiated from the flames at her back, but the man holding her heated her more, deep inside.

He was ravenous, holding the back of her neck, forcing her to bend her head to accept his kiss deeper, more intimately than she'd ever thought possible.

His tongue surged inside her mouth, carrying with it the taste of him, hot and sweet and unbelievably enticing. His hunger threatened to consume her. She groaned against his lips as his tongue tangled erotically with hers.

Her heart quickened its pace. She couldn't drag enough air inside her lungs, had to fight to keep the oxygen flowing inside her. She felt faint, wanted to run from her reaction to him. But she couldn't break their desperate connection, and his gentle touch masked a strength that wouldn't allow it regardless.

A rush of excitement surged through her, hot, filled with anticipation that made her sex ache with it. She moaned as his wandering hands found her ass and cupped her cheeks to crush her against him. Her pussy clenched on a hard spasm of desire. Her breasts throbbed at the pressure of his chest, making her nipples harden to painfully swollen peaks. The line of her stomach, molded to his, jerked with each ragged breath, forcing her breasts to rub against his chest and increase the sensuous ache there.

He massaged her ass cheeks, bringing her hard against his groin until the thick erection trapped inside his pants rubbed against her mound with a sensual promise that turned her knees to water.

She locked her hands around him, clutching his silk clad back as if she would fall without support. The corded strength of his muscles made her feel weak, needy in some incomprehensible way.

His lips caressed hers, tasting, savoring, like he couldn't taste her enough. His excitement drove her own to new heights, and she plunged her tongue into his mouth, moaning as he sucked it like a succulent treat.

She whimpered in the back of her throat, dragging her nails up and down his back, rubbing her mound against the ridge of his cock to ease the ache there. It hurt, like an itch needing to be scratched.

He tore his mouth away, trailing brokenly along her jaw. "You taste so good, Maggie," he said roughly against her neck, sucking and leaving cooling wet aches in his wake. "I can't taste enough of you to appease my hunger."

He worked a wet, burning swath up to her ear, tugging the lobe between his teeth.

Chills slipped down her spine, making her skin tingle with awareness. He shifted his grip, sliding his hands into her panties to stroke the bare skin of her ass as his tongue danced in her ear.

"Oh," she gasped on a faint moan. She'd thought she burned before, but the feel of those hard, callused palms caressing skin that had never so much as seen daylight sent her senses reeling.

Her cunt sizzled with hungry need, demanding his touch, his hands all over her, inside her. He burned away her shyness, leaving her wanting, needy for more.

Maggie dipped her head back, biting her bottom lip as he kissed the front of her neck, working a knee between her thighs until it rubbed intimately against her cleft.

The movement spread her, leaving her labia sensitively vulnerable to the hard ridge of his thigh.

She moaned as he sucked a spot at the cords of her neck, cupping her bottom possessively to bring her up hard on his leg. It rasped painfully good against her swollen clit, notching up the need for relief. Her cunt clenched on her desire, wetting her lips in preparation for their joining.

She wanted him so badly. The desperate compulsion to feel him inside her burned her, turned her feverishly hot.

Recklessly, she pulled at his shirt, anxious to feel his skin against hers so that she could burn the fever out of her system.

Sensing her urgency, he stepped back, releasing her

bottom only to rip her shirt up over her head. The loss of connection lasted only a second, and then she was working his buttons, her fingers clumsy in the dimness and with her own desperation.

He chuckled and pushed her hands away, peeling off his shirt as she opened his fly and let his pants fall down his legs. His erection fell into her hands, hot, the thick veins almost seeming to throb to the frantic beat of her heart. It was huge, weighty, and seeing it, feeling it in her hand made her pussy weep anew with a plea to have him inside her.

A sense of ultimate femininity assailed her, leaving her weak in its aftermath. She wanted him stretching her sensitive muscles, deep inside. She wanted him to pound into her, hurt her, anything to take the emptiness away.

"I need your cock inside me," she whispered, cupping his cock in a taut, torturous grip. He closed his eyes a moment, throwing his head back as she boldly pulled him and rubbed her thumb over the head and collected the bead of pre-cum moisture nestled there.

He groaned, a deep, masculine sound that reverberated in his chest with dark passion. Maggie gave his shaft a pull, enjoying her power over him and the barely restrained strength of his passion. She sensed a wildness hovering beneath the surface, a wildness she'd called.

It thrilled her to have him so on edge. The danger excited her implicitly. She didn't feel like herself. This woman was alien, too bold and hungry. But she liked it. "Could you give me everything I need," she said, pumping his dick, moving until the head rasped against her mound.

He opened his eyes, dark, blazing with passion. "I will take you in ways you never dreamed possible."

He didn't give her a chance to escape, not that she would run, but his sensually dark smile made a thrill of warning rush down her spine. Without a word, he pushed her hand away and trapped her in his arms, scooping her off the floor. He carried her to the bed, settling her down before covering her with his body.

His arms locked as he hovered above her, his hair falling

around his shoulders, his eyes gleaming with carnal light. "I thirst for you as I've never thirsted for anyone." He lowered himself until his lips were inches from hers. "Your kiss cannot slake it," he growled with carnal threat.

Maggie whimpered as he descended roughly, crushing her into the mattress as he kissed her. Her nipples brushed his chest, growing engorged and sensitive. If she didn't feel his mouth there she would die. If he stopped kissing her, she would die.

Maggie kissed him desperately, sucking his tongue with her own ravenous appetite. He shifted onto one elbow, fingers stroking over her skin, down the side of one breast, making her want to scream at the achy need he invoked there.

She groaned into his mouth, capturing his hand and placing it on her breast.

He grinned against her lips, nibbling her teasingly as he plucked her nipple.

She jerked in his arms, thrusting her breasts against him. His lips moved from her mouth down her chin. "Danior, you're killing me," she breathed.

"Fair treatment for your torments on me," he whispered before laving a path down the center of her chest.

"Oh god," she said, almost screaming as his lips closed over one nipple and it disappeared into the hot depths of his mouth. He sucked it deeply, his tongue flaying it, flicking it into agonizing awareness.

She almost came right then, her pussy spasming in near ecstasy, making her so wet her thighs felt slick from her desire. She rubbed her legs together, as if that would ease her somehow. She clutched the back of his head, trapping his mouth to her breast, gasping breathlessly as pleasure swirled from the tip through her nerves.

He pushed her panties off with one hand, shifting over her as he freed her from that last constraint. And then his hand was down there, whispering over the hair covering her mound even as he toyed with her nipples, teasing the buds with his tongue and the dangerous scrape of his teeth.

Her heart leapt in her throat. Fear and desire mixed

potently, making her drunk with arousal. He cupped her, dipping his fingers into her cleft to graze her begging clit. Maggie moaned, jerking against him, spreading her legs without conscious volition.

"You are so slick," he said roughly, breathing hotly against her chest as his fingers parted her folds.

The juices of her cunt seemed to gather at his words. Her clit throbbed with need. He circled it, spreading her cream, edging that spot she so desperately needed him to touch. She would scream if he did not. Scream now. Scream as his circle tightened, coming so close. She didn't, couldn't get the breath to expel from her lungs. She jerked her hips, trying to drive herself against his hand, but he moved, spreading his palm over her mound to keep her still.

"Your body hungers for me, Maggie," he growled against her ribs, nuzzling the under curve of one breast as he toyed with her folds.

"Yes," she said, choking back a whimper, digging her hands in the covers to keep from shredding him with her nails.

He rose on his knees, lifting above her. Her thighs rubbed against his, the crisp hair there sensuously abrasive.

Something pushed through her cream-laden folds, probing deep, until it grazed her clit. Maggie's belly spasmed, her cunt jerking, tightening as his cock rubbed against her clit.

"I'm desperate for you," she gasped, writhing beneath him.

"Yes," he murmured huskily, moving, stroking that hot hardness down, smearing her thick cream down her slit and up again. The blunt tip made her womb tighten, gasp with need. Pleasure flared along her nerves.

Her entire body felt like one huge, impending orgasm. Her nipples throbbed, her stomach jerked, her thighs burned. Each brush carried her higher.

He stopped the rough caress, lodging himself at her vaginal opening. He nudged her with his cockhead, probing the edges until they began to stretch.

Maggie froze, inhaling a sharp breath. Her body locked

up, kegels tightening to refuse him.

He groaned, pushing, but her body refused him. Her blood pounded, rushing to her head until she was dizzy with it.

"Look at me," he demanded hoarsely. "I want you to see the man who takes you."

She opened her eyes, meeting his half-lidded gaze, so intense, it made her breath catch.

"I am not him, Maggie." He bent until he could brush his lips over hers. "Let me in, *ma Coeur*. Do not shield your heart from me," he said softly.

He kissed her tenderly, rubbing himself against her moist center in a coaxing caress. Maggie kissed him back, arching, spreading her bent knees out and opening herself to him. She wanted this--him--inside, to take the pain away.

His tongue rubbed along hers as the stroke stopped, pressing into her opening. Her muscles tightened unconsciously. She willed them to relax, accept him. A streak of pleasure and pain flared along her nerves, making her pussy cream with a forceful gush. He groaned into her mouth, probing her, pushing that thickness past her screaming muscles.

She was whimpering into his mouth, clutching his biceps, struggling not to pass out. He stretched her so far that her tight channel burned in protest, spasming in agony and repulsion.

He tore his mouth from hers, growling in fury and pain. "I cannot do this," he said raggedly, withdrawing.

Maggie stiffened, cried out. "Please," she said desperately, locking her legs around his hips.

His arms shook, muscles bulging. Sweat dotted his brow, his arms and chest. "It hurts you too much. I should never have pressed you."

She pulled him further, forcing him deeper inside, gasping, crying at the hurt. "I want you to. Don't stop, I beg you, don't stop."

"I must," he rasped.

Danior groaned in agony, fighting her lure, the siren call of her womb and the sweetness of her body. He held perfectly still, shaking with the effort. Every muscle was taut, stretched to the limits of his endurance. She arched upward, rubbing her nipples against his chest, her cunt clenching and unclenching on his cock.

With a broken cry, his will shattered. He drove into her fully, until his thick erection jutted against her womb.

Maggie screamed, pain overriding her pleasure, but mingling, until her nerves prickled with heated need.

He dropped his forehead against hers, panting, his warm breath fanning across her lips. She tilted her head, kissing him lightly, bringing her hands up to cup his cheeks.

He opened his eyes, looking at her as her sheath groaned with the weight of his cock.

"Make love to me," she whispered, kissing him.

A shudder wracked him, traveling down his spine through his hips. With tender care, he pulled out, inch by inch.

The bulb of his cock rippled through her channel, making her quiver.

"You are so tight," he croaked huskily. "You burn me alive. I feel as though you clutch my heart with your sheath."

He neared the edge of her opening, gritted his teeth, and drove inside again. A strangled cry ripped from her throat as he burrowed so deeply, so possessively inside.

Sweat dampened her skin, making her cling to him, making her feel like she would melt. Her pussy was feverish, burning her up. The pressure there nearly unbearable.

He thrust shallowly, quickly, working her juices up and down his thick shaft until her tightness eased and he set a pistoning stroke that had her raising up to meet him.

Maggie braced her feet on the bed, raising her knees, jerking her hips up with every stroke. He ground down, against her clit, roughing that sensitive spot until shots of pleasure streaked through her veins. She bucked against him, dying with pleasure, nerves going taut with each bumping grind.

She sizzled with need everywhere, gripping his shoulders, tossing her head side to side as he drove into her like a man possessed.

Moans echoed in the room, her own, frantic, desperately reaching for the climax she felt hovered just out of her reach.

He pushed her toward it, higher and higher, his hard thrusts driving her up the bed with the force of his movements. Something had been unleashed in him. Desperate. Frightening. That danger she'd sensed before loomed. He buried his face at her neck, teeth and tongue caressing her there.

He craved the blood. She wanted to give it to him, let him suck her dry if only to prolong the blissful torment impaling her.

He groaned against her neck, sucking at the crook, where she'd been injured before. Maggie moaned, her inner muscles rippling as the pleasure built to a crescendo of fury.

She clutched him, grasping his cock as the orgasm sizzled along her nerves. Screaming, she was helpless to it, crying out again and again as waves of searing pleasure pounded inside her.

Her mind closed down, embracing the feeling. It poured through her, making her cunt convulse on the power.

He arched his head back, shuddering, driving into her one last time as his semen erupted inside her quaking pussy. Her vision went dim and she closed her eyes, going lightheaded from the peak of it, a pinnacle she had never dreamed possible.

"*Ma Coeur. Amour,*" he said, his breathing hard, labored against her neck as he collapsed on top of her and held her, pleasure shuddering through him into her.

After a moment, he withdrew his flaccid length with a soft smacking sound and rolled, bringing them onto their sides as he rocked her close, sheltering her body. Maggie snuggled close, overwhelmed and unable to speak. He whispered French into her ear, lovingly kissing the shell of it, her neck and cheek, anywhere he could reach. His hands moved tenderly over her backside, through her hair and along her shoulders.

She had always been ashamed of her past and how stupid she'd been. But Danior made her forget it. Near him, all she could think about was how *he* made her feel, and he made her feel beautiful and womanly.

She felt new, as though by accepting him into herself, she'd been remade into another woman. Stronger. Someone capable and worthy of love.

Her lips curled in a smile and she kissed his chin, already warming to his tender caresses, craving more of him.

Chapter Eight

Danior studied Maggie as she slept the deep, dreamless sleep of the truly sated. His lips curled faintly on that thought in self-deprecating amusement, but she'd left him in no doubt that he had thoroughly pleased her. He was weary himself after making love to her most of the day, but too tense and anxious to sleep.

She still didn't fully grasp that her own life was in as much danger as his, but then she didn't realize that the council was ruthless, and merciless. As beautiful as she was, they would not hesitate to destroy her. Their rules would be maintained. There were no exceptions.

He'd known that even when he agreed to take her. He'd known, sooner or later, they would learn of it and Maggie's life would be forfeit as well as his own for protecting her.

She would have to accept it. For whatever reason he'd felt compelled to protect her, to begin with--for amusement, or merely a whim--there was no doubt in his mind why that had changed from mild interest to a desperate obsession.

He couldn't go on without her and he had no intention of doing so even if he had to take her by force.

There was no place inside the US safe for them now. The council might have no control outside of New Orleans, but they need only contact the council where ever he might think to go to, and he and Maggie would be forced to flee again.

They must leave for Europe. He could make arrangements for a night flight to New York, but they would have to travel by ship from there since there were no flights that could take them to Europe overnight.

It didn't matter. Once they were outside the US, they would be beyond the control and jurisdiction of the council.

He decided to allow her to rest while he made the arrangements. He had fake passports made, using a scanned copy of her driver's license for hers. He emailed the information to X with instructions to meet him at the airport. He'd used this man, X, in the past, and he was trustworthy enough only in that he could be bought into silence for a price.

They were trusting their lives to him, to make sure that X wouldn't betray them, perhaps for more money, or the threat at losing his life.

There was no way around it, unfortunately. This late in the game, he couldn't afford to shop around for someone else.

Danior called and ordered their tickets to New York and booked passage on the first available ship to Europe. At this time of year, their options were limited to the Mediterranean. He had connections there, however, and would be able to find refuge until he found them a place to make their new home.

Satisfied he'd done all he could at the moment, he crawled back into bed with Maggie, nestling her against his side as he stared up at the ceiling, going over his plans. He wished he could have taken a ship directly from the port here, but it was too risky taking a smaller vessel, and there was nothing else available except a few cargo ships, which wouldn't take passengers regardless. No, there was no choice but to fly to New York. Airport security after the attack there would force him to go completely weaponless, but it also meant their chances of being attacked there were slim. He had only to get there before running into trouble to get her aboard safely.

He prayed that his luck had not run out.

* * * *

"Maggie."

Something tickled her nose. "Unnh," she complained, rolling over. Sore muscles winced at the movement, and she groaned. "Oh. I think I've been injured," she mumbled, curling into a ball.

"As much as I would love to kiss those aches away, we have no time now. You've slept the day away. Dusk approaches."

Maggie bolted upright, stifling a groan as she put her weight on her bottom. "Why'd you let me sleep so late?"

He smiled, looking incredibly sexy despite the danger looming. She almost suspected he was putting on a façade to keep her from panicking. "I couldn't bear to wake you."

Maggie rolled her eyes, smiling as she got out of bed and hurriedly woke herself up. Her thighs were sticky from their lovemaking, and she bathed herself off with a rag, washed her face, and brushed her teeth with the spare toothbrush he'd bought for her.

She changed from her nightshirt into the leather clothing and boots. After she finished, she came out of the bathroom and found him gone.

A brief moment of panic assailed her, but she quashed it, hurrying out and down the stairs. She released a pent-up breath to find him downstairs waiting for her.

"It's safe to go out now. Hurry," he said, taking her hand as he led her out the back. When they reached the door, he stopped, seeming to listen for some sound she couldn't hear. Apparently, he heard nothing to alarm him, and he opened the door, guiding her to the draped car.

He pulled the tarp off, revealing a silver Dodge Viper. Clicking off the alarm, he opened to door for her and shut it once she was inside.

The interior was roomier than she'd thought it would be, and she knew he had to have had it custom built for his height to accommodate his legs.

Getting in, he started the car and revved the engine, flashing her a quick grin as he put it in gear and drove away from the dark mansion.

The drive passed in taut silence. He maneuvered the streets easily, reaching the airport with almost anticlimactic ease. She couldn't believe it had been so easy to get away.

"We're not free yet," he said, as if reading her thoughts, which she realized he could if he wanted to.

As they passed through the electronic doors, and man pushed off from a column and strode purposefully toward them. Maggie tensed, her breathing quickening. This was it. They'd been found.

Danior draped his arm over her shoulder, giving it a squeeze as the man stopped in front of them.

He had bad ass written all over him. From his shaved head and sunglasses, through the black tribal tattoos that covered his body and the black, silver studded leather he wore.

"X," Danior said, nodding a greeting.

"Danior," X said back, giving Maggie a once over before returning his attention to Danior. He fished two passports out of the inside of his jacket. "Do you have my money?"

Danior took the passports and examined them. "As good as always, X." He pulled out his cell phone and dialed a number from memory banks. They waited while he transferred the money to X's account and X confirmed it.

Danior and X nodded at one another again, both in that mode of conversation that could only be comprehended by other men, and without another word, they moved away and checked in for their flight.

Maggie couldn't believe how easy it had been to get away. Once they were on the plane and it had taken off, she finally managed to relax. She wasn't aware before then of just how tight her nerves had been. She had a tension headache coming on, and the cramped space and recycled air wasn't helping it any.

"Where are we going?" she finally asked Danior, who sat by the window with his eyes closed.

He didn't look at her. "New York and from there we take a ship to the Mediterranean."

"Nice. I didn't think I'd ever get another vacation in my lifetime."

He looked at her then, his eyes smoky and passionate. "I hope to do so much more for you for many years to come," he said, his husky voice vibrating pleasurably along her nerves. "I'm surprised you didn't fight me more on this."

He traced a hand up and down her thigh. Even through the leather, he left his impression on her.

"I didn't see much sense in it. It's for the best, and ... I trust you."

His eyes gleamed. He leaned close, nuzzling her neck. "You don't know how much it pleases me to hear you say that," he murmured, running his hand up her inner thigh, up her covered cleft.

Maggie jerked in her seat, clamping her hands down tightly on the arms of her chair. "What are you doing?"

"Mmm. What do you think?"

His fingers moved up, tugging at her zipper.

"No, Danior. I'll never get that zipper back up," she whispered frantically, looking around worriedly.

They were in first class and it was empty except for a solitary man several rows above them, and he was snoring.

"They've made the rounds. No one will come, and I would not let them see," he murmured hotly against her neck before sucking her lobe between his teeth.

Ignoring her silent protests, he pulled the zipper down, baring her panties, which were no barrier at all for him. He slipped beneath the waistband, fluttering his fingers over her mound.

Maggie bit her lip, squirming in her seat as he curled his fingers into the top of her cleft.

"Mmmm. You're wet. I knew you wanted this," he growled softly, thrusting his tongue into her ear as he stroked her clit.

She arched in her seat, thrusting her mound against his cupped hand, fighting to contain the moan that wanted to tear from her throat. She kept her eyes open, looking around for anyone to catch them, afraid and excited at the possibility that they'd be caught.

He dug down, slipping in her slit until he edged her vagina and probed the tight hole, rimming it with a finger before thrusting inside. Maggie took a sharp breath, her knuckles going white to control herself.

"I want so badly to pump my cock inside you, amour," he whispered, laying open mouthed kisses on her neck as he drove two fingers into her tightness.

Her pussy sizzled, ecstasy imminent, rolling toward her as his palm ground against her clit and she rode his hand.

She was breathing erratically, hard through her nostrils, her heart beating a staccato as he drove her to orgasm. It exploded inside her, vibrating through every nerve ending with shattering precision. Her pussy clenched on his fingers as he continued to thrust into her, mimicking the drive of his cock.

Maggie whimpered, burying her face against his shoulder, biting him to keep from crying out.

Slowly, as her climax faded away, he withdrew his hand and zipped her pants up.

He brought his hand to his face, tasting one finger. The movement of his lips and tongue on that one digit had her cleft clenching with want again.

"I love the scent and taste of you, chere. When we are aboard the ship, I plan to taste every inch of your body."

Maggie shivered pleasurably and snuggled close, enjoying the feel of his arm wrapped around her shoulder. The tension she'd had was gone for now though her thoughts still lay in torment.

They had to make it. She didn't think she could bear losing him now. For once, it seemed like she truly had something to live for.

* * * *

Without any need for a watch, or any sign in the sky above them, Maggie knew as they got of the plane at last in New York, that it was nearing dawn. She wasn't certain if it was her vampire senses kicking in, or the urgency she sensed in Danior, but she knew they had little time to get from the airport to the docks.

Danior had arranged for a rental car and directed her toward the door that led out to the parking lot in swift strides. They carried nothing. Except for the clothing

Danior had bought for her, Maggie had nothing in any case, but Danior had checked the luggage they did have when they went into the airport. He'd told her arrangements had been made to transfer it to the ship once they reached New York, but he seemed singularly uninterested in whether or not their luggage actually made the trip with them.

Unspoken was the far more urgent need to be free of any sort of encumbrance if they should meet up with the hunters.

Pushing the door open, Danior held it, catching her when she would have gone through and lifting his head to listen, almost seeming to sniff the air. After a moment, his grip relaxed fractionally. "Hurry," he said in an under voice, placing his hand on her back, along her waist. "Slot 652."

Nodding, Maggie proceeded him, scanning the numbers on the pavement nearest her and trying to determine what direction to take. Danior strode past her, grasping her hand and leading the way once more.

Unnerved by the tension she sensed in him, Maggie focused on searching for the car.

Suddenly, Danior stopped, going stiff. His tense wariness caught her attention, and she looked up, shocked to see a woman standing not twenty feet away from them. Petite and blonde, she was everything that Maggie was not.

"Danior," she said, and in her beautiful voice was a threat. Death emanated from her lips.

"What are you doing here, Tatiana?" Danior demanded, clenching his hands into fists.

"I had to see if it was true." She laughed coldly. "How far the mighty fall."

Danior's lips curled in a chilling smile. "You were ever one for theatrics, Tatiana, but I'm afraid we'll have to miss the rest of the play. We've an urgent need to breathe more healthful air."

She chuckled. "I know, but I'm afraid that won't be possible."

To her left and right, two men cloaked in black stepped out, almost indistinguishable from the dark save for their pale, skin and glowing eyes.

"You led them to me."

Maggie glanced at him sharply at the tone of his voice, or rather the lack of any tone at all, as if he were being excruciatingly careful of his words. She could read nothing in his expression, but she knew, quite suddenly, that this woman had once been Danior's woman. She turned to look at the woman again, fighting the sickness that welled inside her, the jealousy.

She smiled at the look on Maggie's face. "They needed someone who had a blood bond with you. How could I refuse?"

A sense of unreality washed over her. Time seemed to slow, the moments stretching into minutes. She blinked, turning her head to look at Danior once more and seeing nothing but a blur of motion as he launched himself at the nearest man. They collided mid-air, struggling, slashing at each other with their teeth. Cold washed over Maggie as she watched helplessly, trying to fight the shock off, trying to think if there was anything she could do to help. *Should* she try to help? Or would she only be in the way? Would her efforts only distract Danior and hamper him instead of helping?

Cringing away from the fight, she moved her head to see where the others were.

The second man stood where he had been, awaiting a chance to strike. The blond woman, Tatiana was watching the two men who struggled with a smile on her face.

Rage filled Maggie. This woman had meant something to Danior. She knew just from the way he'd behaved that he had been stunned that Tatiana had betrayed him. What had that cost him? Had it divided his heart and mind? Distracted him from the strength and purpose he needed to defeat the hunters who'd come to kill him?

She couldn't seem to will herself to move, however. It was like a nightmare. Every smallest movement required the utmost concentration.

It was almost as if she'd been enthralled.

She knew with sudden enlightenment that she had been. One of the vampires had her. Which one, she wasn't certain. Danior, in an effort to protect her? Or one of the others?

She didn't know, but as she watched Danior slay the man he'd been fighting and struggle to his feet to face his other foe, she began trying to break free of the mind control that held her rooted to the spot, helpless, unable to help Danior.

He was weakened from his battle with the first vampire, bleeding from wounds on his face and neck and hands, bleeding, she saw to her horror, even from slashes that had cut through his leather clothing and into his chest, his shoulder.

She dragged her gaze back to the vampiress, realizing abruptly that it was Tatiana that held her. She allowed her hate to swell inside of her, allowed it to consume her mind. Little by little she felt the control over her slip, like the faint loosening of a binding rope.

Grinding her teeth now with the effort, she focused on the pain this woman's betrayal had caused Danior. She focused on the fact that the woman was the epitome of those women who'd tormented her her entire life.

With an effort that made her break a sweat, she took a step forward, and then another.

Tatiana's attention shifted and Maggie's followed, almost as if she were a puppet.

Relief filled her when she saw that Danior had slain the second man … until she saw that he was too weak from the battle to rise. Even as she stared at him, struggling to break the mind hold so that she could run to him, Tatiana fell upon him, tearing a gash alone his shoulder and neck with her teeth.

She meant to kill him, to finish him off now that he was too weak to fight her.

Without any conscious effort whatsoever, Maggie broke the hold on her and surged forward. Mindless, beast-like, she fell upon her prey. Grasping her by her hair, she tore Tatiana from Danior and slung her away with a strength she'd never known she possessed.

Tatiana struck one of the concrete supports of the garage, wrapping halfway around it. It would have snapped the back of a human. The vampiress landed in a crouch and launched herself at Maggie, her teeth bared in a snarl. Maggie's heart seemed to leap into her throat as she watched the woman flying at her. Ignoring it, she waited until the woman was almost upon her and slung her fist directly toward the oncoming teeth. Pain slid up her fist, her arm, and into her shoulder. It shook her terror from her, however, and, before the woman could recover and scramble to her feet, Maggie fell upon her, pummeling her and tearing at the vampiress with her own teeth until she realized the woman wasn't moving any more.

Gasping for breath, she sat back on her heels, staring in horror at the bloody corpse that she'd made. As abruptly as the animalistic madness had descended upon her, it vanished. She scurried away from the woman's body, crab like, unable to tear her gaze away.

Her stomach heaved bile into her throat and she braced her palms on the pavement, retching until she could do nothing more than gag. After what seemed an eternity the heaving ceased. Wiping her mouth on her sleeve, she spat the vile taste from her mouth and looked around.

Danior lay motionless.

On the instant, everything else vanished from her mind and Maggie scrambled toward him. She didn't even realize that she was sobbing hysterically until she saw the tears dripping onto Danior's face. Scooping his head against her chest, she rocked him, stroking his hair. "Don't die, Danior. Please! Don't leave me!" she sobbed, knowing it was already too late.

But he was warm still, she thought angrily. He couldn't be dead.

When he touched her face, she jerked all over.

Leaning back, she blinked the tears from her eyes and looked down at him. "Danior?"

"It's ... nearing dawn. Go. Save yours..."

"Not without you," Maggie ground out. Shifting, she caught him beneath both arms and thrust upward with all her strength. Her back burned. Her arms burned with the strain, but she staggered back, dragging him with her. It would be easier, she knew to run to get the car, but she couldn't leave him with the others. Someone might happen upon them before she could get back.

When she'd finally managed to drag him into a darkened corner, she leaned down and kissed him, briefly, on the lips. "I'll be back in a minute," she said, fishing the car keys from his pocket and turning to look at the numbers on the parking slots nearest them.

When she returned, he lay much as she'd left him. It took sheer determination, but she finally managed to get him in the car. Once she'd done so, however, she wasn't certain what to do next.

They were supposed to take a ship, but which dock? How to get to the dock? How was she going to get him onboard, in this condition?

Shaking off her doubts, she fished around in the glove box and unearthed a map. He would heal, she told herself. By the time they'd reached the docks, he'd be OK and they could board and everything was going to be alright.

Chapter Nine

Danior was dying. She couldn't see why. The blood had ceased to flow. His wounds, even the worst of them, had closed. Unless … unless that bitch had broken him inside somehow. But everything else was healing.

"Danior, please," she said, cupping his cheek. He felt frigid, impossibly cold. "What's wrong? I need you to tell me how to help you."

His eyelids fluttered.

Dear god, she didn't know what to do. Dawn approached. She had little time to get them on the ship or they'd both assuredly die.

Tears stung her eyes, blurring her vision. She kissed his cold lips, fighting down panic. "Please, love, don't die. Tell me what to do," she whispered brokenly. Pulling him up into her arms, she rocked him.

Something tickled her mind, making her dizzy. Words whispered in her ears like a soft breeze. She focused on them, striving to understand.

He was speaking to her with his mind.

We shared a blood bond, he spoke inside her head, his voice thready, as though his mind could barely connect with hers.

"What is it? How do I fix it?"

To break it is mortal….

No! Oh god, no! Maggie sobbed, clutching him tightly. *You can't die. I'm going to save you.*

You have to leave and find the ship. Before the sun rises. There's no … time.

The connection with him broke. She could no longer feel him inside her, trying to speak.

Maggie cried out. She had to do something--now. Her thoughts were chaotic. She couldn't focus. All she could think about was the thirst. It drove the vampire, fed them, kept them alive. If he had fresh blood, it could save him.

She had no other choice. It was this or nothing, and she couldn't give up without trying.

Without hesitation, she turned her wrist up to her mouth and bit it, wincing as her teeth sliced into her skin.

Choking on the well of her own blood, she hurriedly brought it to his lips, letting the warm red liquid fall onto them. She pried his mouth open, forcing the blood to flow into his mouth.

A weakness washed through her limbs, up to her head, making her dizzy. She blinked, her eyesight going fuzzy, her breath as thready and weak as his.

She collapsed on one elbow, barely registering the suction of his mouth at her wrist. She was so tired of a sudden.

Her head drooped and she slumped over him.

His hands touched her, drawing her wordlessly up his body, until her face neared his neck.

She smelled blood there. The scent awakened her. Her mouth watered as her fangs lengthened. Without conscious thought, she sank her teeth into the crook of his neck, reveling in the blood that welled into her mouth like ambrosia.

Instant fire burst through her veins. She choked on the blood but continued sucking, caught up in a vortex of feeling--emotions and memories flooding her brain and driving it into darkness swirling with raw ecstasy and understanding.

* * * *

Warm lips called her from the night, pulling her out of a slumber so deeply intense, she half feared she'd died.

Slowly, opening her eyes, the world came into focus.

Danior looked down at her, propped up on one elbow.

"Did we die?" she asked, her voice hoarse from disuse.

He smiled, stroking the backs of his fingers up her cheek. "No, thanks to you."

"I don't understand."

"You blood bonded with me when you shared your blood and took mine. I didn't think it was possible to share such a bond with another vampire after it had already once been given, but your strength drew me back from the edge. You kept Tatiana from pulling me into death with her."

Maggie sat up, studying him uncertainly. She hated to ask, but she had to make sure. "Are we ... are we safe?"

"Yes, *amour*, we are."

Maggie breathed a sigh of relief, throwing her arms around him to hug him tightly. The dread was gone, the uncertainty, all of it, leaving nothing but this huge swell of happiness. She could hardly believe what had happened, but she wouldn't question what fate had brought her. "I love you," she breathed against his neck.

He stiffened in her arms, pulling back to study her face, holding her gaze for a long, silent moment. Finally, he smiled and pushed her back onto the bed, covering her mouth in kiss that made her toes curl and her insides heat to the point of combustion.

He broke from her mouth, breathing raggedly, staring down at her with intense, passion laden eyes. He ran a thumb across her bottom lip, curling his fingers along her cheek. "You are everything to me, Maggie. When I lay dying, I could think of nothing but that I would never see your face again, never touch your lips or kiss your hair. You have brought me back from an empty abyss I've lived in for a thousand years."

He kissed her again, softly, so sweetly tender it brought tears to her eyes.

"I love you, Maggie," he whispered against her lips, pouring himself into each word and kiss so that she was engulfed in the rapture of his love.

The End

BORN OF NIGHT

Chapter One

The streets raged with the dizzying sounds and scents of Mardi Gras in full swing. Women and men laughed, twisted and writhed to music, singing lyrics known only to themselves. Beads jangled like hollow bits of wood. Torn, dyed feathers floated in the air on a lazy breeze that carried with it the ripe smell of too many people too close together. The voices of drunken revelers warred with the exciting tempo of a zydeco band playing on one corner and a blues band on another. An alto saxophone and a clarinet played a moody, mellow song that stirred the blood of those close enough to hear it above the dull roar of carousal.

There was no other city quite like New Orleans, cozy as a small town with all the amenities of a metropolis. History drenched every street corner, every balcony on high, every facade along the waterfront. Traditions ruled the city with a firm hand, southern justice was always in effect, but everyone turned a blind eye when it came to the decadence of the holiday.

No, there was no other experience to be had like that at Mardi Gras.

It was dangerous times for the unwary, though. He'd never seen so many vamps prowling the streets, hunting prey, getting fat and drunk off the careless and ignorant. Not that anyone would believe an underground war raged in the dead of night. The truce that had held long before he was born was as shaky as a long tailed cat in a room full of rocking chairs. The Lycan territories were breached, and the feuds had spilled over onto the neutral grounds of the historic district--into the main heart of the city.

Since the vampire lord's disappearance a month or two ago, things had turned from shit, to rancid shit.

Gabriel Benoit snickered at that thought. The pack thought he was crazy for braving no man's land, especially at night. He didn't let little things like caution get in his way though. He was just cocky and confident enough it didn't bother him to think of being outnumbered. Some would call it stupidity. He called it weariness of denying his appetites.

Vamps traveled in packs, and when they could, they supped on Lycan. One bite was enough to take a Lycan down, paralyzed with their venom. If two struck, it was wolfie for dinner. Their potent, Lycan blood was the whole reason this damned war had been started in the first place, and frankly, Gabriel was tired of ceding hunting grounds and territory to the blood suckers. It was getting to where no decent Lycan could even roam the streets or bayous alone anymore--except during the daytime.

If he could've, he'd give up all his Lycan powers to just be normal and not have to worry with the bull-shitting politics and wars, the never ending battles that always seemed to flare and stir up the natives. It was just a damn miracle some tabloid hadn't caught on and got the humans started on a vamp and Lycan hunting season.

Gabriel sighed. He just wanted a simple life, with a woman ready, willing, and waiting in his bed ... and a car that stayed running more often than not. That wasn't too much to ask.

Still, Gabriel relished the thought of taking on a pack of vampires, found it invigorating as only a man with too much time on his hands could. Thus, he'd come to the "party" looking for action ... of one type or another.

Moths clinked like tinny music against the heated light above him. The light flickered, making him almost annoyed enough to move--but not quite. Gabriel leaned against the lamp post, his arms crossed over his chest, lazily perusing the crowd with an easy grin and the heat of spiced rum flowing through his veins.

Even without the risk of battle, the others would not have come to the festivities. They felt alienated from the humans, too obviously different. Gabriel suffered no such qualms, himself. But more and more, it seemed they grew more animalistic and less human as time wore on. He would be worried except for the fact that that was what had allowed them to survive through the centuries to start with.

A woman smiled as she walked by, catching his eye. She giggled, hooked her hands under the hem of her shirt, and flashed him before running off. Gabriel grinned, shaking his head.

He never denied himself this pleasure. This was his favorite time of the year, when the underbelly of the city exposed itself and its impurities were reveled in as only proper sinners could appreciate.

Plus, he enjoyed seeing women flash their breasts for something so trifling as beaded necklaces and a smile from an appreciative man.

He'd been lounging against the cool metal post for some time, enjoying the sweet blues spilling from a local bar and lost in his thoughts, when a scent tickled his nose, strange yet familiar. His beast leapt instantly to life, ruffling the hair on the back of his neck.

Gabriel straightened suddenly, sniffing the wafting air. Past the cloying alcohol and perspiration, he caught it again on the wind. Faint, it uncurled with a spicy sweetness in his senses like a rare perfume.

He dropped off the curb and pushed through the crowded street through sweat slick bodies, following the scent. It teased, taunting, drawing him in until he was helpless to do anything but follow.

Pale skin flashed before him as revelers begged for beads from those standing above in balconies. He ignored them all, intent on his quarry, stopping only when he found the source of his affliction.

Gabriel looped and arm around an iron lamp post, gaining height over the crowd, watching her. He knew instinctively she was the one ... the one that taunted unawares.

She was trapped in the throng, walled in by bodies. She looked mildly worried, as though she was claustrophobic but determined to have a good time regardless.

She looked like a china doll: fragile porcelain skin, baby blue eyes, a pink blush tingeing her cheeks. She smiled and pushed back a loose tendril of pale blonde hair behind her ear. One pert breast lifted with the action, and even with the distance he caught the slight pucker of her nipple beneath the thin cotton.

He rubbed one thumb against his bottom lip, drawn by her movement and imagined sensation.

An instant fog of lust clouded his brain. She was in heat. Never had he smelled a woman so ripe for fucking. The scent and knowledge threatened to burn away all rational thought. His hands clenched into tight fists, his fingers digging into his palms. His arms bulged with the effort to restrain himself. For a few minutes, he could think of nothing but taking her and laying her on the street, pushing her legs apart and burying his cock deep inside her.

The knowledge that he was reacting as an animal didn't stop the feelings raging in his blood. If anything, they worsened. His balls tightened, his cock throbbed. He gritted his teeth, pained with the hot surge of blood in his groin.

Slowly, his beast backed down when it realized it would get no satiation. Thoughts churned like sluggish clock wheels, and he finally realized something had tamed the waves of pheromones fanning off her, or else he would have been driven to nothing but pure animal instinct. He didn't flatter himself by thinking it was his strength of will that had kept him in control.

For the first time since he'd been turned, it had nearly slipped. He didn't want to think about what could've happened.

He continued calming himself, watching her dance, sip her drink. One of thousands, she was more precious than she could ever begin to imagine. And he'd found her. He wondered where she'd come from, how she'd gotten here.

She could not have been in the city long or else she'd not be standing here, but be trapped in some alley, her skirt up to her waist with a slick cock thrusting into her.

His groin spasmed at the illicit thought, of parting her soft thighs and smelling her want of him, of feeling the thick cream that would ease his passage inside her.

Had the spicy musk of heat been in full effect, he and any other Lycan would've been on her like the pack of beasts they were. He knew he could not allow that to happen--and it would if she wasn't careful.

He growled low in his throat, animal instincts surging to the surface once more. Then and there, he determined he would take her ... before another could. She was his, and he had every intention of staking his claim to her, tonight.

Now.

* * * *

Someone jostled her elbow from behind, sending her plastic cup flying from her grasp to clatter dully onto the ground.

"Hey!" Jessica Talvert yelled, whirling around to deliver a blistering tirade.

A hand snaked out and snatched the necklace from her neck. Her throat burned as the chain snapped under the pressure. The thief took off through the crowd before she could even raise a hand to stop him.

Jessica gasped in outrage, following the thief without thinking. The necklace was her only physical link to her past. She was never supposed to take it off--*never*. She couldn't lose it!

Jessica pushed through the milling throng, running after him as best she could. He stayed ahead of her, slippery as an eel, weaving through the bodies effortlessly while she was hemmed in. She soon lost him, and jumped up to look over the crowd, ignoring the angry looks she got. She spotted the hooded figure running toward an alley squashed between a strip club and a bar.

Heart pounding with adrenaline, Jessica squirmed through the closed bodies. It was like trying to squeeze through a crack in the wall, and she wondered how the thief had managed it so quickly and easily. After a minute, she broke through and raced past a man hawking naked girls and went into the alley.

An immediate feeling of danger clutched her chest, squeezing her ribs like two gods snapping a wishbone.

A narrow band of light stretched through the center, leaving the sides in utter blackness. Garbage littered the cracked pavement. A clatter of cans sounded deeper, stirred by wind or fleeing feet, she didn't know. She heard the sounds of a scuffle, of meaty fist strikes and the crash of metal.

Jessica stopped halfway down the alley, catching her breath, wondering what kind of shit she was in now. Was it worth it? She thought the necklace was, but there was no way she could take on a grown man by herself. Or whatever was fighting up ahead.

Suddenly a man stepped out of the shadows and walked towards her with a cocky stride. Had she run headlong into more trouble? Jessica instinctively backed up a step, remaining wary and tense ... until she saw what dangled in his hand.

The silver medallion twirled on its chain, glinting in the failing light and the glare from a distant street lamp. Startled into immobility, Jessica looked blankly up from her necklace to the man. Whatever questioning words she'd had fell forgotten from her mind.

A tension seemed to fill his body, belying his easy, relaxed stance. His left thumb was hooked in his waistband in easy confidence. He held her necklace with his right hand, playing with it as he watched her steadily with an unblinking stare that missed nothing and seemed to see straight through her clothes. Jessica didn't stop to wonder why he was standing there, or what he'd done to get her necklace back. She should've been grateful. She should've demanded that he return it to her. But she couldn't do anything but stare at him, dumbfounded.

The spunk she'd always prided herself on possessing deserted her. She blamed it on shock, on unfamiliar surroundings, on being practically attacked. But those were lies. She'd been all ready to kick ass and chew bubble gum until she saw him. She felt like she'd been kicked in the gut and all the breath knocked from her lungs.

He easily outdistanced her own height, standing at least 6' 2", but that wasn't what had her entranced. He was naked from the waist up, and though she'd seen plenty of practically naked men and women running around the streets, this man put them all to shame. Thin, silver studded rings glinted wickedly from each nipple. His sculpted chest was sparsely covered with hair, hiding none of the beautiful planes, and it moved in a straight, purposeful dark path down his rippled belly and into his jeans--which were tantalizingly unbuttoned, as though he'd hastily thrust them on after carnal pursuits and raced out into the night.

That alone was enough to fuel the coldest woman's fantasies--even her own. She'd never seen a man with pierced nipples. She wondered what they felt like. Her fingertips prickled with the need to flick those rings.

The shredded, torn jeans he wore fit him like a glove and left little to the imagination. What they covered had her mind racing to find out his secrets, and hoping he'd slip and fall and tear the jeans the rest of the way off. A patch of skin on one hip showed, and one lingering glimpse at it told her he didn't wear anything beneath those jeans. If the zipper slid a little lower, she could see everything....

She'd been schooled to at least make a pretense of being a lady, to quash baser instincts. Lessens of 'good girls don't' and 'bad girls do' seemed to mesh in one confusing jumble, and she couldn't for the life of her think of why any good girl wouldn't *do* a man like this.

Jessica swallowed, working moisture down her tight throat as she tore her eyes away from his groin. Her eyes felt indelibly seared by that prominent bulge, just waiting to burst out at any moment. Slowly, she worked her astonished way back up to his face. The hard line of his jaw came into view, sharply outlined with black stubble. Full lips quirked at her in a cocky half-smile.

He closed the distance between them, but Jessica barely noticed, only knew he was coming closer. All the better to see him.

She frowned at his amused lips, then peered straight up at his eyes. Sleek, inky hair clung to his throat and streamed over his forehead in rakish abandon, looking mussed and incredibly sexy. Bedroom hair. Smoky bedroom eyes. Brown and flecked with gold, they were mesmerizing and glowed with sensual promise from the light behind her. He appeared to have trace Spanish blood in him--as did many of the locals, giving them darkly sensual looks and deep, bronze skin.

He looked as delicious and sinful as chocolate ... but with bite to it.

He was definitely a heart breaker. Women probably fell all over themselves for one peep at him ... just like her. She tried to be annoyed, but irritation was the furthest thing from her mind.

He held her gaze, watching her intently beneath heavy, straight brows, eyes reflecting the tension in his body.

Jessica blushed so brightly under his intense, knowing stare, she was sure she glowed in the dark. She tore her eyes away from his and focused on his lips, blushed again at her errant thoughts, and dropped her gaze yet again to his chin. Her eyes kept straying down that belly to his unbuttoned fly. His fly bulged impressively, and she wondered absently if anything was going to jump out and bite her. And if she'd really fight it off if it attacked.

"Like what you see, *chere*?" he finally asked in a velvet drawl, breaking her out of her stupor.

If she'd had fur, she was sure it would ruffle and prickle under that stroking, baritone voice. With an effort, Jessica dragged her gaze back to his, hating that her interest was so damned obvious. Hating more that she continued to blush. She was so hot, she felt like she'd break out in a sweat at any moment. What did she expect? She'd probably been drooling at him like he was a juicy steak for at least five minutes.

Something changed in him, and his look turned to one of amusement at her perusal. His gaze dropped to her feet, and he roamed his way up her body, leaving her strangely flushed and aroused. She hadn't thought it was possible to become aroused just looking at someone, let alone a stranger, and she didn't like the feeling one bit.

Get a grip, she told herself, and fixed him with a stern stare. "Did you see someone run by here?" she asked, then immediately thought about how stupid that probably sounded. She didn't know how long she'd gaped at him, because her brain was strangely foggy, but he was holding her necklace and she'd heard the brief fight.

Dammit. She normally curbed her impulse to ask dumb questions. It was hell being a blonde. Society just had no idea the burden they placed on already burdened minds.

He didn't seem to notice her dumb blonde moment.

He leaned back on his heels. "I did. I found sometin' you lost, *cherie*," he murmured, cocking that smile again. He held up his hand, dangling her necklace before her eyes. The medallion glinted and twirled on its chain.

His husky, drawling accent caressed her ears like a melody, sending shivers up and down her spine like smooth silk. Jessica shook herself with an effort. It was time to stiffen her spine and stop thinking between her legs. She was as bad as a man. "Thank you." She reached up to take it, but he snatched his hand back.

"No' so fast, *cherie*. Don' your champion deserve sometin' in return?"

Maybe she did owe him something for the trouble ... but she wasn't so sure about just giving in to his demands though. "What kind of rescuer would demand payment?" she asked, propping her hands on her hips.

His teeth flashed in a wide grin. "One who's smitten with your beauty, *chere*."

Jessica rolled her eyes, trying not to laugh. Why did all Southern men lay the charm on so thickly? "Oh puhlease."

He looked hurt that she doubted him. "You wound me, *chere*. Have you no heart? I have risked my life only t'please, and you begrudge me so small a token as a kiss?"

"A kiss?" she exclaimed. Her heart tripped in her chest, staggered up, and started to run.

He rubbed a thumb against his jaw, measuring her. "Your name and ... a kiss."

Jessica released an exasperated breath, trying to block out the breathless feeling in her chest at the idea of letting those sultry, pouty lips touch hers. She wasn't going to play these games. She'd give him what he wanted all right. "It's Jessica Talvert, and here's your reward." She stood on her toes and kissed him on the cheek. She dropped down and gave him a syrupy smile of satisfaction at outwitting him.

Who said she was a dumb blonde?

"Sweet, but I'm no' your brodder, *chere*," he said in a voice brimming with enough sensual menace a delicious primal shiver skated through her body. He caught her arms about the same time she realized his intent, blocking her defensive ball busting move with one knee and her titty twister with an unbreakable hold. Before she knew what was happening, she found herself whirled around and thrust against one wall, hauled tightly against his body.

Shadows cloaked them, spilling across his face. He seemed a lot bigger and more dangerous so tightly against her. She should've abandoned her necklace to him. "Some hero," she gritted out, squirming in his hold, trying to free a hand. Despite her struggles, she insanely anticipated him stealing a kiss from her. Didn't it make it all right to enjoy herself if she didn't *really* give in? That was a rule somewhere, she was sure.

Something dark and predatory flashed in his eyes, like a slumbering wolf had been awakened. Her breath caught. All the silly little, nervous thoughts washing through her brain froze. He smiled ferally, then bent his head to claim her lips.

Jessica gasped, partly in outrage, but mostly from a surge of heat so sharp and drastic, her heart stopped for a breathless moment.

He seized the break in her defenses and plunged his tongue into her mouth, filling her with hot persuasion and the stroking glide of his tongue. He tasted spicy, like cinnamon and rum and something infinitely wilder and more dangerous. Jessica wanted to bite him, to fight him off, but he rubbed sensuously against her own tongue, silky, slick and rough. It took only moments for vengeful thoughts to disappear entirely and be replaced by the seductive call of desire. Jessica gave a shocked whimper when he retreated and sucked her tongue into his mouth.

She tried to pull back, but he captured the back of her head with an easy, merciless grip, holding her to the thrall of his mouth and his hungry, sucking kiss. Slowly, she began to realize a pressure that had never been there before built low in her belly. Arousal cramped her pussy with a jerking spasm of pleasure. She gasped into his mouth at the piercing, sweet agony, the awakening of some long slumbering beast inside her. His mouth drove her wild, made her respond in a way she'd never dreamed possible. Heat rippled through her.

He cradled his body into hers, stroking those rough jeans against her trapped slit, melting her core until she felt her wet arousal trickle between her thighs. His groin nestled in the juncture of her thighs, so incredibly close to where she *needed* it, unbearably hard and erotic, wrecking what little resolve she still possessed. At some point, he'd freed her hands to draw his around her waist and bring her tighter against him, slipping them down to clutch her buttocks and mold her to the hot tightness of his cock.

Jessica clung to him, her fingers stroking his satiny skin and muscled back. She squirmed in pleasurable agony as he thrust against her, fighting the thrill that surged in her blood at his possessive hold and the knowledge that she'd conjured his lust.

She couldn't seem to get enough air. She felt dizzy with it and the tingling pleasure between her thighs. Her lips and tongue felt gloriously bruised from his kiss, so sensitive she could orgasm if only he'd continue devouring her.

He broke away from her mouth suddenly, leaving her gasping for breath and her knees weak.

"You're so sweet, *cherie*," he said with a drowsy, heated look, rubbing his thumb across his lips and licking the moisture lingering from her mouth off the pad.

Jessica swallowed. Hard. She felt dazed and not herself, and her pulse still raced with something akin to heat. The loss of control unnerved her. "My necklace?" she managed to say past her throbbing lips. She held out her hand, palm up, encouraged by her ability not to melt in a puddle on the ground at his feet.

He gave her an unreadable look and dropped the necklace into her hand, closing her fingers over it. "It's broken. You'll need t'fix it," he said, releasing her hand.

She resisted the urge to rub where he'd touched her. She felt positively branded all over. By the way he was acting, it seemed to be just her reacting so heatedly to the kiss-- which was infinitely embarrassing to say the least. Jessica looked down at the broken chain. "Yes, it is." But she'd already known that. The thief had ripped it from her neck.

"It's not somtin' you wanna wait on, *chere*."

Jessica looked up, distracted from her unwanted physical response by the intriguing tone of his voice. There was warning there. And something else she couldn't quite identify. "What do you mean?"

"Jus' what I said. There's a shop jus' a ways from the corner of Bourbon and Canal--Mikel's. They can fix it for you there. You wan' me t'show you?" He grinned in the half light, his teeth flashing white against his bronzed skin.

"Thanks. I can find it on my own." She hadn't noticed any shops on her way down here--mostly just hotels and the like. A few bars. Her own hotel was on Canal Street.

"You're not gonna go, are you, *chere*?"

Whether she did or not wasn't any of his business. She shrugged noncommittally.

"Jus' remember what I tol' you."

His advice brought the warning her adoptive parents had given her fresh into her mind. *Never take this off. Never.* She knew her neck was ringed with paler skin, the chain having long rested around it ... for as long as she could remember. She half wondered if he knew something she didn't, but she shrugged the silly thought off. He didn't know her or anything about her. She'd gotten paranoid since coming to New Orleans.

Jessica turned to go, then stopped. "What's your name?" she asked, glancing back at him over her shoulder.

He smiled lazily, propping one shoulder against the building in confident male fashion. "Gabriel Benoit, *petite*. At your service."

"Nice to ... uh ... meet you," she murmured and turned away before he could see her blush again ... or draw her into further conversation. She put his disturbing presence and even more disturbing kiss out of her mind.

She wasn't here to get involved with any man, especially not one like him. She knew the type--players. Always charming, good looking, and absolutely horrible on a woman's self esteem when they left and chased after the next piece of ass. She wasn't going to be any man's conquest. Not that Jessica had ever fallen for a player, but she damned well knew *now* why women did.

She still felt hot and bothered as she set off for her hotel. She glanced back to see if he followed--not because she wanted one last look at temptation incarnate--but he wasn't to be seen. She quickly lost sight of the small alley as she made her way toward Canal street and left the Bourbon revelers behind. Soon the only sounds on the street were the hum of car engines, the wind, and her own footsteps. It was a long walk back to her hotel, and she was contemplating catching a cab when she noticed the obscure shop Gabriel had spoken of.

It was practically invisible, overshadowed by the giants around it, but the shuttered, double doors were thrown open to let a cool breeze inside. Obviously, they were open, even at this late hour. Jessica approached it, and the jangling music of wind chimes grew louder as she neared. A man was inside, sweeping the rugs covering the tiled floor. He looked up as she passed through the door.

"Are you closing up?" she asked, stopping inside the threshold.

"Not just yet," he said, setting his broom aside. "What can I do for you?"

Jessica held up her necklace, looking around and feeling like she'd been duped. The shop didn't look like a jewelry repair place. "Someone mentioned I could get this fixed here," she said with a doubtful tone to her voice.

He took it from her and gave her a startled look, quickly shuttered. "Yep. I'll get this fixed for you in a jiffy. Have a look around. I'll be right back."

Jessica nodded and watched him go through a door into the back, then wandered around the cluttered shop. There were racks of charms and potions on one side, including a row dedicated to nothing but essence of garlic of varying sizes and potencies. Weapons lined the walls out of reach near the ceiling: crossbows, long bows, swords, and arrows with silver and wooden heads. There were others she couldn't identify, but that looked almost like maces.

Jessica continued looking and found an umbrella holder filled with short wooden stakes and another with mallets. It looked for all the world like some bizarre, witch hunting shop ... or rather, one dedicated to vampire hunting. The movie Blade popped in her head. Really, being Louisiana, she would've thought they'd have more voodoo paraphernalia.

The man came out again, moving behind the front counter. He laid her necklace on the clean surface. "That's a fine warding medallion you have. Been a while since I've seen one so old."

"Warding medallion?" she asked, walking up to the counter to check the work. She couldn't even tell it had ever been broken.

"Yes. Well, it's an old, cryptic language. Most people wouldn't recognize it. See these markings here?" He flipped it over and showed her a scrawling script. She'd always thought it was some kind of ornate design--not words. "It's protection against the wolf."

Jessica was intrigued. She leaned on the counter, looking between him and her medallion. "What kind of protection?"

"It depends on the wearer really. Now, if you were a vampire, it would ward werewolves away ... supposedly."

Jessica laughed. He wasn't serious. "Okay, you got me. There's no such thing as vampires and werewolves."

He chuckled, watching as she put the necklace on. "I'm not joking around. I would've thought you'd heard of the war by now."

"What war? Does it have something to do with all this stuff in here?" she asked, waving an expansive arm, playing along.

He propped an elbow on the register. "Of course. I'm just a supplier, mind you. I don't take part, but I'm partial to the Lycan side of things."

"Why's that? I mean, I don't see why vampires and Lycans would fight."

He rubbed his jaw, considering it. "It must've been in the early part of this past century. The Lycans rebelled against the vamps using them as food and slaves ... but they mostly objected to being eaten, and still do. Must've been a sight to see them tearing into the vamps--if you were on the inside, that is. I've always been partial to the underdog, so I supply them when they come in."

Jessica was completely unnerved and fascinated by his story. She didn't doubt but what there were plenty of nuts running around claiming to be a werewolf or a vampire. She guessed anyone had a right to make a living selling to them. "So is this war still going on?" she asked, amused.

"It flares up every now and again, but they usually stick to their territory. Just stay clear of anything Southwest of the Ponchartrain Expressway. Especially the warehouse and Garden district."

Jessica nodded, humoring him. She was going there to check out the cemetery where her birth parents had been buried--at least that's what she'd managed to dig up. Jessica paid him and turned to leave, but he stopped her with one last warning.

"You'll remember what I said, right? I can tell you're not from around here and don't know about the territories just yet. I wouldn't want you to have a run in with those bloodsuckers. There's only so much protection that warding medallion will give you."

Chapter Two

Gabriel stood in the shadow of a doorway, watching as Jessica left the shop and walked up the street, completely unaware of his presence. Her senses were too dulled from human living, but he could change that. And he would. Even with the distance, he sensed the necklace about her throat. He was grateful she'd heeded his advice and gotten the chain fixed. A warding medallion was no real worry to him, but he hoped its power would keep the others from sensing her presence in the city a while longer. He'd staked his claim with that kiss, but there were too many to challenge him.

Given what she was, he had little doubt she would be allowed to choose a mate, and better him than another. The fact that he had little remorse for his action proved just how Lycan he'd grown, but it mattered not.

He waited until she'd gained some distance on him before pushing away from the door jam, following her, keeping her within sight. The streets here were empty of other pedestrians. He couldn't smell Lycans or Vamps nearby, but that didn't mean they weren't out there, prowling the streets. Still, he was satisfied they were relatively alone.

He hooked his thumbs in his pockets, rubbing his fingers on the rough denim. They still burned from holding the chain, but no more than the studs in his nipples. If anything, it served as reminder of the kiss he'd taken.

His cock tightened at that thought, and the sight of her hips swaying gently as she walked only worsened the sweet pain. He smiled darkly. She remained oblivious to the fact that he followed her. But wasn't that how he wanted it? She was blissfully innocent, and he knew the warning Mikel had given her had fallen on disbelieving ears.

She'd become a believer soon enough. It was amazing how quickly a person could change their mind when confronted by living, breathing evidence. Seeing with her own eyes would banish that last, clinging ignorance.

Now that she was here, the warding power of the medallion would grow weaker and weaker, until it lost its power completely amongst the overwhelming presence of his brethren.

Gabriel almost regretted what she'd go through. But she should not have come to New Orleans. Now that she was here, he wasn't going to deny himself the pleasure of seducing her. The subtle nuances of her nervous desire excited him immeasurably: the breathless sigh, the pulse in her throat, the fight against her own base appetites that mirrored his own. He could still taste her on his tongue, feel the rounded firmness of her ass in his palms. His groin felt imprinted by the cloaked heat of her femininity.

He couldn't remember ever feeling so frustrated in all his life. He wondered if fucking both their brains out would satisfy the lust boiling his blood, or if it would only worsen, make him insane with lust. He wondered if it was worth the risk in tempting the beast. Could any woman be worth so much?

She stopped suddenly on the sidewalk. Gabriel ducked into a doorway, waiting to see what she would do. He watched her indecisive profile, as she crossed and uncrossed her arms, kicked at a ball of trash on the pavement. Finally, she made up her mind and moved forward and into a local bar.

Apparently, she wasn't ready to give up the night just yet.

He grinned and trotted up the sidewalk. Just his kind of girl. He liked a woman who didn't know when to quit.

But she didn't need to be out too late. He couldn't sense any danger, but that didn't mean it wasn't out there. He wanted to make sure she got to her room okay.

He chuckled, thinking of a few ways to wear her out and entertain her if she was feeling restless.

Gabriel waited a few minutes before sauntering through the door. Inside was darker than out, almost smoky-like. A live band took up a space on a far, center wall, and most of the light and noise came from there and the crowded dance floor. Looking around the hazy space, he saw mostly tourists, probably from the nearby hotels. Their scent gave them away--they were missing that certain spice that only natives had to them, not like his Jessica though. She was a force unto herself.

Gabriel sidled up to the bar, got a beer, and turned around, propping his elbows on the bar as he scanned the crowd for her. He spotted her at a table, nursing a drink and giving a brush off to a man hitting on her. His ears prickled to hear her soft rebuttal, barely audible, even to his own keen ears.

Doesn't like to dance?

A challenge, and she didn't even realize it. She was damn well in the wrong place, not to be a dancer. Music was a part of life here, dancing in the blood, necessary as air or water to live. He was going to introduce her to one of the finer points of Louisiana living.

* * * *

Jessica just wanted to watch. She liked watching people dancing, drinking, talking ... flirting. Interaction had always fascinated her for some reason, even after she'd become disillusioned with society. She just liked the atmosphere, especially down here. Of course, just because she liked to watch didn't mean she wanted to do it herself--especially not with some slush who could barely stand and reeked of stale beer.

A chair scraped behind her. Jessica mentally rolled her eyes and shuddered. She sensed more than saw someone come up behind her elbow.

Much as the guy deserved a hit to the gut, she wasn't going to get physical. *Dammit!* She'd tried to be nice. Repeatedly. There was just no way to be nice to people any more. Courtesy had disappeared fifty years ago, along with manners. She hated being mean--it always made her feel like a dog when she got through.

Jessica swiveled in her chair, her stomach clenched with the rebuttal she was going to have to deliver.

She stopped, stunned to look up and see Gabriel Benoit standing before her.

Her brain only took a few seconds to jump-start this time. She was getting better at recovering. A few more times seeing him and she might even act normal. Her eyes narrowed with suspicion. Before she could demand to know what he wanted, he surprised her by speaking first.

"You followin' me, *cherie*? Dere's laws against stalkin', you know," he said with that husky, lilting tone that made her want to melt to the floor in an orgasmic puddle.

She recovered as the words sank in. Jessica sputtered at his audacity. "Me? Are you serious? You're the one following me!"

He shrugged. "Don' matter. Law's the law. What you gonna do about it?" He looked down her blouse with a mischievous gleam in his eyes.

Jessica slowly followed his line of vision, saw her neckline gaped, and put a hand to her chest, gasping in outrage. She managed to find her voice and said, "What makes you think I'm following *you*? Who approached who's table here?"

He looked disappointed that she'd covered her chest, but only briefly. Really, as little as she had up top, she didn't know why he acted so interested.

"I only came ta save you some time, *cherie*. You don' gotta go through all dis subterfuge to get me." He held his arms up and open, like he was there for the taking. "I'm all yours if you wan' me."

Jessica grinned despite herself. The man really had some balls. She gave him a once over. "Thanks, but I have toys at home."

"I guarantee, no' like dis toy."

Jessica laughed. "But mine come with an independent power supply. Can you keep going and going and going...?"

One thick, black brow arched. A dimple appeared on the side of his mouth. He crossed his arms over his chest, looking smug in a supreme male sort of way. "I can give you more'n you can handle, *petite*."

Jessica snorted very unladly-like, secretly excited--not that she would ever admit it. "I somehow doubt that."

His voice dropped an octave, and all amusement left his face. "Don' make me prove it."

Hot shivers stroked up her spine. The room suddenly felt too small, too private. She was insanely aware of how fast her heart beat, how rapid her breath came, and how damn good he smelled. It was a struggle to remember how to use her voice. All the moisture had fled her body and pooled in one central location. "I don't think so," she said inanely.

He smiled crookedly, baring a dimple. "All mouth and no action. You don' know what dose lips are for."

She didn't want to think about her lips. All she could do was stare at his and wonder about what tricks he could perform. The kiss he stole in the alley came back full force--all the heat, the uncertainty, the rough force of his body pressing her into the wall. She wasn't acting like herself. She should've been scared or nervous, but the only things her nerves were doing were coming to life in anticipation.

Jessica swallowed with effort. Her face flushed with heat. She stood up abruptly, not liking his height advantage over her. She could tell he wasn't nearly as affected as she was. She also couldn't think of a thing to say to him, nothing challenging or witty. He had to think she was a moron, some dumb little thing ripe for the taking. The blonde curse was striking, leaving her open and vulnerable.

"You know I'm right, don' you? Would you like me to show you what lips can do?" He grabbed her arms suddenly.

She looked down at the manacles of his hands one stunned moment, marveling at the contrast of bronze against her pale skin. Erotic images flashed in her mind, of cream and golden bodies entwined, rough and soft. The contrast of his flesh against hers seared her mind's eye. She looked back up at his face, wondering frantically if he could read her mind, wondering a breathless moment if he was going to kiss her like she wanted to be kissed.

What the hell. She didn't care what anyone in the bar thought. For once, she just wanted to give in and enjoy herself. She shrugged mentally, closed her eyes, and leaned in.

His arms closed around her, and suddenly he was moving her backward. She stepped back, instinctively keeping her balance.

Coming out of the fog, Jessica opened her eyes and blinked up at him in confusion. She was still a little dazed when he took her hands and began guiding her on the dance floor. She stiffened instantly when she realized his intent.

"I don't dance," she gritted out and tried to pull away. She felt like everyone was watching her and her two huge left feet. They knew she couldn't dance. They were just waiting for her to fall on her face.

His hands tightened at her waist, his fingers locked on her hand. "It's jus' like makin' love." He moved his hips against hers, making her feel weak. "You rock with it."

"That's original. I must be really bad in bed then." She felt like a robot, all stiff and cumbersome and obvious.

Gabriel melded her to his body, his heat melting her resistance until she felt mellow and relaxed in his arms. If dancing was an indicator of love making, Gabriel had to be an exquisite lover. Just feeling his body move against hers made her weak in all the right places. She could barely keep her feet under her. All she wanted to do was lay her face against his chest and feel his arms around her.

"It jus' takes d'right partner," he murmured huskily against her hair, his breath sparking a chain reaction of pleasurable responses.

He swayed and took her around the dance floor, keeping her distracted from her flighty nervousness with subtle strokes from his fingers at her waist, on her wrist, his lips at her temple, his breath at her ear. Every pore of her body sighed with pleasure. The dance felt too intimate for public, but wasn't that part of the appeal?

He'd managed to do what no man had ever done before--got her to enjoy a dance. She could get used to this kind of treatment.

The thought was like an ice bucket dumped on her head.

Jessica stiffened and attempted to pull back from his relaxed grip. Her efforts failed. He continued moving her on the dance floor, paying absolutely no attention to the fact that she was trying to get away.

"I need to get back to my hotel."

"I'll take you," he said, looking down and giving her a smoky look that spoke volumes.

She knew exactly what he was thinking. "I'm not going to sleep with you."

He arched one brow, looking amused. "Who said anythin' bout sleepin', *chere*?"

The iciness from moments before melted in a puddle at her feet. He flustered her with such ease, it was disturbing. She tried to cover it with a sarcastic tone. "You know what I mean."

"Maybe I don'. You tryin' to gi' me a hint? I tell you what, I don' see dem so good. Maybe you need to be a liddle more direct. If you don' wan' to sleep, what do you wan' to do?"

"Not what you're thinking," she said, frowning.

"How do you know what I'm thinkin?"

"I can tell by--by...."

He grinned. "I'll make it easy for you, *chere*. You can have me if you wan' me. How bout dat?"

Jessica harrumphed under her breath. "Thanks," she muttered. "You could just hit me over the head and make it easier all the way around. Let me go, and I'll turn around so you can do it."

He chuckled, one hand roaming around her back and creeping too close to her ass for her comfort level. His eyes gleamed with wicked mirth. "And here I thought you an *ange*. You really *diabolique, petite*. You like things a liddle rough, no?"

He was being deliberately obtuse, probably all in an attempt so he could continue feeling her up. "I'm suddenly exhausted," she said wryly, trying to loosen herself from his hold.

He finally relented and released her, looking disappointed. "Ah, too bad. You sure you won' let me take you to d'hotel?"

Jessica held up her hand, stopping him. "No, thanks. I'm used to taking care of myself." She was the only person she could rely on. It wasn't safe for a woman to put faith in a man these days. They didn't protect, they didn't take care of--all they did was use until a woman had nothing else to give, and then they threw them away for the next sucker. She was better off being single.

Jessica beat a hasty retreat back to her hotel, leaving Gabriel in the dust before he could use any more of that lethal charm on her.

One thing she knew now: Cajun accent + dimples + good looks = loss of brain function. She felt like a cat hooked on catnip, and there was no way this pussy was going to play and rub all over *that*.

Chapter Three

Jessica had just looked at her watch. She thought for one stunned moment of confusion, and embarrassment, that she had walked into the wall. Then two hands gripped her biceps, steadying her as she drew back.

A faint smiled curled Gabriel's lips. "But, *cherie*, we hardly know one anodur."

"What?" His accent confused her for several moments, but even when her brain finally interpreted the unfamiliar pronunciation, she was still all at sea.

"Las' night you didn' even wan' t'kiss me, now you rush into my arms?"

Jessica sputtered indignantly and looked up at his eyes. "I did no such thing!"

"So, you forget your reward already?"

"What are you talking about--wait. *My* reward. You're really full of yourself. It was *your* reward for rescuing my necklace."

One dark brow arched beguilingly. "So what do you give me for savin' you from a fall," he murmured, leaning too close.

Jessica pulled back so sharply she almost fell, and it was exactly the opening he was looking for. His bare arms wrapped around her, the hair sprinkled skin abrasive against the portions of her back bared by the strappy sundress. Did the man never wear a shirt? She couldn't think straight with all that potent male flesh exposed to her view and the skin of her palms.

Her fingertips tingled as his muscles played beneath them, moving as he trapped her. He tightened his hold, pulling her close, closer. Jessica flattened her palms on his chest, ignoring the fluttering in her stomach touching his bare flesh aroused, and pushed away. It did nothing to stop him. "Gabriel, we can't do this here in the middle of the hotel."

"Perhaps we cou' go up to your room?" he whispered, brushing his lips against the delicate shell of her ear, his warm breath ruffling her insides with delighted shivers.

"I don't think so." She gasped as his tongue thrust, wet and hot, in her ear, sending goosebumps chasing over her skin. He withdrew it, then tugged her earlobe with his teeth before swiping a wet path behind her ear.

"Mmm. You taste good. I cou' eat you right here, *chere*."

"Please don't."

"You don' soun' sure. You soun' like maybe you think yes."

With an effort, Jessica reined in her careening libido. "I think I said no, Gabriel. You're embarrassing me."

He pulled back and studied her with mirth in his eyes and a lazy grin. "I hardly got started. Ah dis color is a blush? It looks sweet on you, *chere*. Such a preddy face, why you hide from me?"

Jessica's face flamed even more at that remark. She was gratified when, reluctantly, he released her. She resisted the urge to wipe her kiss dampened skin, cooling in the climate controlled air. He grinned at her as if he knew exactly what she wanted to do.

Jessica glared back, then her eyes narrowed. "You didn't just happen by, did you?"

He looked wounded. "You don' trust me, *chere*?"

"I don't know you," she said indignantly. "Why should I trust you?"

"Because I am your champion. And I have decided to sacrifice my day and pu' myself at your disposal. I will show you Nawlins."

"That's so thoughtful of you. But I have a tour guide. I believe I can find my way around." She brushed past him and strode from the hotel. He fell into step beside her, not looking the least perturbed by her determined efforts to brush him off.

"We shou' go for coffee, and luncheon at the Bayou Cafe. And then you mus' tell me what sites most pique your interest."

Jessica stopped and stared at him. The truth was, she really *didn't* know her way around New Orleans, and it had occurred to her before that knowing a local would help her in her quest. She couldn't really afford to hire a tour guide-- not if she wanted to continue having a hotel room or things to eat. "All right. I'll have lunch with you. But I warn you, if you try anything, you'll draw back a nub."

He smiled that toe curling grin again and made a sweeping gesture with his arm. "After you, *cherie*."

She stopped in her tracks and gave him a once over. "Wait a minute. Are you going like that?" Never in her life had she seen a restaurant that would allow patrons to go in half naked.

"Sometin' wrong? You don' like what I'm wearin? I'm hurt, *cherie*."

"Well ... uh ... there's just so much of you ... exposed." Jessica blushed as she realized she was staring at his crotch. Not that it was exposed. She probably wouldn't still be standing if it had been. She was sure the sight of *that* would make her faint.

"No' exposed enough for what I'd like to do," he said, full of promise.

"And what would that be?" she asked and immediately regretted it.

He grinned. "Gimme some time, I show you."

"That's not necessary. I'm sure it's pretty--" She looked pointedly at his chin, trying very hard to be good.

"And fun to play with. You ever slid down a pole?" He hooked his thumbs on his pockets, emphasizing the object of their--his discussion.

She blushed straight to her roots and realized all attempts at not being a pervert had failed. She was too curious by half about how he looked without his clothes on. Why did she feel like a prude all of a sudden? "I'm not even going to think about what you just said. Can't you at least button your britches?"

He looked down at himself, fingering the half open fly deliberately to make her look at it. "Scared d'serpent gonna break free and bite you? I promise, he jus' nibbles. He likes warm hidey holes bedder anyway."

Jessica strangled on her saliva and coughed with embarrassment. She took a deep breath to recover before giving him a hard stare. "Well, it isn't getting anywhere near this hole. I thought you were going to behave?"

"You started it. I'm jus' waitin' for you to move so we can go."

Jessica spared him a warning glance and stepped outside, waiting for the doorman to hail them a cab to take them to Bayou Cafe. Gabriel said nothing as they made the five minute drive through traffic, but it wasn't like she could ignore his presence. He seemed to fill the confined space and wind her nerves tight, until she felt ready to spring at any moment. He watched her constantly, as if eating her with his eyes, and Jessica had the unnerving notion that he could see straight through her clothing.

The cab stopped and Gabriel paid, then held the door open for her as they entered the cafe. The scent of sausage and spices filled the air with a tangy nip, and Jessica's stomach began to rumble with hunger.

"Mmm. Smells good," she said, taking a seat at a booth.

"Dey serve d'bes' gumbo in town," he said, sliding in beside her.

"Can't you sit on the other side?" she asked, trying to scoot away and get some distance.

"I cou', but I won'."

Jessica tried to ignore him, but it was nearly impossible when he slipped his arm on the back of the booth, right over her shoulders. Jessica cleared her throat noisily, trying to warn him off, but he recognized hints about as subtle as he flirted. Finally, she looked over the menu while he played with a lock of her hair, wiggling her shoulders as he tickled her with it.

A waiter came up and offered her a brief reprieve. "Are you ready to order?" he asked.

"I'll have d'gumbo special, a coffee, and a glass of water."

"I'll have the same," Jessica said, setting the menu aside.

Gabriel gave her a look. "Bedder bring us a pitcher of water." The waiter smiled and walked away. "Can you stand the heat, *chere*?"

Jessica wiped her hands nervously on her skirt, squirming to get comfortable and failing. "I could probably handle it better if I wasn't so close to the fire."

Jessica saw that sultry grin from the corner of her eye.

"You have no idea, *chere*."

She thought she probably did. Changing the subject, she asked, "Why'd you send me to that shop last night?"

"Mikel's?"

"Yes."

"He's good, no?"

Jessica fingered her necklace, playing with the medallion. "Very. But I just get this feeling you wanted me to do more than just get this fixed."

The waiter came back with their water, and Gabriel took a sip before answering. "Did Mikel tell you a story?"

Jessica twisted in her seat to watch him suspiciously. "Don't tell me you believe that crap too? Wait, this is a trick, right? Some little thing y'all do to the tourists to bilk them   out   of   money?"

The food arrived before he could answer, and she soon forgot all about it as her mouth caught on fire. Gabriel dug in to his meal with gusto, while Jessica nibbled at hers. Her tongue burned like a torch, and she had to take two sips of water for every bite of food. She didn't know how he could stand it.

He paused, studying her. "So how do you like gator gumbo, *petite*? Too spicy for you?"

"Alligator?" Jessica's stomach protested instantly. She dropped her spoon in her bowl.

"*Oui.*"

Despite her sudden ill feeling, the delicate meat she'd thought was chicken was actually quite tasty. "It's good. But yes, it's too spicy for my tastes." She pushed her bowl away and fixed her coffee, heavy on the cream and sugar.

"I cou' show you a bedder spice. It goes down smooth as silk and heats you from d'inside."

Jessica chuckled despite herself. "You're incorrigible. Shut up and eat your food."

Gabriel finished off his *and* her gumbo and stretched out his legs when he was done, rubbing his stomach as he sipped his black coffee.

Jessica looked at his hands wrapped around the mug and wondered if everything on him was as big. She blushed at the thought and knew he'd begun to corrupt her.

"So what are you doin' down here, *chere*?"

She didn't see much harm in sharing her past or why she'd come. "I came looking for my birth parents. I didn't find out until I got here that they died years ago." It pricked her heart that she'd never known them, that they'd given her up. Maybe it was too personal information to give to a near stranger, but she thought it would help her feelings having someone to share with.

"I'm sorry, *chere*. What were their names? Nawlins can be an intimate place."

"Shelly and Jacques LaValle."

He stiffened and straightened in his seat, setting his coffee down.

Jessica noticed his strange reaction, getting her hopes up. "Do you--did you know them?"

"No, *chere*, no. I'm sorry."

Jessica felt downhearted. She was going to find answers, somehow. If she hadn't cleaned out her adoptive parents' house after their death in a car crash, she would've never known she *wasn't* their child. Sometimes she wished she'd never found that damn birth certificate in all that junk. Sometimes she wished things were as they had been. But wishing wasn't going to get her anywhere but smack in the middle of depression. "Any way, I'm going to the cemetery to see them today."

"Which one?"

"It's in the Garden district. I thought maybe I'd take a tour if I find a cheap one."

"You shouldn' go dere."

Jessica blinked at him. "Huh? Why not?"

"It's dangerous for you."

Jessica rolled her eyes, finally getting what he was hinting at as she was brought full throttle back to the question he'd conveniently failed to answer. "Don't tell me you believe that werewolf and vampire crap."

He didn't say anything.

"You do!" And here she thought he was normal except for wanting to get in bed with her. Her ego suffered a serious blow. She should've known it was too good to be true.

"It's against pack law for me t'go dere," he said finally.

It was a shame, really. He was so gorgeous. A beautiful man like that always had to have something wrong with him. "Well, you don't have to come along. In fact, I'd prefer to be alone when I visit."

"As you wish, *chere*. I jus' hope you can handle yourself. Before you go runnin' into trouble, why don' you let me show you aroun' a liddle?"

Jessica was sorely tempted. She sipped her coffee, considering it. It was still pretty early, not too long after noon. Hell, she could probably talk herself into anything as far as he was concerned--he didn't have to be charming. "Okay, but you'll remember to behave yourself, right?"

"I s'pose that depends on what you mean by behavin', *chere*. Dis ol' dog don' do tricks without a treat." Gabriel left some cash on the table and slid out of the booth, eyeing her appreciatively as she got up, as well.

"This girl doesn't give them unless she sees something really special."

Gabriel looked affronted as they headed out. "You sayin' I'm no' sometin' special, *chere*? You don' like my tricks so far?"

Jessica suppressed a laugh and walked along the building shaded street. The wind flirted in her hair and skirt, flashing a length of thigh. She caught him staring, and a little thrill shot through her. She grinned, feeling unaccustomedly saucy. "You remind me a little of Pepe Le Pew."

He choked. "I stink?"

Jessica burst out in laughter. "No. You smell really good, actually--maybe too good." And maybe she shouldn't have admitted that. "No, I feel a little like the poor cat is all."

He grinned, moving closer. "Hunted? Loved?" He caught her hand. "You wan' me to kiss you all over and whisper French into your ear?" His kissed up her arm to her neck, making noisy smacking sounds.

Jessica screamed and giggled, and pulled her arm free before running down the street. He chased after her, ignoring the strange looks others cast their way. He caught her before she could elude him, took them into the shelter of a doorway.

Jessica felt breathless from her run and looked around, saw that they were virtually alone, and the shop was abandoned. He had a knack for finding cozy, lonely spots. She glanced up at him to see him grinning down at her.

He leaned back on the opposite side, keeping some space between them.

"You gonna start callin' me Pepe now?"

Jessica chuckled. "It crossed my mind. I'm mean, aren't I?"

"Maybe a liddle. I like a mean woman though."

"Hey! You're not supposed to agree with me." She mock kicked his shin.

He rubbed his leg with his opposite foot. "Ow. You know how to kill d'romance, *chere*. I don' mind a liddle beatin' now and den, but dis? Aren' you s'posed to tie me up first before you have your wicked way wid me?"

Gabriel really knew how to implant a mental picture. Just imaging him naked, tied, and spread-eagled on a bed gave her hot flashes. "Uh. I'm not into that. And you, you're changing the subject. Admit it. Don't you think you come on too strong?" Truth be told, it wasn't him that was the problem, it was her. He was perfect. She just wasn't used to a hot pursuit, particularly not from a man she actually *wanted*.

He shrugged. "I got to work fast. No time to take it slow." He gave her a sultry grin. "Besides, it's workin', ain't it?"

She had no idea what he meant by that statement, but that smile said enough. She wasn't going to admit just how much he tempted her to do all the wicked things she shouldn't be doing. "No. As a matter of fact, you're really just wasting your time."

The look on his face said he didn't believe her. "Why do you fight so hard, *petite*? Why can' you jus' feel?"

Jessica's humor vanished. She was forcibly reminded of past mistakes, of letting people get too close. Her self-esteem was bad about getting beaten, but she preferred to think of herself as a realist. Beautiful people stuck with other beautiful people, and she most definitely wasn't in their class. "I'm afraid I'll get addicted," she admitted, slanting him a look. "Guys like you don't stick around, especially not with girls like me."

"You sell yourself short," he said softly.

Jessica shrugged. She wasn't when it was the truth. "It's better than getting hurt."

"Livin' in a shell ain't really livin' at all"

Hadn't she heard that over and over again? She shrugged again, trying to be nonchalant. "I'm used to it. I like not feeling anything, especially with men. I like my life simple and uncomplicated. Love is so messy."

"Some say it's no' good if it ain't dirty and sticky."

"Yeah, well, not me. I'm a clean freak. And I like freedom."

As she talked, she sensed a growing tension in Gabriel, like some dark cloud building for a storm. She didn't know what she'd said to piss him off, but she was definitely getting that vibe from him. Unfortunately, she couldn't think of a way to dig herself out of her hole without really knowing what she'd done--only dug in deeper with her rambling. Finally, she dared to look up at him and saw his face had gone hard, his eyes cold and angry.

He stared at her a long, drawn moment, knotting her stomach with nervousness at his continued silence. It seemed he'd listened to every word she'd said--and he hadn't liked a one of them. "When I kiss you, you don' feel nothin'?"

She swallowed past the sudden lump in her throat. "No," she lied.

He was on her before she could blink, trapping her with an arm on either side of her head, his face inches from her own. Energy seemed to vibrate from him, forcing her still, forcing her insides to react. She could feel the heat of his breath on her face, felt enveloped by his subtle, masculine scent. Every nerve ending reached out to him, reached to feel his body press tightly against her. He didn't close the distance, didn't meld to her. Somehow, that near touching had her reacting more than if he'd been right up against her.

His voice low, husky, and full of promise, he said, "If I kiss you like dis, your breath don' catch?"

He settled his mouth over hers before she could stop him. Soft, coaxing, he pulled at her lips in a hungry, nibbling kiss that had her muscles quivering in response. Jessica moaned softly, her mouth parting, willing his tongue to play with hers. He refused to oblige, teased her maddeningly, licking and sucking at her lips, keeping her hovering on the edge of anticipation. She couldn't ever remember wanting to be invaded so badly in all her life, and he wouldn't give her anything.

He retreated from her after a moment, a lazy, satisfied smile curling his lips, as if she'd reacted exactly the way he'd wanted her to. She wanted to growl in frustration, reach up and force his head back down.

A small gasp escaped her throat as he brought a hand down from the wall, trailed his fingers through her hair and over her shoulder, brushing against the side of one breast. "If I touch you here, your heart don' race?"

It did. Without even touching her, he made her heart gallop. A look, a smile, the way he walked--it was like some dream come true that he could be interested in her. Blood roared in her ears from the heavy pace. The only sound she could hear above it was his velvet drawl tormenting her with soft words and husky breath.

A thumb grazed over the soft peak of her nipple. She gasped at the faint touch, her pulse quickening, her nipple hardening as he moved in a slow, taunting circle. She tried to brace herself against the sensation, failed miserably. Her breast begged for more. She bit her lip to keep from asking him to touch her. He sensed her struggle, smiled, closed his hand over her breast. A piercing stab of pleasure arced through her as he massaged her with a possessive hand, as though he had every right to bend her to his will and make her want him.

His lips brushed against her earlobe, so soft, so teasing. He freed her breast, and she felt like crying out as he flattened his hand beneath it and moved a steady trail down her stomach, over her hips. His lips played with her lobe, sucking at it, tugging the flesh with his teeth as his fingers skated up and down her hips.

Jessica's hands clenched with the effort not to reach for him and tear the jeans off his body so he could take her right there. She wanted to hold onto something, but if she moved, she'd break down--nothing would be left. She felt distracted, touched everywhere. She closed her eyes, tried to focus ... and it intensified the riotous feelings a hundred-fold. When his hand slipped up under her skirt, she hardly noticed, only felt that callused palm on her thighs, so deliciously rough, making her feel so sensitive. He teased the edges of her panties, and she trembled with excitement and trepidation.

No, this wasn't what she wanted. But deep inside, she did. She wanted to open her thighs to him, but a voice of self-preservation nagged like an annoying gnat. Her legs closed against his hand, but he was insistent, moving inexorably toward her moist folds. The fine hairs on her thighs prickled with unfamiliar sensation.

"And here...." he whispered hot against her ear, arousingly invasive.

His fingers pushed past the flimsy barrier of her panties, delved into the top of her slit in one bold move, rubbing sensuously, achingly close to her clit. Jessica's eyes flew open with shock. She found him watching her, lust in his smoky eyes. A rush of raw heat flushed her body. She pushed at his chest, pulled at his arm, squirming and unable to get away.

"You're wet for me, *petite*," he said, his voice tight and hoarse. "Dere is no denyin' it." His muscles strained against her. His arm felt hard against her belly, his fingers foreign. This wasn't supposed to happen.

"Stop it," she whispered, trying to look away, at the street, at the shop, anywhere but him and his knowing eyes.

"Why?" Do you feel sometin'?"

She rose on her toes, arching her head back as one finger flicked against her clit. A chain of pleasure unwound inside her, fierce and breathtakingly sudden. "No," she said through gritted teeth, fighting the feeling when all she wanted to do was surrender. She couldn't. Not here, not out in the open where anyone could happen by at any moment. He shouldn't make her feel so tempted to give in.

"I think you do." He straightened from her as abruptly as he'd begun, leaving her feeling achingly unfulfilled and pissed that he'd begun something only to make a point.

"I never figured you for a coward," he said, watching her straighten her dress.

Before Jessica knew it, she'd slapped him. Her palm cracked across his face, slamming the satisfied, challenging look right off it. She looked at him in horror, unable to believe she'd actually done physical harm to him. She hadn't hit him hard enough to leave her hand print, but she'd struck him all the same. She looked from her hand to his face and back again, feeling numb from shock.

A dark fury settled over him. It was as obvious as the sky turning black and the wind howling through the trees.

Here was a man you didn't mess with. She'd done what her mama had always warned her not to do--never get physical with a man. Cold dread slid down her spine.

Rough hands grabbed her biceps, forced her back against the wall. Male strength crushed against her, taking the breath from her body--muscles hard and angry against her soft curves. Jessica gasped in surprise as he brought his mouth down on hers, thrust his tongue past the part of her lips, deep inside. She tasted the anger in his kiss. Her lips burned under the heavy pressure, the rough glide of his tongue, in and out, leaving no space untouched. He was ravenous, consuming her silent pleas to stop ... to go on....

Potent, male excitement pervaded her senses like flood gates thrown wide. He growled low in his throat, thrusting his hips against her as if in emphasis that he controlled her. She was his to do with as he willed and nothing would stop him. His hard cock rubbed against her in rough warning. One wrong move and he'd take her, willing or no.

Thrilling fear moved in a heady rush through her limbs like a shot of ecstasy. Her heart hammered in her chest. She wanted to cry out when he forced her legs apart with rough hands, but his mouth muffled her cries, kept taking and taking until she couldn't give any more, and still he kissed her. She couldn't breathe, could barely think. All the blood pooled between her thighs, rushing to that hot, insane place that wanted him, wanted the angry, hard feel of his cock deep inside. She pushed against his arms, needing to be free before she completely lost her mind, but one stroke against her sparsely covered cleft had her digging her nails into his flesh in mindless pleasure.

He tore his mouth from hers, gasping hoarsely against her throat, pumping against her in short, rough strokes, his fingers digging into the backs of her knees. Jessica scraped her nails down his back, arching into him, shaking her head as he dragged his teeth down her throat and groaned with pure satisfaction. It rumbled through her, her body echoing with primitive response.

"How much you wan' me to push you, *cherie*?" he asked hoarsely against the base of her throat. His tongue snaked out, bathed her. Her skin felt on fire as he lathed her collarbone and sucked against the crook of her neck. Hard.

She jerked to instant awareness, opening her eyes. Her hands went still as he stiffened against her. "It's not a contest, you bastard."

He met her gaze, his eyes unbelievably dark. His chest heaved, his arms shook with the effort to control himself. Slowly, with effort, he dropped her legs. "You fool yourself if you don' believe life is a challenge. Dere's only one prize in d'end."

Jessica pushed away from him, wiping her mouth and neck. She could smell him everywhere. Taste him. It made her weak. She couldn't afford to be weak. "Just leave me alone. This is a mistake."

"Why? Cause maybe you like me too much?"

She turned away from him. "I'm not answering that."

Gabriel made a soft clucking noise as she walked away.

She could've ignored it--she should've. It might have just been her imagination, but she knew by now that Gabriel was a man to push a person's buttons. He was determined to push her to her limits. And this was just too much. She'd damn well show the damned goading, confident bastard what she was made of.

She turned around, found him watching her expectantly, almost as though he was eager to see what she'd do. She took the two steps back to him, pressed one hand against his chest and pushed him back on the wall with little effort. She reached down and cupped his cock. His eyes widened, his mouth opened. Jessica wrapped her hand around his neck and forced him down for her kiss.

She gave him everything she had to give, forced her tongue into his mouth, massaged his erection, rubbed her body sensuously against his as she thrust in and out of his mouth. His whole body when rigid. He sucked her tongue as though starved, and she could feel the beat of his heart quicken against her breast, felt his cock jump and throb against her palm. He groaned, reaching for her, but she wouldn't allow it. When his hands touched her, she released his groin. His hands smacked against the facade, making him helpless, vulnerable and wanting of only what she would give.

A triumphant thrill went through her, to have him under her control. Heady pleasure rocketed through her. Her palm burned with the feel of his cock trapped in her hand. She rubbed her thumb against the bare patch of skin exposed by one tear. He stiffened even more, sucked her tongue harder, hungrier, groaned into her mouth.

She pulled back before she could get too caught up in the moment, before she could lose her point. When she was done, it was him leaning back against the wall for support.

"I think I just won the game," she said.

He was breathing heavily, watching her with a mixture of wariness and appreciation. "I think maybe you did too."

She allowed herself one victorious smile and walked away.

Chapter Four

Jessica deeply regretted not heeding Gabriel's earlier advice. It seemed like he'd delivered it days ago, but it had really only been a few hours. She also regretted everything that she'd allowed to happen between them. Jessica shook her head, trying to block the thoughts, the guilt. She didn't want to dwell on it. She'd never been one to hash and rehash what she should've done then, what she shouldn't have done there. She just put the whole thing out of her mind and resolved not to feel guilty for anything. At least, that's what she'd do in an ideal world where she had ample self-control.

She didn't. She didn't have any self-control at all. Gabriel sucked it all out of her--literally.

After only a short time, he occupied her thoughts far more than he should've. She half wondered if she'd developed an obsession or something equally disturbing. Surely normal women didn't feel and think so much about a man. Just remembering his kisses sent her into instant lust. She swore she could still taste him, like spicy gumbo and warm, creamy coffee. His scent definitely still lingered on her, rubbed into her neck like a cologne--not a strong smell, but potent in its own subtle way.

Everywhere she walked, when the wind picked up, she caught just a hint of him, in her hair, on her clothes, like a finger making the come hither motion right under her nose. If she hadn't known better, she'd swear her nose was more sensitive. Everything seemed more ... sensorial now, scents sharper. Even the wind had it's own distinct fragrance.

Her imagination was running overtime.

What she really should've done was gone back to the hotel and washed his scent off her skin. But she'd become so embroiled in her quest for the day, and smelling him on her gave her such a secret thrill--she hadn't allowed herself the time.

It was nearly dark by the time she'd found out exactly where Shelly and Jacques LaValle were buried, and longer still to make it through the holiday traffic over there.

The cemetery was an above ground one, as most were in this part of the state due to heavy rains and soggy ground. The dusk created eerie shadows between the small mausoleums. Jessica walked along the path, broken shells and rock crunching under her sandals. She picked up her pace, eager to get out of the cemetery before dark. She knew she should've just come back tomorrow, but she didn't think she could wait that long.

A feeling grew in her, a warning to get out of Louisiana as fast as she could. She couldn't explain why the feeling persisted, only that it did. Nothing had happened to her to cause it, but just the same....

Being in a cemetery didn't help matters, and she was sure her imagination had gone into hyper mode. She'd never felt superstitious before, but there was something inherently creepy about dark cemeteries that she'd never noticed. A hush settled on the grounds, expectancy that she couldn't quite comprehend.

There wasn't anyone around--everyone inside had been entombed long ago, but the silence, coupled with hazy, failing sunlight worked together to give her the willies.

She shuddered and called herself names, rubbing her arms as she continued on her way, eager to get this done and be gone.

The mausoleums created a labyrinth of narrow passages, standing above her head to block her sight of other lanes and surroundings. It was almost like walking through a tunnel, except she could still see the sky. In the dark, it would probably seem more like catacombs.

Just when she'd decided to call it a night, she finally managed to locate her parents' tomb. It was younger than it's neighbors, like they'd lucked out and managed to procure the single remaining spot in the cemetery. A morbid thought, that, thinking of their "luck."

Above the mausoleum stood an angel with her arms outstretched, her marble face tear stained from decades of rain.

Jessica touched the sun warmed marble, as if to assure herself it was real, that she'd actually found her parents' final resting place. The stone was smooth, worn only slightly by time and weather. Peering closer, she could just make out the engraving on the tomb in the failing light. There was no testimony to their life together, or the child they had created. No haunting poetry. Merely their names and the date each was born and died.

Her mother had died June 2, 1978. She swallowed past the lump in her throat and looked at her father's life date. He'd died on June 3, 1978. A sliver of fear slid down her back bone, raising her hackles. She shivered with foreboding. Her mother died the day she was born. She could understand that, that maybe she'd died in childbirth or complications arising afterward. But why had her father died the day after?

The tomb gave her no answers, only more questions. She felt more disturbed than ever before. In her heart, she knew something terrible had happened to them. She was grateful for the life she'd lived, for the love of her adoptive parents, but her life had been upset by the discovery. And now this.

Her entire life seemed a mystery, her roots hidden from her with no hint as to why. Regret and disappointment sat heavy in her stomach.

She wondered who she really was.

Jessica desperately needed to know what had happened, but she'd run out of ideas to try and make sense of things. If this was a secret, and she knew it was, how was she to uncover it? It occurred to her that a library might possibly be a good place to start. She might even be able to learn something, pick up some clue, from the department of records.

She walked away, heading toward the exit. She was contemplating just how she was going to find out more about her parents' death when she stepped out onto the main path and saw three men hanging around the front gate. Jessica stopped. Her heart quickened to a breathless pace. She tried to get a grip on herself, to reason that she was overreacting, but something about the way they stood there made fear prickle along her neck. There was no reason in the world why she should be afraid of a small group of men--but there it was.

They hadn't seen her yet. She could almost breathe with that grateful thought filtering into her stricken brain. She could find another way to get out and get back to her hotel. And for all she knew, they were just three guys hanging out and having a good time.

She just wished she believed that.

Jessica slowly backed up, keeping her eyes trained on them. One step back. Another and another. She started breathing regularly again, almost home free. Just as she'd reached the narrow, shadowy alley of one mausoleum row, they looked up as though they'd heard her mental sigh of relief, and spotted her. They grinned and straightened, moving forward like a pack of wolves, coming straight for her.

Jessica whirled and ran, her heart in her throat. She disappeared into the shadows, running over the irregular path, praying she wouldn't trip over broken cobblestone or a protruding root. She didn't know when it had gotten so dark. It hadn't seemed that way only minutes ago.

She couldn't see anything with the tombs above her, couldn't hear past the steady, rapid thud of her pulse in her ears. She had a good lead on them. She could lose them in the maze of the cemetery if she just kept her wits about her.

Something howled in the night, like an animal. Excited pants carried on the air behind her.

They couldn't have gotten to her this fast!

Jessica wanted to scream, wanted to turn around and fight. She hated being chased, hated the helplessness of being prey, but she couldn't fight against them, not without a weapon of some sort, and she dared not slacken her pace to find one.

A pain stabbed her side, her lungs labored to drag air inside, to keep her from passing out. Jessica tore through the grounds, keeping to the deeper shadows, weaving through the tombs. She dropped her purse, left it, kept going. She headed North, hoping there was a back exit somewhere, or maybe a lighted street or a late running cemetery tour.

Why, *why* hadn't she brought Gabriel with her?

Something growled right behind her, a wet, slathering sound that sent fear careening through her vitals. She could feel his hot breath on her bare back, and she did scream then.

It tore from her throat, loud and long and ripping through the air like a siren just before the man grabbed her and threw her to the ground. Jessica landed hard, rolling with the impact, broken shells grinding into her shoulder, scraping her tender skin. She couldn't feel any pain, nothing but the sense of weight and pressure--her body went numb with shock.

She kicked out, missing her attackers, wishing she wore heels. She couldn't see anything, could only hear him circle her. Pebbles sprayed out, striking her shoulders and legs, her face. Someone ran up from behind, two of them, where she couldn't see, but she could hear heavy, excited breathing.

They didn't rush her. It was like they were waiting for her to react. Like they were thrilled by the chase--as she knew they must be. Jessica struggled to her knees, planting her palms on the ground, clutching two handfuls of grit and shell as she rose to her feet.

The scuffle of feet told her one lunged, and she threw a handful of dirt at his face, whirling to throw it at another. They cursed, growling almost inhumanly as she dashed past them, guided only by sound and touch now. The main path opened before her, so close she could taste freedom and safety.

A hand closed in her hair, yanking her back. Rough hands groped her breasts, her waist, her hips, everywhere on her body. Jessica screamed in fury and fought them, but they were all around, holding her arms, holding her legs as they brought her to the ground.

One of them lifted her skirt and tore her panties away, burning the flesh of her hips as the thin fabric gave way. She kicked at him, satisfied to hear him grunt with pain as she connected with his cock, and then her legs were hauled apart.

Jessica screamed again, snapping her teeth at the hands that held her, rising off the ground as she bucked against their hold. Rough jeans slid up the insides of her thighs. She smelled the musky scent of bare cock and thought she'd throw up.

They were going to rape her.

And there was nothing she could do about it.

* * * *

Gabriel's wolfen senses burst to life a second before the faint scream echoed on the night air like the cry of a dove. His head snapped up, his pulse hammered, his body went tense with sudden, repressed violence.

He knew instantly who the cry came from--Jessica. The sound of his chosen one in danger reverberated through his being.

He cocked his head, centering on her location, though her voice had faded away. She was in the cemetery, where he'd told her not to go, where he'd followed her anyway. He was close, but not close enough.

He threw his head back as the wolf inside growled, erupting from his throat in fury, a haunting challenge that carried on the air.

For the first time in his life, he was out of control. He wasn't near enough to her. She could be dead even now.

He refused to believe that.

He took off at a run, low to the ground, lower, leaping over obstacles in his path until he was flying with the speed of strength borne of desperation. The quickening surged in his blood, spread through his muscles, invading his every pore. The beast was eager for blood, eager to protect its claim. He recognized the cry for what it was--the sound of prey.

Someone hunted his woman.

He would kill them for hurting her.

Chapter Five

The man bent over her. Hot, fetid breath spilled over her face and chest. He stank like a dog, his feral stench turning her stomach. He growled and nuzzled her breasts roughly, as if she'd invited him to touch and taste.

She strained against her fleshly bonds, but the hands holding her down yielded nothing, allowing her not even the slightest movement.

Hopelessness crept into her, growing like a cancer.

Jessica gnashed her teeth, unwilling to succumb to it. She swore to kill them if given the chance.

In the distance, a dog howled at the moon. She wondered dimly if it was one of Gabriel's werewolves prowling the night. She'd never be so lucky.

The man on top of her halted suddenly, sniffing the air. He snarled, growling deep in his chest, like a Doberman giving warning to a trespasser. Jessica felt her heart and lungs freeze--there wasn't enough air to breathe.

One of the others snapped his jaws, growling in response. The hairs raised on her skin, shivers crawling over her like swarming ants. Why didn't they speak? Their animalistic behavior kept pushing her to the edge, panic dulling her mind. She swallowed against the rising tide, trying to keep calm.

The man between her legs stiffened, twisting against her thighs. He released her abruptly as something came crashing through the night with the force of a barreling semi. The hands holding her arms and legs disappeared, ripped away. Jessica gasped at the bruising wrench, the sudden freedom. She scrambled upright, pushing her dress down, peering into the shadows. She couldn't see anything. She felt like her eyes were closed, like this was a nightmare come horribly to life. Jessica continued scrabbling back, until cool stone pressed against her back. She kicked her feet out, waved her hands in case anyone came near.

In the dark, the men snarled and growled like pit bulls at a dog fight. Jessica didn't know if she was more scared or relieved. Had some guard dog come to defend her? Feet scuffled on the worn path, grunts echoed meaty strikes.

"It's because you are pups I don' kill you for dis," a voice growled in the dark to the accompaniment of heavy thuds.

Jessica's bones nearly melted from her body at the velvet drawl she'd recognize anywhere. Gabriel. Somehow, he'd come for her, known she was in trouble.

Jessica huddled on the ground, not daring to move lest she distract him. She wanted to help, but she couldn't see a damn thing and she was too scared she'd injure him if she entered the fray.

Something liquid splashed against the ground next to her feet, and the coppery scent of blood filled the air as the beatings continued, interspersed with painful groans and shouts.

Finally, after what seemed like an hour of unbearable tension, someone touched her shoulder. Jessica startled, looking up to see the faint, star framed silhouette of a man above her.

"*Chere?*" Gabriel asked.

"Gabriel!" Jessica breathed in relief, getting to her feet. She hugged him fiercely and felt her thin dress soak through with sweat or blood or both--she couldn't tell. He ran his hands against her back in soothing circles.

"Did they hurt you?" he murmured against her hair.

"No. Nothing I can't handle." She pulled back, wishing she could see him. "Thank you, Gabriel. I don't know what I would've done without you."

He stifled a groan and slumped heavily against her.

"Oh my god. You're hurt. Gabriel, where is it? Where are you hurt?" His silence unnerved her. Jessica felt around his body, but she couldn't find anything that could have weakened him so much--unless it was something internal. The thought galvanized her. "We have to get you to a hospital."

"No," he said and pushed away from her.

"Yes."

"No," he said emphatically. "You can ... take me ... home."

He sounded like he was just before passing out. She couldn't blame him. He'd run off three men nearly as big as he was, and from the sound of them, they'd been insane. She didn't have time to be impressed. They had to leave before the thugs had a chance to come back. "I'll take you home. But first we have to catch a cab or something."

"My car is out front," he said, and leaned into her for support.

Jessica stood under his arm and they hobbled their way to his car--an old Camaro, its color indistinguishable in the faded dark.

She followed his directions, and he fell asleep as she drove up the Ponchartrain Expressway, getting off once they'd passed the fair grounds. A wooded area came into view, and she stopped at the first house as he'd instructed: a sprawling two story Victorian with a gazebo and porch swing on one end, interconnected with the porch curving around the house.

Jessica didn't stop to admire the house, pulling the Camaro onto the lawn along a roughened patch of dirt until she neared the front entrance. She stopped the car and switched it off, giving Gabriel a concerned glance before she got up and went around to help him.

He came awake as she opened the door and got out on his own, but Jessica fussed and continued to help him walk. It was just like a man to try and be macho about serious injuries. She didn't know about his, but she wasn't about to take any more chances than he was already forcing her to take.

The front door was unlocked, which she found oddly trusting considering the state of this day and age, but she pushed it open and went through. A long, wide hallway shot straight through, past the narrow staircase, to the back door, and large rooms parted off from each side.

"Dere's d'livin' room," Gabriel said, pointing to the right tiredly.

Jessica shuffled to it, feeling on the wall for the light switch. She found it easily enough, flipped the lights on, and guided him onto a worn, leather couch facing an old TV. He collapsed on it, closing his eyes and throwing an arm above his head. He was wearing the same basic outfit she'd seen him in before: Jeans and no shoes or a shirt. Blood smeared his chest and throat, and she knew she had to clean him off to properly to assess the situation.

Jessica left, in search of a bathroom or a kitchen. She found the kitchen in the back of the house on the left. A small cupboard above the sink revealed clean dish rags, and she pulled several out and wet them before returning to Gabriel.

She stopped in the doorway, watching him a breathless moment as she waited to see the rise and fall of his chest. Breathing a silent thanks, she went in and dropped onto the hardwood floor on her knees, leaning over his chest as she slowly wiped the blood away.

There were no wounds anywhere, not even the beginnings of bruises. She kept wiping at him until she'd cleaned his chest, then moved up to his throat and face. Gabriel slept through her ministrations. Still, she found nothing, no wounds to explain his weariness. She changed rags and cleaned his arms and hands. His knuckles were only slightly reddened, when she'd expected to at least find them split open. She frowned down at him, wondering how he could be unscathed after a fight like that.

Some residual blood clung to a patch of skin bared by a rip in his jeans, and Jessica wiped it away, flushing as she realized how close she was to his groin. She looked back at his face to see if he'd woken up, and nearly choked when she saw him watching her with a hungry look to his eyes.

He looked at her with such heated interest, she could almost swear she knelt before him naked.

"Gabriel, are you okay?" she asked with a breathless little whisper.

He said nothing as his hand snaked out and grasped the hand still holding the towel, lingering near his groin. She dropped it and it rolled down his hip into the cushion of the couch. Jessica gasped as he pulled her toward him, closer, until she was laying splayed atop his bare chest, her mouth inches from his own.

His faint, warm breath made her insides quiver with anticipation. If felt good to lay on top of him, with her breasts squashed into the hard planes of his chest, her belly melded to his rippled, washboard abs. She felt as malleable as molten metal.

His mouth curled into a satisfied smile. Jessica was caught between the urge to strangle him for making her worry, and the urge to kiss him breathless and wipe the grin from his face.

"You weren't even hurt, were you?" she asked with an exasperated, accusing breath.

"I was wounded more than you know, *chere*, t'think you cou' be harmed."

The reminder of what had almost happened made her shudder, and his eyes darkened until they appeared almost black. A primal look flickered in them, strengthening as he pulled her head down to greet his lips.

Jessica gave in to him, her concern weakening her defenses. Her lips throbbed under the insistent pressure of his mouth, and an electric thrill of excitement rippled through her veins, dancing like heat lightning before a storm. He nibbled her lips, coaxing her, running his hands over her back. Her skin sensitized to the pressure of his hands, and suddenly she had too much clothing on. She wanted to know what it would feel like to mold against him, skin to skin. His whispery touch made her burn, sent her blood pulsing through her body.

He hooked a hand firmly around one thigh, pulling it up and over his hips to settle against the opposite side, hoisting her off the floor until she lay on him completely, pressing him deep into the soft folds of the couch. Her dress rode up from the movement and position until she felt air in places that had never seen the sun.

His mouth grew rough, hungrier to have her above him. Her pulse thundered, echoing in the tight clench of her pussy. His right hand eased around her back, a thumb skating against the side of one breast. Jessica trembled with excitement at his daring, the steady pull of his hand on her thigh, the touch at her breast.

Jessica moaned as her legs parted and his jean clad erection connected with her bare cleft. He thrust upward with rough, sensual promise. She'd forgotten her panties were gone ... until his hand slid up her thigh and he cupped one bare buttock, slipping his fingers in the bottom cleft of her cheeks. Her skin suddenly sensitized, his possessive fingers lighting a sizzling fuse in her body.

Heat curled through her slit, and Jessica gasped at the feel of those callused digits strumming a heady tune on her nether lips, dangerously close to the core of her femininity. He played with the wetness he aroused, smoothing it on her lips to cool in the air, skimming through her swollen folds as though she belonged only to him. Jessica whimpered into his mouth, jolted with the white hot pleasure shimmering between them.

Distantly, her subconscious railed against giving in, but she could no more resist him than she could cease breathing. She was helpless against his devouring mouth, helpless to keep from drawing further under his spell.

She groaned and plunged her tongue into his mouth, rubbing her body against him, eager to put the fire out that raged in her blood. Her clit throbbed with the rough abrasion, the frantic movement of her hips. He tasted addictively sweet, as delicious as chocolate, as potent and stimulating as coffee. She drowned in his scent and the molten feel of his muscular body trapped beneath her.

Gabriel growled and sucked her tongue, digging his hand into her ass cheek, slipping his fingers into her pussy from behind. She wanted to scream from the pleasure of it, the tight stretch of two fingers pumping inside her, curling into her with deliberate, probing strokes.

Jessica broke away from his mouth, arching her head back as he kissed along her throat with sucking, nibbling kisses. He scored her flesh with his teeth. Shivers chased over her skin.

"Your scent drives me mad, *petite*. I wan' to taste you all over," he whispered, his voice hoarse with passion and need. He nipped her throat, marking her with tongue and teeth and lips. Jessica's nerves jolted down to her core. Her body wept with the fierce, demanding need.

Small, harsh whimpers escaped her, marking a change in him, a ravenous intent that hadn't been there before.

An animalistic growl vibrated from his throat as he thrust his fingers into her again. Harder. Her pussy creamed with the forceful drive. She felt the excess trickle down her parted folds to her clit, soaking her, soaking his jeans. Her womb contracted with a hard, violent spasm of pleasure. The strength fled her muscles. She moaned mindlessly, rocking her hips on him, trying to envelop him in her heat. She was empty deep inside, where not even his fingers could reach, needing the thick heat of him within her, begging for it with every jerky move, every shaky breath.

Her clit throbbed with achy want, engorged to the point of pain. Each brush against his hard cock had her pussy spasming near ecstasy.

Her mind shut down to everything but the steady, driving pump of his fingers, pushing her toward rough climax. She felt herself getting closer, and moved on him with mindless abandon.

A harsh voice interrupted them like a dowsing of ice water. "What is this?" it demanded gravelly.

Jessica came off Gabriel so hard, she landed on the hardwood floor with a bone jarring thud to her knees. She ignored the pain, pushing her dress down her legs to stare up at the intruder, wide-eyed with shock.

If god had any mercy, she would have died of embarrassment on the spot. Her pale skin turned bright pink, the heat of desire changing to the burn of shame.

Gabriel sat up on the couch, giving the intruder a look to kill. "What are you doing here, Nardo?" he ground out, standing, his chest rising and falling with sharp, angry breaths. His hands fell to his sides, clenching and unclenching with repressed violence.

"Your demands are not important...." He trailed off as Jessica stood and moved beside Gabriel.

The man was huge, looking like nothing so much as a muscle-bound wrestler. His insolent stare lingered on her breasts, and Jessica covered them uncomfortably, moving closer to Gabriel as if she could melt into his side. She wanted to slap the knowing look right off the man. She worked up her anger, eager to put her embarrassment behind her.

"I have as much say in the pack as you do ... and every right t'claim a mate," Gabriel ground out.

The man laughed, grating on her nerves, keeping his eyes trained on her. He looked like he would jump her at any moment, and what desire Jessica'd had quickly slipped away as nervous fear took over.

His laughter subsided, and a cruel glint entered his black, soulless eyes. "Gabriel," he growled, "did you really think you could keep her from us?"

* * * *

Nardo "escorted" her and Gabriel outside, keeping steady watch on them both as if expecting them to bolt at any minute.

Outside on the lawn behind Gabriel's Camaro, a truck waited. As they came out, the driver looked up at them and started the truck. It came to life with a deafening roar, and a chug of smoke rose from the tail pipe, clouding the air like city smog.

"Where are we going?" Jessica asked, wanting nothing so much as longer legs or faster feet ... or a gun. She despised this feeling of helplessness and not knowing what was going on.

"A meeting's been called. You're the guest of honor," Nardo said behind her, snickering. She felt his eyes bore into her back and buttocks, and it took supreme effort of will not to cover her cheeks with her hands. Or turn around and knock his head off.

Gabriel said nothing to Nardo, but his tension was evident in every move of his body and the angry clench of his jaw muscles. He seemed ready to snap at any moment.

Jessica didn't know what to think about what was happening. That intuitive warning she'd ignored before came back full force. She should not have ignored her inner voice. She should've left town without answers. But then, she would likely have never met Gabriel....

Nardo pulled the back gate of the truck down, and Gabriel helped her climb up. She settled down in the back, the metal cold against her back and buttocks, making her shudder. Gabriel climbed up and sat beside her, wrapping an arm around her shoulders, pulling her tightly against him. His heat made her feel better, warmed her when she felt unaccustomedly cold. Jessica appreciated his comforting, protective gesture, but she didn't know how much good it would do them.

Nardo closed the gate and sat across from them, ever watchful. Jessica drew her knees up to keep her feet from touching him. He noticed her movement and sneered at her before turning slightly to the driver. He tapped the back window and the driver took off, heading West, further down the road that passed in front of Gabriel's house. The truck picked up speed, bouncing them in the bed and sending plumes of dust into the air like a thick fog.

The dark swallowed them whole as they left the lighted yard and drove down the oak shrouded road. The moon's light pierced the thick canopy marginally as they progressed, and Jessica gave up trying to keep up with where they were going, since it didn't seem to make any difference--they were headed in a straight line.

She snuggled against Gabriel, comforted by his presence and fearful of what would happen. The nervous fear had her stomach tied in knots. She hated the feeling.

Normally, she could handle herself pretty well, but there was something infinitely bizarre about the whole situation. She was completely out of her depth. If she'd known from the start what trouble she would dig up by trying to find her birth parents, she damned well would have brought her gun ... and enough ammo to take out an army of Rambos.

Jessica closed her eyes and tried to ignore the piercing stare across from her, not that she could see him, but she inherently felt that he could see her. Her skin prickled like she was being watched. She felt like throwing dirt in his eyes just for the satisfaction of it.

The truck slowed and swayed as it turned, and Gabriel tightened his arm around her. He still hadn't said anything, and hadn't tried to kill their abductors. She wasn't sure if that was good or bad, but she'd rather see anyone's blood but their own spilled.

They moved down a road narrow enough the tree branches scraped the sides of the truck. She thought perhaps they were going down some hunter's trail, or possibly a long, winding driveway. The truck stopped after several more minutes of driving. Jessica looked around but even with her eyes adjusted to the dark, she could see nothing but trees and more trees, and little patches of light striking the ground.

"Get up," Nardo said roughly, kicking the gate open and jumping down.

Gabriel hopped down and Jessica sat on the edge, her legs dangling. He wrapped his warm hands around her waist and lifted, helping her gain her feet on the ground.

A woman came up, startling Jessica with her sudden presence. "I'm to take you with me," she said in a cold, angry voice, grabbing Jessica's wrist with a bruising grip.

She'd never felt more violent in her life than she did tonight. Everywhere someone attacked her. She'd had enough of it. Screw being a lady. Jessica pulled back. "No."

"You mus' go with her, *chere*. It's d'only way. I'll come for you soon," Gabriel said reassuringly.

Jessica didn't feel the least bit reassured. "I said no."

"You don't have any choice," the woman ground out, tugging her forward.

Jessica dug her heels in, grabbing Gabriel with her free hand. She was just before ripping the woman's hair out.

"Please, *chere*, for me."

She sighed and released him. "Okay. You have to come back for me. I don't want to be wondering if you're dead or alive all night."

"You know I live ta please, *cherie*," he said, and she could hear the smile in his voice.

"I'll kick your ass for you if you're lying." She felt a little assured that he wouldn't run off and die on her. But not much. She refused to dwell on it.

Grudgingly, she went with the woman, who pulled her through the woods at a pace too fast for her to easily keep half blind. Brambles tore at her exposed legs, dirt and pebbles skittered into her sandals and under her heels. She kept up as best as she could, since she had no other choice.

She said nothing as the woman brought her to a lighted tent that looked big enough five adults could easily spread out inside.

The woman released her and opened the flap, gesturing for her to move inside. When Jessica didn't move fast enough, she pushed her. Jessica tripped over the opening and fell on the floor, sucking in a sharp breath as her knees bruised on the hard ground.

Jessica whipped her head around, giving the auburn haired woman a scathing look. "You bitch," she gritted out, her hands clenching with the need to rip that shiny red hair from her skull. She'd taken as much of this shit as she was about to take.

"Fuck you," the woman sneered and raised her hand to slap Jessica.

Jessica lunged for her, her fingers curved into claws, digging into the woman's legs as she dragged them out from under her. The woman went down and rolled instantly, slashing at Jessica with her nails. She growled primitively, missing Jessica's eyes by a hair's breadth.

Jessica drew back in a split second, crouching on her haunches, sidling past the center pole of the tent, keeping the woman distant. She eyed the tent opening, wondering if she could make it past. She decided to risk it. She dove for the opening, running into the dark. The woman's fingers scrabbled at her dress, pulling her back just as Jessica ran into a meaty wall.

Cruel fingers dug into her arms, making her gasp as she fought the hold. Jessica kneed him in the groin, and he barely grunted before crushing his fingers into her biceps.

"Lavinia, can't you do any fucking thing you're told? Are you so weak you can't hold on to a *human*?" the man sneered the last word like it left shit in his mouth.

The woman, Lavinia, came up behind her and snatched her hair, pulling her head back until she thought her scalp bled. "Kiss my fuckin' ass, Lado," she ground out and dragged Jessica back inside.

Jessica growled in impotent fury as her arms were forced behind her back and tied to the center pole. She kicked out as Lavinia came around her, connecting with her shins. Lavinia cursed and grinned maliciously before slapping her hard across the face. Bright light exploded on the left side of her face, and Jessica tasted blood as her teeth rattled.

The woman chuckled and tied her feet together while she sat there, stunned. Lastly, she gagged Jessica, then zipped the opening closed as she left.

Jessica blinked the pain back, focusing on her surroundings. There was nothing inside but sleeping bags rumpled from their fight. She craned her head around, looking for a weapon or something to cut the cord, but still found nothing. The tent was empty of anything even remotely useful. Obviously, they'd been expecting to house her inside it. The thought left her cold and miserable.

She couldn't sit there and worry about it. She *refused* to worry about it. Worrying caused more harm than good.

Jessica wiggled her fingers, thankful the rope was at least loose enough the blood flow hadn't instantly cut off. No amount of wiggling could free her, however, and trying to rip her hands loose only made her shoulders and muscles ache. She tried pushing against the tent pole, but the post was so secure, it didn't move no matter how hard she pushed--almost like it was mounted in a cement foundation. If that was true, then they routinely stayed out here ... or held prisoners inside.

She fervently wished she could do something useful, like dislocate her shoulders and slip her hands under her feet. But the pole would still be in the way even if she could do that trick. She considered her options and came up empty. With the gag tight on her mouth, she couldn't work it off and chew on the ropes.

She sighed heavily through her nose, shaking her hair out of her face.

There was nothing to do but wait and see if Gabriel would uphold his promise to her. She just hoped he didn't do anything stupid--like getting killed before he could rescue her.

The wry thought did little to ease the tension cramping her belly. In all honesty, she knew she had no one to rely on but herself. Smart people didn't trust their fate to others. The urge to let Gabriel play her hero and sweep her into his arms went beyond tempting, but it was completely irrational. More than likely, they were outnumbered, definitely weaponless, and in the middle of nowhere.

She was going to have to get free by herself and try to do something. She just wasn't sure how much she could do if someone didn't come back inside ... and by then, it would probably be too late....

Chapter Six

Nardo pushed Gabriel roughly, driving him ahead to the luna clearing where the pack met each cycle, when the moon sat fat in the sky and pulled them to shift with near irresistible force. Gabriel stumbled from the forceful push and whipped around, his voice a menacing growl, "You push me again, I'll kill you, *mon ami*."

Nardo returned his menacing look, his eyes flashing in the dark, but he said nothing. He did not touch him again as they walked.

Gabriel thought of Jessica being taken away by that bitch, Lavinia. He hoped she did nothing so foolish as to hurt Jessica, for if she did, she would regret it.

His fury rolled inside, like the flames of a white hot blaze. He should have expected this. He had, but not so soon, and not when he was with Jessica.

His brains fled to his cock every time she was near. Had he gotten a handle on his lust, he never would've been so foolish as to take her home, or any other place he'd ever been. The pack could sniff him out so easily. He should have known they were waiting to take him.

Gabriel felt like hitting something. His fists tightened with the urge. He knew he'd soon have the chance to satisfy the bloodlust.

They crossed the guardian-like trees into the clearing, moving toward the center. Nardo parted from him silently as they reached the center, moving back into the shadows of the trees. Gabriel stood in the placement of the accused. A mark of shame for the worst trespass on pack laws, the accused stood surrounded by the pack, yet alone.

The last time the pack had met to try an accused had been a few months back, when Raoul had trespassed into vamp territory to claim a human woman.

Gabriel had done much worse, and he knew it. He didn't expect to fair as well as Raoul.

He expected to die.

A dead calm settled over him. No matter their decision, he would not allow harm to come to Jessica. They'd taken her father. They would not take her too.

Regret left a bitter taste in his mouth, vanquishing the lingering sweetness of her kiss. He'd wanted so much more, and he had no right to those desires. No right to her....

Gabriel angrily thrust the thought to the corners of his mind, preparing himself for judgment. To help her, he must remain clear, focused. He could not allow thoughts of her to distract him in an already deadly contest. One false move could prove instant death ... no chance for survival.

Yet still, she entered his thoughts. He knew little enough of her, but even his limited contact had him distracted to the point where he thought of nothing else. He resolved to destroy those urges. He couldn't have her, but neither would anyone else. He would see to it.

He looked up at the sky a brief moment, feeling the energy of the moon course through him. The moon shone down clearly, gilding his muscles with silver, days from ripeness. Had the moon been full dark, he would still have known he was not alone. Gabriel needed no light to see his brethren move from the shadows and into the circular clearing, ringing him until there was no opening for retreat.

Low, feral growls carried on the air, angry rumbles of dissension. His beast tensed at their challenging voices. The air vibrated with their energy, moving like chain lightning through the crowd. His beast answered their challenge, eager to face them, unmindful of the odds. His brain clouded as his beast threatened to take control. It stretched inside, uncurling through his limbs, making his muscles jump with power and barely checked violence.

It seduced, promised the euphoria only animalistic existence could provide ... the high of the fight, the rush of wolfen speed ... the taste of kill.

Gabriel closed his eyes and gritted his teeth, his hands clenched tightly. The lure was as seductive as a woman, stronger, in a way that insanity beat the sane.

With effort, he fought it back, until he was panting for breath. He opened his eyes and faced his pack as he would an enemy. What he saw confirmed what he'd already suspected. A shudder of remorse surged through him.

They were all naked. Ready to shift.

Ready to kill.

He knew it with absolute certainty.

More than anything, that fact brought home how serious his situation was--as if he could have ever been in doubt. And still, he did not regret finding Jessica, nor staking his claim to her. He regretted not warning her away from New Orleans, for not fighting her stubborn streak and getting her out of the city while she was still safe. The warding medallion would never hold now. It was a miracle the power had lasted as long as it had. Without it, she would be in danger wherever she went ... any place that neared a Lycan stronghold. She might not ever be safe again. She needed a mate able to fight for her, able to secure their place in the world. Perhaps an army would not even be enough....

He told himself he could have made her go, even though it was foolish to think she would have believed anything he said.

The menace of the pack quieted as their leader came forth, moving with stealth through the parted bodies and into the clearing.

Gabriel faced him, shielding the anger from his eyes, tamping down his sudden, fierce urge to shift. Gabriel did not speak. Instead, he waited to hear what the charges were. They were not animals--not yet.

Deron, pack leader, had forced them to retain some measure of humanity in the pack structure. He'd ruled them for over two decades, taken control when it looked as though the vamps would wipe out their race entirely in these parts. They'd been easy prey then, solitary. Deron had forged them into a group. Now Gabriel wondered how far Deron's humanity extended. Ideally, Gabriel would be allowed to face his accusers and deny their accusations, and would be granted a fair trial by his peers.

He nearly sneered at that thought.

They were eager for blood, anyone's blood--especially one who'd found someone precious and rare ... and dared to deny them equal chance to pursue it for themselves.

The hunt for women able to survive Lycan mating was fierce, and usually deadly for the female. He'd heard of some Lycan communities to actually hunt their females in a competitions of sorts, where only the fastest and strongest won and the weak perished.

Deron raised his arms, quieting the angry murmurs around them before he began to speak. "Gabriel Benoit, you stand before the pack charged with attacking fellow pack members John, Michael, and Cruz, and for claiming a female without fair contest. How do you plead?"

"I am no' guilty for attackin' John, Michael, and Cruz. For claimin' the female, I am."

The pack roared with disbelief, deafening him with angry howls and shouts. A wind rose, ruffling his hair, seeming to echo their fury.

"Silence!" Deron yelled above them. The noise reluctantly died down. "Explain yourself, Gabriel."

"I found d'female held down by the three members. Her legs were spread, and Cruz knelt between dem, his cock hard and ready. They were going to rape her."

Cruz spoke up from his right with a nasty growl, "She's in heat. The pretty cunt begged for what I had to give her. She didn't want you--"

"Enough, Cruz," Deron said quietly, cutting Cruz off as effectively as if he'd slapped him. He turned his attention back to Gabriel. "The attack was only in the woman's defense?"

Gabriel nodded, feeling his tension abate somewhat. Perhaps he would be given fair treatment. "She will attest to that fact if questioned."

Deron studied him several minutes before finally nodding. "This satisfies."

The crowd rumbled, but Deron cut them off with a fierce frown. "Do any here challenge my decision?"

No one spoke. "Very well then, my decision on the attack stands. Now, Gabriel, what have you to say to the second charge of taking the female without consent?"

Gabriel met his gaze steadily. "I am guilty. But I will no' allow her to be taken from me. I issue a challenge here and now, to be settled tonight." Gabriel straightened his fingers. Claws sprang from his fingertips like ivory knives, dull in the moonlight. "I will fight anyone here who thinks t'claim what is mine," he said, his accent fading with deadly soft menace.

"In his form, the challenge stands. No shifting. Let it begin," Deron announced and stepped back from the clearing to watch the games.

No challenge such as this had been issued in decades. The pack rumbled with excitement, the air charged with anticipation.

Gabriel stripped his jeans off and flung them away, out of the clearing lest they trip him in the heat of battle. He waited for the first challenger, his beast rolling inside with expectation of tasting blood this night.

He gave in to it, the swelling power, the quickening of his blood. It roared in his ears like a tempest. Strength bled into his pores, stretched through his every fiber in preparation for the fight. Some called the change the madness, for it was like that, animal instinct blotting out the human half's rational mind. Even partial shifting was dangerous. He felt it now, felt the call of the moon and the wolf inside burning to be unleashed.

His senses heightened ... smell, sight, hearing. The soft sound of crushed grass drew his attention to the right. He shifted his gaze and watched as the bodies of his brethren parted.

From the shadows, Nardo stepped out. He looked bigger without his clothes, obscenely muscled. Naked as Gabriel, he rolled his neck and shoulders, stretching in a confident move as he strode cockily to the center of the ring.

Gabriel crouched slightly, centering his body as he tensed and awaited Nardo's attack. Nardo grinned, releasing his claws as he feinted at Gabriel, circling and feinting, circling and feinting.

Gabriel's nerves tightened, winding taut with each false move. He bided his time, preserving his strength for a long night, keeping wary. He knew Nardo's style, knew Nardo relied more on brute strength than skill. Even his size hindered him somewhat, though Lycan grace had saved him before.

In a predictable move, Nardo suddenly turned a feint into a full blown lunge. Gabriel caught Nardo as he hurtled toward him, stepping into the move with a sweeping kick that took Nardo's feet out from under him and sent him crashing into the ground. The ground ruptured under Nardo's immense weight, grass and dirt flying out from beneath him. Gabriel was on him before the chunks settled. He straddled his chest, pinning his arms with his knees. He bent low and pierced Nardo's throat with the barest tip of his middle claw. A drop of blood trickled down Nardo's neck, pooling in his clavicle.

"I won' regret killin' you, *mon ami*. Do you yield?" Gabriel whispered with a deadly voice.

Nardo's chest heaved with his breathing, and he tapped the ground with his right hand. Slowly, remaining wary, Gabriel moved off him and helped him to his feet.

Nardo shook the dirt from himself and strode angrily away without a word. Gabriel had humiliated him for taking him out so quickly.

No sooner had Nardo left the clearing then the three youths came on to the field. Their hatred at being beaten on all fronts was palpable, evident in the tension of their bodies and the black looks they gave him.

Gabriel cast a questioning look at Deron. Deron nodded, giving the go ahead.

They surrounded him, claws extended, moving their hands constantly in a blur of motion to distract him. Their claws cut the air with the sound of wood ripping on a saw. Whipping the air with their own currents, they closed in, blocking him on all sides. Cruz stayed out of reach, the general commanding his troops as John and Michael converged on his flanks in a coinciding rush.

Gabriel ducked beneath their swinging arms, felt the sprinkle of slashed hair fall in tickling strokes onto his back. Air rushed by his head. Talons dug into his exposed back as he twisted.

Fire lanced down his spine. Sweat broke on his skin in an instant wave, salt driving into the wound. Gabriel roared, moving into the roll, continuing on his path. He came up under John, the claws still embedded in his back, deeper. Gabriel's teeth clenched against the pain, and he drove his hands up, up into the exposed length of John's belly. John's face froze, his arms flew back, freeing Gabriel. He tried to catch himself, failed, fell back onto the ground, coughing up blood as he landed. The blood was black in the night, like thick oil, coating everything.

Gabriel had no time for regret, no time for thought beyond that of survival. He turned toward Michael, caught him standing and looking down at John in stunned immobility. A strangled snarl came from Gabriel's left, capturing his attention. He turned, ducking.

Cruz lunged. His feet left the ground as he leapt over John, driving for Gabriel's throat. Michael came back to life, took him suddenly from behind, trapped his arms so he couldn't move.

He was a fool. A god damned fool for not moving quicker, for ignoring Michael in favor of Cruz. Fingers dug into Gabriel's biceps. Nails sliced his skin, deeply. His body healed itself, but not fast enough to prevent the flow of blood from escaping. Cruz smiled in triumph, twisted and raised his hands as though going to bat, moving into a death strike.

Gabriel saw it in his eyes, saw that he meant to kill him, that there would be no mercy, no yielding in this game. He would have to kill the stubborn bastard, maybe the others too. He relaxed his weight, heard Michael grunt in surprise right before his grip failed. Gabriel slipped from his hands, dropping to the ground, his flesh in ribbons from the razor-like claws. He landed just as Cruz swung. Claws whistled through the air, unable to stop, unable to do anything but slash above his intended victim.

Above, blood poured like heavy rain, saturating everything in its path down to the ground. Michael groaned, stumbling back, clutching his chest.

Heart pounding with the fury of his beast, Gabriel flattened between Michael's legs, driving razor tipped fingers up the thick meat of his thighs even as he kicked out and knocked Cruz's feet out from under him.

They each landed with a crash, bodies tangling in one heap of dirt and blood and torn flesh.

Gabriel could think of nothing but Cruz kneeling between Jessica's thighs, ready to impale her, beat her, even kill her. It built his fury, drove it to a fever pitch that blinded him to anything but the need for blood on his hands.

Gabriel gained his feet just as Cruz freed himself and faced him. They looked at each other a bare moment, hatred emanating from each.

They circled each other, panting heavily. Michael and John had crawled away, freeing the clearing of everything but the slickness of their blood on the ground.

Gabriel jabbed, puncturing Cruz's side, his arm, always darting back out of reach before Cruz could connect. His legs and arms ached, his back was on fire, trying to repair the damage. He felt his wounds cease to bleed, felt the flesh knit and heal itself, but it left his skin hot and feverish. Sweat and dirt and blood coated him.

Mosquitoes feasted on his blood, but Gabriel could think of nothing but taking Cruz down. If it was the last thing he ever did, he would keep that bastard from touching Jessica again. She could not go through that again. He wouldn't allow it.

It sent his blood to pounding, his head swimming hotly. He stumbled on the muddied ground.

Cruz snickered, growing in confidence.

Gabriel knew Cruz thought him weakening, thought him an old man. He was, the healing sapped his strength with every passing moment. His steps slowed more and more, his arms grew heavy, his feet leaden. But he was not so weak he couldn't take out this pup.

Gabriel jabbed at Cruz, moving past him with purpose, falling to one knee with a cry of agony that rippled on the night air. Cruz saw his opening, exposed his vulnerable heart as he swung his arm wide to take off Gabriel's head. Time seemed to slow. The wind moved at a snail's pace against his face, shaking off droplets of perspiration as he twisted from the fall.

His own growl sounded heavy in his ears, deeper than his own voice. It grew in intensity, becoming wild as he drove his hands up Cruz's chest. He felt the flesh give way, the sudden cessation of movement. Bone crunched, crumbling beneath his claws as he dug deep inside to the rapid beating heart. He sliced it, feeling repelled, sickened at killing one of his own, knowing there was no other choice and hating the need to kill or be killed.

Blood rained, hot and slick, streaming down with the force of a river unleashed. Gabriel pulled back, looking away from the dead eyes of his enemy. Without support, the body dropped to the ground with a heavy thud.

Gabriel stood over him, a knot in his gut. The fool had needed killing, deserved it with years of menace, but he despised being forced to do the deed. Cruz was a vengeful bastard--one of them would have died eventually, and Gabriel preferred it be Cruz to himself.

Jessica was safe from him now. It would have to satisfy his guilt for this night. There had never really been any other choice but the path he'd chosen.

Two pack members came and hauled the body off before the next challenger came into the clearing.

Gabriel sighed and wiped the blood from his hands on the grass.

He stretched his kinked muscles before facing his newest attacker. The night promised to be long, and by the line forming, he had little confidence that he would win.

Chapter Seven

Someone was at the tent opening. The soft sound of a zipper sliding slithered through the tent, evoking terror as if a snake glided toward her. Fear flashed through her, pumping her adrenaline until she verged the line of panic. Her breath came harsh against the gag, puffing her cheeks, flaring her nostrils. Her heart thrashed, threatening to beat through her ribs. She tried to get a hold of herself, to think clearly so she could escape, so she'd have some chance rather than none. She'd been here so long, and instead of time dulling her apprehension, it had only increased with each agonizing minute.

The tent flap opened. She jerked against her tethers, desperate to free her hands before they could come inside and kill her....

It was Gabriel.

She knew him the instant he entered, though his head was bowed and his hair fell down, obscuring his face in thick wet locks. She wanted to scream in relief, rail against him for giving her such a fright ... and throw her body against his until the tremors racking her ceased. The dizzying race of her blood abated to a dull roar.

The door flapped down behind him. He stood up once he passed the shallow entrance, standing straight and jerking his head back to toss the cloying strands away from his face and eyes. He froze as though pinned when he saw her. He looked at her. She looked at him.

He was naked.

The information filtered through the chaos of her thoughts to that one coherent whole. She didn't know why he was--didn't care. The relief alone of seeing him was enough to make her feel giddy. That he was naked changed everything, heightened senses that had been blunted previously by unease.

She was scared, yes, but it didn't stop her brain from functioning, stop her eyes from taking in every glorious inch. She wanted to tell him to get her the fuck out of there, but she hadn't moved past her initial shock at seeing him nude. It was her first time seeing him with nothing to bar her view. The adrenaline pumping through her system, the fear of before, it rushed in her head, made her careless, intoxicated. He'd looked good before. He was devastating now. So much skin, so bronze and beautiful. Muscles, everywhere, gleaming with droplets of water running in beads down his skin like liquid gold.

She wanted to feel him against her. Cold shock chilled her, made her shudder with appalling weakness. She'd never felt so needy in all her life. She should've been outraged, horrified at the turn of her thoughts, but all she wanted to do was feel his heat inside her, until it thawed every pore and banished the chill seeping from her marrow.

She wanted to look down, see *all* of him, but she couldn't. She wasn't ready, knew she should die on the spot for daring to think of sex at a time like this. She tore her gaze away from his belly up to his face. Hair clung damply to his neck and cheekbones. What captured her attention was the expression on his face--drawn, hard, his jaw clenched until the muscles stood out. Black stubble shadowed his face, lending him a rough, untamed look she hadn't seen before.

But his eyes ... they were hunted, wild and fierce. His black eyebrows were drawn down to two hard, straight lines. He looked ... haunted.

Fear shot through her once again, more potent now than ever before. What gave him that look? What had he done? What had they done to him? It terrified her to even think of it. The charming rogue of before looked vanished, wiped away and replaced by a savage stranger with hungry eyes that saw too much.

He dropped suddenly to his knees before her, kneeling at her feet as he untied her ankles. The binding came free and she rotated the joint, drawing her legs up as he moved forward between her legs.

Her breathing grew harsher the closer he came. Heat radiated off of him, until it felt like he touched her, pressed intimately against her skin. She flinched as he drew closer ... could practically feel the head of his cock looming close to her sex. A spasm seized her cleft, drenching her with sudden, liquid lust. God, she wanted it so badly. She was tired of fighting, tired of running. Her clit throbbed with aching need so fierce, she thought she would die from it.

He stopped a moment, his nostrils flaring as his breath quickened, as though he could smell her arousal. He held her gaze steadily heart stopping seconds. She saw war in his eyes, a battle that waged for control. His face went tight with need, his jaw tense. His lids lowered, heavy with carnal appetite. Lust glittered in his eyes, quickly masked as he dropped his gaze.

She'd seen it, knew that he sought to hide his need, but he couldn't hide the potency of his desire from her. Danger had heightened her senses, until she could feel the hunger emanating from him, practically hear the blood rush to engorge his length.

He said nothing as he leaned close and reached around her head. She felt like she would melt into the pole at that heated flesh so close to her own. Her skin tingled, her nipples tightened, like buds seeking the warmth of his skin. He removed the gag before moving to her hands, acting as though nothing had changed, that he couldn't sense the begging of her body.

"Oh god, Gabriel," she whispered, trying to find the strength of her voice. Her lips felt numb, her throat and mouth dry. His arms slid against her arms, raising the hair with delicious goosebumps on her skin. She shivered at the sensation. "I thought you'd never come."

"I made a promise, *petite*," he murmured, his fingers brushing against her as they worked on the binding.

Jessica worked her jaw muscles, stretching them. The rope on her hands came loose and her arms fell forward, her shoulder joints pinching with a dull ache. The pain didn't matter. She had to touch him herself, know that he was real, whole and unharmed. She wrapped her arms around him, hugging him fiercely. "I thought you were dead."

He went rigid all over, stopped breathing. "Don' touch me," he said, his voice hoarse and rough, as though he were in agony. They'd hurt him somehow. The knowledge spread an ache through her chest.

He sat back on his heels, hooking his hands under her arms, trying to push her away.

She tightened around him, refusing to let go. "No," she said, kissing the side of his neck, breathing against his ear, breathing in the clean scent of him that was so familiar when everything else seemed to have changed. She needed this. Her body tightened all over, needing to feel him touch her all over.

He shuddered, his breathing loud in the sudden silence, harsh and ragged. Against her chest, she felt the race of his heart, beating hard and fast. He pushed again, with less force this time--resolve weakening. "Stop. Don' touch me, *chere*, please."

"I can't not touch you. I don't want to let you go." She ran her tongue up his neck, reveling in the subtle tremor that raked through him. She didn't know what was happening to her, instincts guided her. An inner impulse wanted to taste him, smell him ... touch him ... everywhere....

He growled suddenly, thrust one rough hand in her hair and pulled her head back. Jessica gasped, her eyes wide, her mouth open and waiting for him. Like a storm, he descended, giving her no chance for retreat. He kissed her violently, his mouth savage, so hungry and rough alarm shot through her veins. Hot need welled the instant his bruising mouth touched her, blooming heated and wet between her thighs. Something was different, something had been unleashed.

God help her, she liked it.

The fingers gripping her hair hurt, burned her scalp. Her skin prickled from the abrasive stubble around his mouth. Jessica flinched at the pain, making a soundless cry into his mouth. His tongue thrust inside with a sharp growl, stroking wet against her limp tongue, coaxing and commanding until she was helpless but to join him. He missed nothing, encompassed, wouldn't let her withdraw.

Her tongue eagerly mated with his, stoking the arousal that gripped her body. Her stomach contracted with a hard spasm, reverberating deeply in her womb. Lust so intense it hurt lanced through her pussy, pulsing wildly in her clit. Jessica sucked his tongue hard, taking him deeper, as though it would satisfy the sudden aching emptiness of her core.

Rough excitement rumbled in his chest at her capitulation. He jerked with it, crushing her against him. The bruising pressure of his body, the molten sweep of his tongue spiraled through her body, drenching her sex with lust.

Jessica whimpered into his mouth, clawing at him for more, wanting so badly to feel the pleasure.

Her movement startled him awake. He tore away from her as though he'd been bitten, releasing a strangled, frustrated groan. His chest heaved, his eyes were black with violent longing. His face was hard with barely repressed desire. The intensity of his look frightened her, made her insides clench with fear and hunger. Her heart struggled in her chest.

They were inches apart. He devoured her with his eyes, drew them down her body as though he would eat her. Her sex spasmed at his heated look.

He closed his eyes suddenly as if pained. He shook his head.

Jessica allowed him no respite, closed the distance and locked around him. He stiffened again. She hated and delighted in his resistance.

"No. No. Sweet Jesus." His voice broke. He closed his hands around the underside of her ass, fingers digging into her flesh, drawing a ragged groan from her. She squirmed, brushing her breasts against his chest, her nipples hardening more than she'd ever thought possible.

He groaned, long and deep and pulled her without warning, hard, sliding her so suddenly up his lap she had no time to react. And then the heat of his cock was there, tight against her parted lips, slick against the wet heat of her cleft. Jessica jerked at the probe, tightened her knees around his thighs, gasping as the unyielding ridge of flesh slid through her soft lips across her clit in one agonizing motion. Her wet cleft jerked with pleasure against the silky smooth thickness of his erection. Every rigid, engorged vein tormented, sent pleasure soaring along taut nerves. Her muscles contracted involuntarily, wanting what he wouldn't give.

"They'll kill me for dis." His hoarse whisper into her hair sounded tortured. He shuddered, tightening his hands on her ass.

"You're killing me," she managed, hating the desperate need that held her in thrall. Jessica clenched, tremors of pleasure working through her. She rocked, unable to sit still, needing to move on him.

"Oh god. Don' move. Don' move!" he ground out.

She rocked again, unable to stop herself.

He sucked in a sharp breath, his eyes squeezed tight. "Stop. I'm gonna cum all over your preddy body if you don' stop!"

Her hips jerked at the rough growl of his voice, the harsh promise.

He was hard all over, tension bleeding from every pore, muscles standing at attention, ready to break control at any moment. She felt that he was on the edge, his hold tenuous. His cock throbbed against her, scalding her flesh like a red hot poker. She ached to feel that rigid heat inside her. Her entire body whimpered with need. She couldn't stand it. She had to move, couldn't stop herself. She rocked against him again, and an anguished moan tore from his throat.

Gabriel was dying. His mind raged with lust. Every muscle screamed with pain, screamed with the need to ram, to lay waste and conquer. The cream of her body felt like hot oil on his cock, making the nerves jump. He was engorged to the point that the slightest movement, the softest brush of her labia had him groaning in agony.

Time meant nothing to him now, when it should. Each second near her felt like an eternity of sensual torture. He could see nothing but her, feel nothing but her skin, smell nothing but her musky, sweet desire. Her cunt promised ecstasy, liquid fire that would devour his soul. A hard shudder wracked his body. His beast raged, his cock spasmed to be inside her. She consumed him in every possible way ... and they would die because of it.

He had to let her go. He commanded his hands to release her, to thrust her away ... commanded his legs to move, to run and not come back. Touching her was madness, stretched his sanity to the brink.

She moved on him, sliding her pussy up his shaft, drawing out the torture until he was near mindless with the urge to ram inside her. His control slipped a notch every second. Her breasts rubbed against his chest, her body pulled against the burning rings in his nipples. Pleasure and pain raced through him, mingling, racketing through his body out of control.

He sucked in a sharp breath, willing his cock to lay still, his hands not to move. His fingers dug into her cheeks, palms sensitized with the woman's flesh filling them. He couldn't be gentle. He'd hurt her before, knew he had. He hadn't been able to stop. The hunger raged in him now, unleashed by the beast and the fights. He was close to turning, anything could push him over.

If that happened, he could kill her.

He fought the beast back, felt it hovering beneath the surface, always there, always waiting for any sign of weakness.

The musk of her sex intoxicated him, heightening the danger.

Oh god ... just one thrust inside her, it was all he wanted, all he needed. He knew it wasn't enough, that he had to have her completely, fuck her again and again until his body was dry of its juices. And then he would fuck her again.

The thought rang savagely in his soul, burning him alive. He wanted more than that, wanted her to surrender herself in every way.

"Please, Gabriel," she whispered, begging, her voice seducing him out of his wits.

They'd smell it, know what he'd done, know that he'd fucked her without the right of a mate. "I ... can't."

"You can," she breathed, kissing his jaw, running her fingers through his damp hair. "Please, if we're going to die anyway, I want to have you inside me, just once."

His cock throbbed unbearably at her words. The selfish impulse grew, wresting control. He wanted to be her first Lycan, the first to mark her in their way. He couldn't fight it, not any more.

An anguished growl escaped him and he went down with her, crushing her against the ground, her legs still wrapped around him. Her feet dropped to the ground as they landed, and the breath fled her lungs. He kissed her, long and hard, moving one hand between her legs, guiding his cockhead to her pussy.

She was so wet for him, he thought he would explode.

His fingers slipped against her wet folds, smoothing her cream against his flesh as he nudged her opening.

Jessica whimpered into his mouth, spreading her legs wider, squirming under his touch, unable to bear it ... unable to move away. The huge head of his cock touched her entrance, burrowing through her swollen folds. The edges of her cunt tingled, burning with the hard press of his cockhead. Pressure built, climbing higher, anticipation an agony in her womb. The fiery sensation was almost more than she could bear. Jessica sucked his tongue as though she would eat him alive, incapable of restraining the hungry pull of her mouth, the rapid stroke of her tongue.

He broke from her mouth suddenly, bracing above her on his arms. His biceps bunched with power, veins bulging, climbing over his forearms as he held above her.

She looked up at him, a tremor of fear and excitement rippling through her. His eyes were dark, unreadable. His arms shook as though he could barely contain himself.

She wanted that loss of control, wanted him to love her with no restraint. The wildness thrilled her, banished the guilt that always ate away at her.

Jessica arched, begging with her eyes and body. He shuddered violently, arching his head back as he thrust his hips forward and drove to the hilt deep inside her, ripping past the barrier of her body. Pain lanced through her. A cry ripped from her throat at the invasion. Tears stung her eyes.

Her body bucked, muscles clenching as they fought to accommodate the thick length of him. She hadn't expected him to be so big, so thick. She hadn't expected it would hurt. She hadn't even realized it had still been there--not at her age.

He stopped in an instant, but it was too late to go back, too late to stop the destruction. She didn't want it, she wanted him to use her ... wanted to use him, keep him deep inside her forever. He cursed in French, his voice harsh and strained.

Jessica weakly opened her eyes, looked up at him past the watery blur. He looked accusing, angry. The lines of his jaw and shoulders were taut, muscle clenched with repressed passion.

His shaft jerked inside her, a rod of heat and pain. Waves of mingled agony and pleasure rippled through her, enticing. She wanted more, she had to have more. If this was their one chance, she would have it--consequences be damned.

"Damn you," he ground out, voice thick, his gaze penetrating, seeking the depths of her soul.

She shuddered uncontrollably. "Don't stop. Please, don't." She wrapped her legs around his hips, digging her heels into his firm cheeks, urging him on.

He held her gaze, his eyes shadowed by heavy lids. Slowly, he pulled back, drawing his thick length from her depths. White hot bands of pleasure twisted inside her, writhing through her veins. He pulled until only the thick, mushroomed head of his cock remained inside. Emptiness gnawed her insides. It was unbearable torture.

"No," she gasped, moving her hips, trying to force him back inside her. "Don't leave."

"I couldn' if I wanted to," he said through gritted teeth, then forged a hot, raw path deep inside her core, stifling her scream with the crush of his lips.

Swift, sweet pleasure exploded through her body like fireworks. Jessica felt like she was melting, burning alive. He anchored her, stoked the flames, thrusting heavily into her until she was panting into his mouth. She drew her arms up around his shoulders, desperate for his support. He stretched her to overflowing, exciting her with a burning stroke that forced the muscles of her sex to flex and clench in blissful response.

He shuddered as she gripped him, groaned fiercely into her mouth, thrusting his tongue inside as he withdrew his cock and pushed forcefully into her again. He couldn't control himself, she knew she'd pushed him too far. She was wild for it, kissing him back, locking her legs around his hips to keep him there, moving inside her.

He moved again, setting a rapid stroke that had the tissue of her pussy quaking with desire, creaming in abundance. Every thrust had her jerking in response, had the nerves of her pussy screaming with scalding pleasure, begging for release.

Pleasure and pain traveled through her body, closing her in warmth until sweat dampened her skin. Her hips bucked with his thrust, moving higher, tilting up for the thick, glorious intrusion.

Her body sucked at him, screaming, pleading. The rhythm of his strokes had her heart tripping over itself. Her thighs tensed around him. Her blood sizzled in her veins, tightening her chest until she could barely breathe. It was too much, not enough. Too hot. Too fast. She was going crazy, mindless, undulating against him, trying to melt against his skin. Lights danced behind her eyelids as she fought to hold onto consciousness.

She bucked against him, fighting to drive him harder, deeper, knowing if she didn't climax she'd die. Her clit throbbed with every grinding stroke. The hair of his body rubbed with rough abrasion, making her skin tingle in response. She whimpered, wanting to scream, dug her nails into his back as the pleasure engulfed her body in agonizing wave after wave. Her kegels contracted with the rapture, sucking his cock deeper inside her.

He groaned into her mouth, his muscles gone rigid, his heart beating so hard and fast, she felt it in her bones. His hips jerked involuntarily as her bliss forced him over the edge. He swallowed her cries as the rapture swelled. His orgasm ruptured inside her, jerking with echoing force in her pussy. Hot cum jetted into her, so slick and delicious inside her. She milked the cream of his body, his heated release exploding in the depths of her core until her every nerve centered on the rippling vortex of ecstasy swirling through her flesh and pulsing in her clit.

Gabriel tore his mouth away from hers, heaving for air, collapsing on top of her, shaking with the explosive force of climax. Her body was melting, dissolving into the hard ground. Jessica sobbed with relief and fading pleasure, quaking as he pulled away from her, his cock breaking the suction of her body with an erotically wet sound.

She closed her eyes, trying to reform the pieces of her body. She was so weak ... bruised ... raw ... satisfied. She should've been ashamed--she wasn't.

He recovered while she was still gathering herself, trying to think of something she should say or do. He gently kissed the slope of her shoulder before moving away. The loss of his heat and presence resonated through her.

She lay still, knowing he watched her expectantly, waiting for her excuses. Jessica couldn't look at him. She felt the heat of his gaze on her, knew he was pissed. His anger crackled in the air, as palpable to her as a slap. If she opened her eyes, she'd see it for certain. She couldn't take condemnation now, not after what they'd done, what she'd begged him to do.

"Look at me, *chere*," he commanded. His voice was deadly soft.

Slowly, she opened her eyes and saw him standing above her, studying her with an expression that had her quaking inside.

He narrowed his eyes. "Why didn' you tell me you were a virgin?"

Her heart thumped hard in her chest. "I didn't think it mattered that much."

Gabriel bit off a curse, his French unable to soften its rough violence. His hands shook as though he meant to touch her again. He ran them savagely through his hair, his jaw knotted, his muscles tense.

Jessica swallowed hard, sat up and immediately saw the blood on her thighs. It was pink with the mixture of semen and her own creamy juices. She felt ill all of a sudden, raw inside. She pushed her dress down before he had a chance to see it.

He did. He looked more angry than ever. "I would never ha' touched you--" He broke the words off with a furious growl, as though too pained to utter them. He rubbed his face, shielding his eyes from the sight of her.

Jessica stood on her knees, reaching for him, ignoring his semi-soft erection and smeared groin. "I don't regret it, Gabriel."

He flinched away from her, grabbing her wrist before she could touch him. Warning glittered in his eyes, roughened his voice to a growl. "If you don' wan' me to fuck you senseless, don' touch me."

The coarse hue of his voice made her tremble, rubbed against her insides like the hot, hard stroke of a tongue. Oh god, even now, surrounded by danger, aching inside, she wanted him again. The explosive climax had fried brain cells. She felt like an addict, in need of a fix, desperate to have it again. She withdrew her hand from his hold as though burned. The intensity of feeling frightened her, set warnings to ringing in her head.

He turned his head, sniffing the air. "You have t'go. Now. I can hold them off long enough for you to escape."

Jessica stood, alarm heightening her reflexes and lending speed to her muscles. She wouldn't do it--he didn't deserve to face this alone, though she had no idea how she could help him, or how many foes they would face. She shook her head, resolute. "No. I can't leave you here to die."

"They won' kill me, *petite*. They will if you're here to confirm what we done. You can' erase my mark on you."

He was lying. The bastard wanted to protect her. He was crazy. *She* was crazy. "Why is this happening? What do they want?"

He was quiet a long moment. She could see he battled himself, striving to contain something, some secret. Curiosity burned in her, stronger than her desire to flee.

He grabbed her chin, forced her to look straight into his eyes so that she couldn't escape what he was going to tell her. She flinched at his hard grip. His eyes softened and he eased his hold.

"You're Lycan, as I am...." He drew in a hard breath, continuing on before she could respond, "Werewolves, Jessica. I didn' want to tell you before. I knew your father."

She slapped his hand away, feeling sudden, immense betrayal. "What? Stop lying to me!" She wanted to scream, kick something, rip something--anything to shreds to satisfy the hurt searing her mind.

He grabbed her, halted the violence shimmering inside as he hugged her fiercely. He forced her to feel the comfort of his body. He laid kisses against the top of her head, moved through the tangle of her hair to her ear, speaking in a soft, strained voice. "It's no' lies. He didn' want dis life for you. Your mother died in the birthin'. He sent you away in secret that night, to keep you from changin', to keep you from bein' our whore. The pack found out, imprisoned him. He killed himself to protect you, so no Lycan cou' ever find you."

Gabriel shuddered against her once the words had spilled out. He breathed brokenly behind her ear, ragged against her neck--her pain his own.

Anguish, raw and severe, grated her mind. She closed her eyes, swallowing past the lump in her throat. *Suicide...?* It couldn't be true. None of this could be true. Gabriel couldn't be much older than she was, maybe thirtyish, he couldn't possibly have known her father. It wasn't possible. He was insane ... or a liar ... or both.

"I don't believe you," she whispered, pushing away from him, missing the heat of his arms already. She was weak, too needy, too vulnerable to him. She didn't want to believe him, couldn't. It was too hard to stretch her imagination so far, no matter how much her conscience told her he spoke the truth.

The look he bestowed on her was hurt, radiating regret. The anger had seeped from him, leaving the haunted man she'd seen briefly before. Guilt assailed her, twisting in her gut. She felt as though she'd plunged a knife into him, as though it wasn't she who'd been delivered devastating news, but a reversal. What fate had conspired in her life to deliver such agony, such fierce desires and aching loss?

"Believe wha' you will," he said softly, painfully. "D' truth will come, soon enough. Now you mus' go."

Gabriel turned his back on her, striding from the tent. She knew he was going to his death, and there was nothing she could do to stop him.

Chapter Eight

The ground was littered with death traps and mutilators; roots, rocks, prickly pears, and other objects and obstructions she couldn't place with her limited senses in her nearly blind state. The moon had already begun it's descent, glowing gold above the treetops, filtering through the canopy like scattered rain. Her feet and legs bled from her headlong rush, but she ignored the pain, running through the woods at an insane pace, praying she wouldn't fall and break something.

She had to get help. They were going to kill Gabriel, possibly even come after her. But that didn't matter nearly so much as what she imagined him to be going through, what tortures they'd devised. Thinking about it quickened her pace, stole the breath from her lungs, made her heart gallop in her chest. She knew for certain now that they were some kind of cult, and being in the middle of nowhere, there was nothing to stop them from doing exactly what they wanted to to Gabriel.

Jessica realized it didn't matter what Gabriel or she believed, the danger was still real. He could be saved from their brain washing, but only if she could get to the police in time. She bit back the exhausted sobs, trying to stay focused, calm. Hysteria loomed under the surface, threatening to consume at any unguarded moment.

The moon guided her, dipping in the sky, foretelling the late hour. It had to be after midnight, probably later. The streets would be dead in town. She kept the moon's position fixed and headed east, always glancing past the tree tops to make sure she hadn't strayed off course. She didn't dare try to find the road and follow it, even if it would speed her progress. They could be looking for her, even now. The road would be a death trap.

The wind picked up, rustling through the trees with a whistling rush. Branches rattled above her, shaking dried leaves to flutter to the ground. Her hair twisted and writhed in the breeze like a live thing, flying into her face and mouth until she was blinded completely by the thrashing tendrils.

A howl rippled through the night like the toll of a death knell, spelling her doom. The wail rose again, undulating on the air like some foul caress, followed by an excited call--words indistinguishable but instantly recognizable for what they were.

Fright froze her to the spot, clenched her heart in a painful, breath stealing grip. Ice flooded her veins, swallowing her, replacing calm with instant, dread panic.

Jesus! Oh god, oh god, oh god.... They were after her. The howls, the howls were coming closer, everywhere, all around. She shook her head, covering her ears, trying to block the noise, fighting down the mind numbing panic.

But muffling their calls only worsened her fear. She dropped her arms, cocking her head, trying to gain their position, heard them above her.

Something fluttered in the treetops, briefly blocked her view of the stars. It had to be a bird, an owl, something-- anything else. She was going crazy, it wasn't possible. Men couldn't fly, the woods were distorting the sound.

They had to be behind her.

Jessica tore off in a run, ignoring the stitch in her side, the stinging, tearing brambles, the grate of bark on her skin as she ran into trunks and pressed on. Her lungs froze with the crisp air. Her throat felt raw from dragging each breath in, fighting blackness that swam in and out of her vision, threatening unconsciousness.

Wind roared around her, whipping her hair and dress into a frenzy, forcing debris into her eyes. She shielded her face, kept running, tried to listen past the thundering in her ears, but the forest had grown deathly silent, giving no warning.

She ran into a trunk, bouncing off it onto the ground. The breath knocked from her lungs at the impact, forcing her to drag in shaky lungfuls of air. Her body felt bruised, battered beyond belief. She blinked the dirt out of her eyes, laughing hysterically at herself, forcing the macabre giggles back.

It was then that she saw the legs.

* * * *

She was surrounded. The hysterical laughter died in an instant, replaced with quiet wariness. She cringed at her weakness, despising herself, despising that she hadn't run fast enough, that she had no way to protect herself. She was so weary of being hunted, almost to the point where she sadistically willed them to end her constant, excruciating anxiety.

There were three of them, possibly more that she couldn't see. Their faces and arms were white, almost glowing and paler than her own skin, seeming disembodied with the darkness and their black attire.

One of them broke off from the trio, approaching her and reaching for her face. Jessica hesitated on taking off his fingers with her teeth, waiting to see if by chance she'd merely over-reacted in her panic. She raised her eyes and looked at him unflinchingly as he gently brushed the hair from the tangle of her lashes.

"This is no Lycan," he said, turning to the others with his hand lingering in her hair.

The word aroused instant, gut-wrenching pain. *Lycans....* They knew of Gabriel's group, were possibly members themselves. No, that didn't seem right. She shook her head, trying to make sense of her thoughts, but they jumbled around in her brain. Her ears buzzed, whining like the hum of electronics.

They closed in, sniffing the air as though scenting some delicacy had been pulled from an oven, ripe for tasting.

One of the men snatched her hair, twisting her face toward the sky. Jessica gritted her teeth against the pain, raking her nails down his arm until he released her. In a lightning-fast move, his hand snaked out and slapped her, drawing blood from her mouth. Her lips throbbed with biting pain. She spat out the sickening taste, resisting the urge to rub her mouth to ease the pain.

He snickered, shaking his arm. "She bleeds. I say we eat her and then continue on to their gathering place. This hunt was not nearly as satisfying as I wished."

Another audibly sniffed the air. "I smell Lycan cock and pussy ... and blood. The hunger gnaws, I agree."

"You will not touch me," she ground out, holding her hands as weapons.

"There is no one to stop us, not even your Lycan lover."

The words were a slap in the face. They couldn't know what she'd done, but they did. She didn't believe they smelled it--they must have come from that place. "What did you do with him?" she screamed, struggling to her knees. "Where is Gabriel? Did you ... kill him?" Her voice broke. She choked down a sob.

"She cries," a male said, snickering.

One of the men spoke up, "We'd be happy to oblige you by killing him if you'll show us the way."

"Her pussy smells sweet. Lycan coats her skin. I wonder if the little bitch tastes as good as she smells. I say again, we should eat her and let the master find his own kill. The night grows short." Menace dripped from his voice.

She knew in that moment that she was dead. And she was damned well going to take some of them with her. The savagery of her thoughts empowered her.

Blistering rage surged inside her. Jessica jumped fluidly from her knees with a snarl, running at him with her fingers curled into talons. He laughed, pushing at her as though she were no more threat than an gnat. The laughter died on his lips as she ducked past his arm and came up again, gouging her fingers into his eyes with a scream that scored the lining of her throat. Blood spurted from his lids, lukewarm as it hit her face and rolled down her cheeks. She ignored the instant, fierce nausea, continued crushing his eyes, digging in, trying to find his brain.

She wasn't going to die without a fight. She'd hurt them, make them sorry they ever touched her, ever hunted her.

He screamed and knocked her back. Her brain rattled as she hit a tree trunk. Her head thunked wetly against the harsh bark. Hot blood seeped instantly onto her scalp, tingles crawling through her hair like biting ants. Her eyes crossed, making her dizzy. She closed her eyes against the sickening bile that rose in her throat with a burning tide. She'd become an animal and it had done her no good.

The vamp she'd attacked screamed again and snarled, "I will kill her now!"

Something stopped him from attacking--she didn't look to see what. She was too ill to feel grateful.

"No," another said, "This one intrigues. She smells and acts almost ... Lycan. We take her to the master."

Someone grabbed her arms suddenly, hauled her roughly to her feet. Her legs were weak, unable to support her weight. She struggled to keep her feet under her as she opened her eyes to another wave of nausea, and then felt her heart stop as she looked at the blood blackened face looming above her. He snarled at her, baring sharp teeth that gleamed in the light, but that wasn't what sent the icy dread slithering through her bloodstream.

His eyes ... his eyes were back.

She'd crushed them, felt them pop beneath her nails. Her fingers were covered in sticky gore.

He grinned at her, as if reading her thoughts, snapping his jaws menacingly at her face. Jessica struggled against him, frantic to get away, clawing at his arms, his neck, anywhere she could reach. His hands tightened on her, cutting off the blood flow to her hands. She winced from the pain.

She knew then that Gabriel's tales had been true. There were monsters in the night. And she was their prisoner.

* * * *

No one knew what he'd done, that he'd marked Jessica in the most primal of ways. Gabriel had sliced his thigh and smeared his own blood on his groin, masking the scent of her before rinsing off once more.

Unbelievably, it had worked. He'd felt invigorated from their joining, fiercer than ever to defend his right to claim her as mate.

The fights came faster, easier, but they still wore him down.

Now he'd accomplished something few had ever seen in their territory--he'd triumphed over every challenger without serious harm to himself.

Gabriel was weary beyond belief, his mind was spent, exhausted. The tight warmth of her body, the sweet taste of her kiss glimmered in memory alone, swallowed by the effort to survive. Every blow made Jessica safer, every strike insured she covered more distance.

He stood now, in the clearing, alone. After what seemed like an eternity, the challengers had ceased to come. His chest visibly rose and fell, pronouncing the taut line of his body, his rigid, wary stance. Blood dripped from his fingers, trickled from lacerations in his flesh, slowly healing with feverish sped.

Deron stepped forward into the clearing, regarding Gabriel with clear admiration. "You have done well, Gabriel." He looked around the circle of their brethren. "Are there no others left who wish to challenge him for the right to the girl?"

They were silent, as one. The challenge was over.

"Claim your woman," Deron said to Gabriel.

The pack roared with approval, calling to his inner beast. A wind sighed through the gathering, carrying with it a sense of completion and victory. He tilted his face and looked toward the setting moon, wondering if he could find Jessica again, unbelieving that the ordeal was finally over.

The stars blotted from the sky a brief moment as a black shape crossed his line of vision.

Gabriel ducked and rolled as it swooped over his head, coming up baring his claws. He growled in warning, tensing to jump.

"Peace, Lycan. I bring a message for the one called Gabriel," the vampire said with barely repressed amusement.

"I am Gabriel," he snarled, his hackles standing on end. Never had the vampires dared to invade the luna clearing.

The vamp looked him over. "My master bids me to tell you we have your woman. If you wish her return, come to *le Ventre de le Diable* in Vieux Carre tomorrow night. If any Lycan should be seen before then, we will kill her."

Before Gabriel could wrap his hands around the smug vampire's throat, he leapt into the air and disappeared in the black sky.

"She is one of ours. You cannot face them alone," Deron said. Muffled agreement followed, excitement building with each passing second.

"Dey seek to slay us once and for all," Gabriel murmured, watching the sky. *The Devil's Belly*.... It was one of the largest resting places of the vamps--that they knew of.

"Tomorrow we take her back and end this," Deron said, his voice carrying over the crowd.

It was what they had dreaded and waited for--open battle with the vamps. And Jessica would be right in the middle.

Chapter Nine

"What do you want with me?" Jessica demanded, glancing around surreptitiously for a weapon. The room they were standing in was perhaps twelve foot squared. The walls floor, even the ceiling seemed to be made of stone. A single door was set into one wall, but the man stood between her and that avenue of escape. The only possibility she could see was a tall candelabra holding a couple of flickering tapers almost within reach.

A faint smile touched the vampire's bloodless lips. "Why, to eat you, my dear."

"Very funny," she said. "Ha ha."

He showed her his fangs. Jessica felt her heart stand still. "My, what big teeth you have."

Mordecai smiled thinly. "The better to drink your blood," he responded wearily, beginning to feel some annoyance at her flippant responses.

"I don't think so," she said and leapt toward the candelabra, grabbing it. She discovered she couldn't lift it.

"It's bolted to the floor," Mordecai said dryly.

Not to be outdone, Jessica grabbed the tapers and threw them at him. He raised an arm to shield himself. Once she'd distracted him, she dashed past and threw open the door. Beyond lay utter blackness. She ran down the smotheringly dark corridor, blindly feeling the walls for guidance. Her breath, rasping in and out of her lungs in fear, deafened her to pursuit, but she thought she detected little whispers of sound, like the tiny scurrying feet of rats.

The corridor ended abruptly in what seemed to be a far larger room than the one she had left behind. She couldn't know that for certain, but she sensed a vast emptiness and damp currents of air swirled through the room.

She paused, catching her breath, trying to listen for any sounds of pursuit. She wasn't really comforted when she could hear nothing. After a moment, she began fumbling her way through the room, feeling the walls, searching for a door. Her heart leapt when she found one at last. Excitement flooded her when the knob turned under her hand. It was dashed in the next moment when she opened the door and discovered only another corridor--this one lit by a single, flickering torch.

Glancing uneasily behind her, she discovered that the room she had just traversed was filled with coffins.

The hair stood on the back of her neck. Jessica shuddered and strode down the corridor, her shadow casting long before her, melding into the darkness that swarmed the sides of the hall. The corridor turned in a sharp corner and ended with another door, leading into another small, empty room. On one end, heavy velvet drapes covered an opening. Faintly, Jessica could see light filtering through the curtains. Certain that she had discovered a window and the means of escape, she rushed to it, throwing the curtains aside. To her dismay, she discovered the drapes concealed another open doorway.

She was seized by two men the moment the curtains parted. Jessica struggled to free herself, but their hands were as unyielding as manacles around her arms. They dragged her deeper into the room, past huge candelabras filled with lighted tapers.

Ahead of her, she saw a stone throne on a dais. Mordecai was seated on the throne. He did not look happy.

"Let me go!" she screamed, lifting her feet from the ground, trying to break their hold. They led her inevitably to the dais, unfazed by her continual struggles. They stopped, releasing her to her own feet and stepping back just enough to quash any ideas she'd have of making a run for it.

"What do you want with me?" she asked him again. He'd deliberately allowed her to escape, only for the pleasure of capturing her again--and tormenting.

Mordecai tapped his fingers on the arm of the throne in impatience. "You are not as valuable to me as you seem to think."

Jessica swallowed. If anything, her situation was worse than she originally thought. "Then why keep me here?"

The vampire stood, slowly taking a step down and then another, until he was inches from her. "Bait. I seek your

Lycan lover ... and others should they be foolish enough to come."

"He's dead," she said, feeling sick with the words. Her mouth felt tainted uttering them. Her heart pinched painfully. "You're too late."

"On the contrary. He is coming for you."

Oh god, no! She would be his downfall. Everything that had happened to them--him--had been because of her. Gabriel would come, and he would die trying to save her.

Mordecai's hand snaked out and snatched the necklace from her neck. He held the large medallion in his palm. His eyes glittered. "What is this?"

"Protection from werewolves," she said weakly. What she'd needed was protection from vampires too. She thought wistfully of Mikel's, brimming with weapons for fighting the undead.

"A useless trinket." He chuckled, throwing the medallion away. It skittered on the floor and vanished from sight. He caught her with one arm, forcing her against his body, digging his free hand through her hair to grip her scalp. Jessica gasped and tried to fight him, wincing as he discovered the wound she'd sustained earlier. His grip on her hair tightened, forcing her to arch her head deeply to the side.

The blood rushed to her head, pounding with the frightening knowledge of what he was going to do. And there was nothing she could do to stop him. She closed her eyes and screamed when the fangs ravaged her flesh.

* * * *

Gabriel knew before the night was out, many Lycan would die. He regretted it, regretted the necessity of this action, but there was no other choice. If they did not take a stand now, they would be wiped out in their entirety--as a whole at once, or one by one.

By the next evening, when the moon climbed high in the sky like a warped pearl, they were ready.

Some drove to the meeting place, others walked, but all told, over two dozen showed up at Vieux Carre for the showdown. The streets were strangely empty, as though the people sensed something massive was going down.

Their excitement infected the air, crackled between them, connecting them with a hidden energy.

Gabriel led the pack. His rage had not abated in the many hours since first hearing of her abduction. He seethed with fury, angered at himself and them for their daring, so much so that he feared he would be no help to Jessica whatsoever.

They traversed a narrow, dirty alley, keeping watch above for ambush as they made their way to the back of the building. The entrance to the underground was there. There was a garden in the back, with a fountain as centerpiece, spraying water with a soft gurgle of sound. It appeared tranquil, like the home of some wealthy, upstanding citizen, surrounding by other upstanding neighbors.

Gabriel wondered just how many knew what atrocities went on in the townhouse before them.

A vamp at the back entrance motioned them forward, holding the door open for them. They left a few men behind for backup to go for help should they need it, not that he expected there would be a need. They lived or died, there would be no second chances.

The vamp let them in without question. Had Gabriel been in any doubt it was a trap, his suspicions were now confirmed. He knew better than to expect them to keep their word--not with the way things had progressed in the past few months. Either the vampire force far exceeded their own ... or they were foolishly confident and on equal footing.

Another vamp waited inside, leading them down corridors into the belly of the earth. He did not bind their eyes or dowse the lights.

The vampires didn't expect the Lycans to leave.

He caught the faint scent of old blood. For decades, victims had been lured to the Devil's Belly, never to see light again. The cold stone was oppressive. The stink of vampires permeated the walls, like the dried husks of roses-

-a sickly sweet stench, unnoticeable by any but the most sensitive.

They were led through labyrinthine corridors of reinforced stone, finally to a throne room, barren of anything save candelabras filled with glowing candles, a raised throne, and vampires. Dozens of vampires.

Gabriel stopped in the middle of the room, his men fanning out behind him, facing the man seated on the throne. "Where is Danior?"

Mordecai smiled thinly. "I killed him. I am master of this city now."

It explained why the incidents had steadily worsened.

"I've come to trade myself for d'woman. Where is she?"

Mordecai inclined his head, and two vamps pushed through a curtained doorway, dragging Jessica between them. Her head hung down to her chest. She was unconscious. The front of her dress was stained with blood.

"I have marked her," Mordecai remarked, standing.

His vision turned red. Mordecai had fed on her. A violent urge to tear the man apart surged in his veins. "She can' be turned. She's one of us."

"As delicious, as well. Take her back," he said, gesturing toward the men.

Gabriel stepped forward, growling. "Danior kept his word."

Mordecai's eyes glittered dangerously. "I am not Danior."

He didn't have to look to know the vampire's ranks were on the move, closing in. He tried to block thoughts of Jessica from his mind, worries that she was still alive.

Mordecai grinned, showing his fangs. "I ordered in tonight. Tonight, we feast on Lycan."

Gabriel unleashed the beast with a furious howl, answered by his brethren in chorus. They launched at their enemies, ripping clothes, human flesh replaced with fur and fangs and razored claws.

Mordecai launched himself from the dais, straight for Gabriel.

* * * *

Something called Jessica, reached into the corners of her mind with urgent fingers. Howls filled the air, a haunting chorus of bloodlust answered in her soul. She sank deeper into the darkness, blinded, pain scalding her muscles. The pain was everywhere, on her skin, in her bones, spurred on by the incessant howls. Molten oil coated her like tar, oozing over her flesh, sticking to her skin, burning a path over her body.

She screamed, clawed at herself, but she was frozen, unable to move. The pain changed suddenly, mellowed. Ripples of energy rubbed inside her, spreading like tingling waves of ecstasy. Her body jerked involuntarily, seized with rolling, mingling agony and bliss. Senses that could only have been dead before came alive, so clear and sharp, they stabbed her brain with piercing clarity. She smelled blood, buried in the walls, fresh from cut veins; damp stone and flowing water; the burning of candle wax and wick; fear and sweat.... Her ears prickled with thousands of sounds, with grunts and groans; the rip of flesh; the splatter of blood; teeth gnashing; moans of pain.

A canine cry pierced the cacophony, sending instant alarm racing through her heart. It broke off abruptly. Her eyes flew open.

Gabriel. He needed her, needed her help. Jessica rolled off her back onto her hands and knees.

Something ... was ... wrong.

Her hands were no longer there.

* * * *

Jessica could not tear her eyes away. Fabric pooled around her feet, her torn and bloody dress and a satin robe. She flexed her fingers, watching the claws distend and retract from the blunted tips. The sounds of fighting faded, drowned out by the roar of blood in her ears.

Fur coated her arm, supple black dusted silver that extended up as far as she could see. Her hands were no longer hands--they were paws.

She'd become a wolf.

The realization exhilarated her. She stretched, feeling power move through her limbs. Everything Gabriel had told her was true. She was Lycan born, of his people.

A savage growl caught her, drawing her attention to Gabriel. He fought the man who'd bitten her, Mordecai.

Part wolf, part man, shadowed by black hair--she knew it was Gabriel, felt it by some heightened, inner sense that connected her to him.

They were locked together, tearing at each other with their hands. The vampire had changed somehow, grown until he dwarfed Gabriel. Her heart leapt in her throat as Gabriel was forced down to his knees. He arched his back, groaning in pain and fury. Mordecai kicked him, sending him sprawling on the floor.

Jessica yelped, a canine cry--her voice gone. Mordecai's head snapped up the instant she called. Hè turned toward her and smiled, red rivulets streaming down his face and hands.

In a lightning fast move, he rushed her. Before he could reach her, Gabriel raised from the floor and grabbed him, pulling him abruptly back in a flip with sheer strength. Mordecai screamed and whirled in the air, landing on the ground, Gabriel atop him, his hand poised to rip the vampire's heart from his chest.

"I yield!" Mordecai yelled, holding his hands up to defend himself from Gabriel's claws.

Gabriel regarded him warily a long moment, still caught in the blood lust of his beast, torn between the urge of the beast within and the human side that told him truce had been offered and must be respected. Finally, he stood, releasing the vamp leader. The others had ceased their battles, as well, at Mordecai's words. The room was still, waiting.

Gabriel turned and faced them, gazing around at the carnage. They had lost two of their brethren, but decimated the vamps by more than half. A sense of triumph raced through his blood, quickening the beast. It was the beast that warned him, that sensed that Mordecai had risen behind him, warning of the threat inherent in turning his back on any vamp, particularly one who'd shown he could not be counted upon to keep his word.

Too late, the subtle change in the air warned him of the vamp's underhanded ruse. Even as he turned to meet the death strike of the vamp, he heard the call of his mate.

Jessica leapt through the air, driving her claws deep, ripping Modecai's heart from his chest with her claws, shredding it before she'd even landed on the ground.

With a thought, she shifted back into human form and faced Gabriel. Gabriel gave her an appreciative look, glanced at Mordecai's lifeless body, and then looked back at her with a frown.

"That was no' honorable, *cherie*. The vamp had called a truce."

Jessica shrugged. "I'm a woman. I've no use for honor when it comes to dealing with the likes of him. Besides, he would've killed me and you both if given the chance."

He held out his hand. She glanced at it, but shook her head slightly, smiling faintly. Returning to the place where she'd been held, she scooped up the abandoned robe, covering herself. This time when Gabriel, who'd followed her curiously, offered his hand, she took it.

Unhindered, they left that place of death, leaving the remaining Lycans to watch over the surviving vampires. Deron would come and arrange terms with the survivors.

By uniting at last to face the threat, the Lycan had ensured that the war that had raged in New Orleans for one hundred years was finally over.

Chapter Ten

"What do we do now?" Jessica asked once they were outside and had washed the blood from their bodies in the fountain. The crisp air turned the water to ice, forming chillbumps on her skin.

Gabriel's expression washed heat over her skin and made her cleft clench with hunger. "I have faced d'pack and fought for the right to claim you as mate. Do you accept me, Jessica?"

Jessica couldn't find her voice. She swallowed past the lump in her throat, forcing herself to speak. "I do. I've wanted it since I first saw you. But ... is everything okay now?"

"No one can harm you ever again, so long as I live, *petite*."

She felt suddenly breathless at his promise. "What do we do now?"

He smiled wickedly. "Now we find a bed."

He led her in a run to his car. The streets were empty with the lateness of the hour. Jessica followed him breathlessly. She laughed throatily when they reached his car.

She moved along the passenger side, reaching for the door. He grabbed her wrist before she could open it, whirling her around, crushing her against the metal.

His hand closed on the back of her neck, forcing her lips to his as he rubbed his jean clad erection against her pubic mound. He nipped at the curves of her lips, swallowing her passionate cry as he ground against her. Her legs parted for him, allowing him closer.

He swept his tongue into her mouth, tangling with her tongue. She sucked him, hard. He tasted wild, like summer thunder. He consumed her, addicting her with his taste. She loved kissing him, loved that he was hers and she was his. Her breasts pressed into his chest, growing full and swollen, her nipples achy for the heat of his mouth.

He growled against her lips as she bucked against him, forcing her to accept his tongue and the rough grind of his hips. Blood pounded in her veins, in her clit, pooling in the hot center of her until the slightest touch had her writhing in erotic agony.

"I can' wait that long to taste you," he ground out, pulling back to stare at her intently. His teeth skated along the arch of her throat, past her clavicle. Pleasure erupted along her nerves.

He thrust the robe open with rough hands, baring her body to his eyes and the wet heat of his mouth. "I have hungered for dis, *chere*." His lips and teeth nibbled at the top of one breast.

She knew what he wanted. Her body thrilled to his rough sensuality, the sense of danger and exposure. "Oh god, Gabriel, not here."

"*Oui*." His mouth locked over her nipple, enveloping the tip in the hot depths of his mouth. His tongue rubbed the achy bud as he suckled her, hard, harder.

Jessica bit her lip to stifle her cries, moaning as the pleasure moved up her breast and spread through her body.

He broke away, nuzzled her other breast, closing his hand around her still throbbing nipple as he lathed the other. His free hand moved down the curve of her waist, lower, to her apex, playing in the wet curls there. Jessica rose on her toes, grasping his head, trying to anchor herself to the ground.

Her body anticipated the thrust of his fingers, creamed in excess, preparing for the invasion she wanted so badly.

"It's no' enough," Gabriel ground out, breaking from her breast. He rubbed his nose in the valley, moving lower, trailing wet kisses down her stomach. He was kneeling now, pushing her legs roughly apart.

Jessica acquiesced, too eager to stop him now, no matter who might come along. She had to have him inside her or she'd go crazy.

"Will this appease my hunger?" he said hoarsely, looking up at her with intensely dark eyes, spreading her swollen lips with one tender hand. "You are so wet for me, *chere*. I wonder if your cream can slake my thirst."

He forced one of her legs over his shoulder, spreading her wide to his mouth. He reached around and gripped the cheeks of her ass, burying his face in her pussy.

Jessica cried out as his tongue burrowed into her slick channel, pushing past the tight muscles ringing the entrance of her vagina, deeper. Her blood boiled in her veins. He groaned into her cleft with a deep, rumbling sound of appreciation and ate her with hungry, rough strokes. He pulled loose from the suction of her cunt, lapping at the edges of her pussy, up to her clit, circling the sensitized nub.

Her body wept it's juices. She felt them running down her supporting leg, knew she drenched him with her need. She gripped the cold metal car, arching her back, grinding against his face involuntarily.

Gabriel couldn't get enough of her, couldn't taste enough. She was so sweet, so delicious. Desire fogged his brain, taking control. The scent of her beast coated her skin, driving him insane with lust. He drove his tongue into her core again, moving one hand around to skate his thumb against her clit. He rubbed it roughly

Her muscles clenched tightly around his driving tongue. Her pussy trembled with the force of her climax. Her juices increased, gushing on his tongue. She cried out, bucking against him as he rubbed her clit harder and lapped her ravenously.

He was too far gone to be gentle. Need drove him now-- the need to mate with his woman--blinding him to everything else. He dropped her leg and freed his unbearably hard cock in one smooth move, pushing her legs up.

She wrapped her arms around him, digging her nails into his shoulders. She pressed her slick heat against him, driving him out of his mind. He groaned, buried his face against her neck as he pressed his cockhead to her tight hole.

She cried as he drove inside her. His cock jerked, throbbing with hard, violent spasms, threatening to explode from the excruciating grip of her channel. He stopped, trying to reign himself in, wanting it to be gentle this time. His heart pounded from the effort. His groin burned, muscles taut.

She squirmed against him, tightening her thighs at his hips. "Oh god, Gabriel, don't stop now," she whispered fiercely, heaving for breath, tossing her head in agony and ecstasy. She begged him with her hands, the arching of her body, the clench and release of her inner muscles. She chanted his name, pleading, driving him over the edge.

He lost it. All control, all restraint. There was nothing left but the pure animal need now, to mark and claim ... to conquer. He released a savage groan and scored her neck, sucking her flesh, giving in to the violent, feral needs that claimed him. He pulled out and forcefully drove into her. She screamed, clinging to him. He couldn't know whether it was pleasure or pain, or both. His cock burned from her tightness, gripping him like a fist. He set a rapid, driving pace that had his nostrils flaring. He sucked her neck, pounding his hips against hers.

Her cries echoed around him, quickening the pound of his heart, the fire in his groin. She raked her nails down his back, her body trembling as a climax seized her. Her kegels bit into him with crushing strength, pulling the orgasm from his body. He broke away from her neck, his own guttural cries mingling with hers.

His cock jerked and spewed his hot cum into her.

Her feet dropped to the ground as he leaned weakly against her. He nuzzled her neck, stirred to see his mark on her flesh and smell his scent on her skin. They belonged to each other now, always.

"*Je t'aime*," he murmured against her ear, nibbling her lobe.

"Do you mean it," she said breathlessly, tightening her arms around him. "Or is it because you're still inside me?"

He lifted his head, caught her smile and grinned at her. "Maybe."

She swatted his shoulder and laughed. "That's not an answer."

"I think maybe you shouldn' move so much, cause maybe I'm ready to love you more." His cock was already growing hard again, responding to her heat.

"I think maybe we should wait for a bed," she said tartly. "It's just a miracle no one came along."

"I think you'd like dat too much, *ma diable*."

"I am not a devil!"

He grinned, nipping her lips. "You are when you squirm dose delicious hips."

She lowered her lashes with a sultry smile and squirmed against him.

He sucked in a sharp breath. "You'll be d'death of me, *chere*. I don' know how I could love you so much."

"Because I love you," she whispered, brushing her lips softly against his. "And if you don't get me to a bed right now, I'll show you just how much of a devil I can be."

His eyes flashed with heat. "I'm no' so sure dat's d'right incentive to ge' me ta move d'way you wan'." He ground his hips against hers with emphasis.

Jessica bit her lip, stifling a moan. "Oh ... uh ... I think I just changed my mind."

The End

Printed in the United States
38475LVS00006B

9 781586 086565